Thresholding

by

Jim Hilliard

DORRANCE PUBLISHING CO., INC.
PITTSBURGH, PENNSYLVANIA 15222

ISBN # 0-8059-4249-1
Printed in the United States of America
First Printing

For information or to order additional books, please write:
Dorrance Publishing Co., Inc.
643 Smithfield Street
Pittsburgh, Pennsylvania 15222
U.S.A.

Table of Contents

Preface

Sunday, November 22, 1992

Today Windsor Castle is burning in London, President-elect Bill Clinton and the Reverend Jesse Jackson are attending Mass in a Little Rock Catholic Church, tornadoes are devastating Louisiana, and funeral arrangements for Joey Balaam are being completed up-river in Dogwood.

Here in New Autumn, Arkansas, the paper boy has not delivered the morning *Democrat-Gazette*. No sweat, because radio and television have already given us the news, and for the most part their prognosticating techniques have also told us what is going to happen in the future. My wife, Vi. loves this gypsy tea leaf reporting. I can take it or leave it as one of the metamorphic changes that has come about since I chose retirement, and am no longer in the fast lane of achievement. That does not mean that the zip is gone, but sometimes the zipper does get stuck. Like the day I drove from the Town Center and there on a big rock in front of the gushing falls in Fish Creek Park sat two retirement-age women. From a distance through my bifocals they looked like duplicates of Copenhagen's Little Mermaid. This prompted me to accelerate the car across the road toward them and call out, "I'd whistle at you but I can't through these false teeth."

With an accent of mermaid mirth, one of them said, "Couldn't you just spewwwww at us?"

Age and retirement are for those who appreciate them.

Vi and I do.

Therefore, when you drop by for a visit at our house, we apologize neither for the shoes which one of us kicked off in the middle of the living room last night, or the afternoon naps which we once camouflaged as "eye-resters." We do wish, however, that we could remember our next-door neighbor's name.

This book is dedicated to the
much better half of *Jim & Vi*

Wife, Helper, Advisor, Counselor
Sweetheart forever

Chapter 1

Metamorphosis

It was springtime. The annual snowpack along the shores of Lake Superior in Michigan's Upper Peninsula was accelerating its ancestral migration toward warmer, more liquid regions of exploration. So it was with Vi and me as we faced that frightening, exhilarating, metamorphic rapture called retirement.

Amid frustrations, traumas and dubious decision-makings, we began liquidating household collectibles, professional responsibilities, social ties, and territorial confinements in preparation for the arrival of the moving van, that heart-rending, bulldozing monster that preys on yuppies and retirees.

Vi picked up the first item we had purchased after the wedding bells.

"Oh, Jim,...."

She did not finish the statement.

"We cannot keep everything," I said, pretending to ignore any feelings attached to that cheap little gadget.

She laid it aside in the "Let Go" pile.

"It'll bring ten cents at the church bazaar."

We both returned to our migratory preparations.

There are nine months of winter in the Upper Peninsula of Michigan, one month of summer and two months of indecision if you count the January thaw. Blizzards can blow you right out of existence or they can hold you gently as a mother grizzly nursing her cub. Like people of the desert regions, survivors in this north country may live quite comfortably in harmony with the surroundings if they have sufficient know-how, mixed with determination. To fight the elements is to dishonor the Mother of Nature.

Vi is a native Finn, born and reared on the shores of Gitche Gumee. Not too many of the thoroughbreds are left up there any more. Mixed marriages have thinned the blood. Many have gone down below[1].

---

[1]South, across the Straits of Mackinac; Lower Michigan.

I was a transplant from the southwest plain lands of rural Oklahoma.

In the north country, one learns that the severity of either the people or the weather can quickly determine one's destiny. I survived by marrying one of their native girls. The marriage has endured perhaps due to the weather as much as anything because those long winter nights do get mighty cold--unless, as I say, one succumbs to the harmony of Mother Nature.

Vi and I worked hard all our lives, and we enjoyed what we accomplished. Then, before we knew it we were taking Geritol, and Social Security began knocking at the door like a Halloween Trick or Treater. The time had come to take the big step.

The monster van arrived sooner than it had a right to. Quickly it gobbled up our belongings and left--left us standing there in that old familiar parsonage, suddenly empty now, hushed and bare, each room echoing its own silence as we tiptoed from one to the other. We felt like strangers, intruders in our own home, infiltrated with feelings so very terribly unfamiliar. For a moment, just a milli-moment, the desperation of cold sweat flooded in upon us. We had done the wrong thing!

Then it passed; that moment of doubt did.

Vi grabbed the vacuum cleaner; I began to take the bags and boxes from the back door to the car.

"Honey, where are the suitcases?" I called from the kitchen.

"They're in the front bedroom," she replied, her voice in harmony with the happy whir of the vacuum cleaner.

"They're not there," I called a bit later.

The vacuum cleaner stopped. So did our hearts.

"The van-man took them," Vi whispered breathlessly.

Sure enough--our tooth brushes, pajamas, socks and deodorants--all gone!

Vi looked at me; I looked at her. It was one of those "you might be guilty even if you're innocent" moments, the kind preachers pick up from the Chairperson of the Pastor-Parish Relations Committee when the Bishop calls for the report on the pastor's annual performance.

Then our hearts began to beat again. Vi and I reached for each other, hugged and kissed, and began to laugh. We knew then that even with this little flip of fate, everything would be all right.

So with that feeling, mixed with all the others, we drove from the parsonage, the parish, and the salary afforded a mediocre minister-and-wife.

We were retiring to Arkansas.

Chapter 2

Threshold

The next day, about mid-afternoon, we crossed the border into the Ozarks. Enthusiasm carried us through the lunch hour as we circled around through the hills and valleys, adrenaline in overdrive. Rain sputtered and splashed intermittently, unable to make up its mind whether to attack the windward or leeward side of the slopes. A silent, daring joy stimulated our hopes for the future as the car circled around from one mountain side to another.

Suddenly, a restaurant popped up, all alone, like an oasis! We slowed down and looked at the old wooden sign. Its peeling white paint reminded us of late springtime in Upper Michigan when the patches of snow melt spasmodically on the weathered fields, making the mottled black and white design seen on a Holstein cow. The sign held onto its post for dear life as it cried out to us with its pitiful message, "Knot Hole Cafe "

"Shall we?" I asked.

"Let's."

We did.

The car muffler scraped raw rock as we bumped over into the space evidently set aside for parking. Momentarily we sat there, a little jolted, contemplating the ailing structure of the cafe, its bone-like posts bent arthritically as they supported the sagging porch overhang.

"Hardly the Detroit Ren Cen," I muttered.

"You can't tell a book by its cover," Vi quipped. "Let's go."

We locked the car doors securely and rechecked them before crunching our way over the wet gravel, up onto the porch to the old weathered door. There we held our breath as we turned the door knob. It kept turning, a free wheeler, not even oiled. Cautiously I pushed against the bar that protected the glass in the center of the door. Nothing budged, so I gave a determined push hoping to give the impression that I would tolerate no nonsense. There was a screech of protest and a scrunch of defiance as, behold, that old antique opened wide, admitting us into a brand new life with an unexpected series of experiences.

When we entered the cafe, two men were sitting on flimsy round stools at the counter talking with a waitress who was aimlessly smoking a cigarette near the three-gallon chrome coffee urn. One of the men was young, neat, and very large from his belt line to the stool.

"He looks like a Valentine upside down," I whispered after we had seated ourselves in a tattered, plastic-covered booth next to a window.

Vi chose to ignore my evaluation. She is good at that sometimes.

The other man was small and wiry, sat straight as a sign post on his stool. Yes, he did have sort of a pointed head; and yes, he did look something like an arrow.

Vi didn't even smile when I said, "Cupid's accessory?"

Eventually the waitress finished her cigarette, came over and said, "Do you wont sumthin?"

"Yes, a menu, please," I replied.

"Up yonder," she said, pointing to the hand-written sign nailed to the wall above the pass-through window opening between the kitchen and counter. The chalk scrawling read: "today's special 2.50."

"I hope your special is Lake Superior trout," I spouted thoughtlessly.

Yankee arrogance! I know that was how she interpreted me--and mine. Deadening silence compounded my sudden embarrassment.

"What is your special?" I asked, trying to sound apologetic.

"Two-fifty plus tax," was the reply with no evidence of surprise that a Yankee couldn't read plain English--written out.

"Tip ain't included," she added.

There was an alarming silence as I reflected upon this living drama with its Civil War lingerings.

Suddenly my brain flashed Thomas Hobson's three and a half century old law[2]. "I'll have today's special," I said, completely satisfied with my choice.

Turning to Vi, I asked, "What would you like, dear?"

Vi considered. Then she reconsidered, as if playing chess. She and menus have that mutual game-thing; it's perpetual. Then suddenly she, confident of the right choice, she said, "I'll have the today's special."

"Two specials," the waitress sighed through the window opening.

There was no sign indicating rest rooms, so Vi asked me where they were. When the waitress brought the flatware and water, I asked her.

"Out yonder," she pointed through the window.

---

[2]Hobson's Choice: an apparent free choice when there is no real alternative. (By permission. From Merriam-Webster's Collegiate® Dictionary, Tenth Edition © 1996 by Merriam-Webster, Incorporated.)

"You go first," Vi pleaded.

I returned, grinning, "You could have gone with me; it's a two-seater."

As we waited, the radio next to the cash register announced: "Thunderstorm Watch is in effect; possible flash floods in the area."

Vi pointed outside the window where two Rebel ducks waddled among the rocks under some sycamore trees. While one of the birds nibbled randomly at grass blades, the other nudged a couple of rocks around as if playing solitary hockey in slow motion. Then having scored to some degree of satisfaction, she settled down over them with a quiver, feathers a-fluff.

When the waitress brought the catfish specials, we told her about it. She shrugged, "Oh shore, that's how we raise so many rocks in Arkansas."

The catfish was good in spite of the heavy coating of grist which, like strawberry seeds, kept exploring the underside of my dentures. The fried okra was a new experience; delicious to Vi's palate. As we eyed the green beans boiled with pork fat, a voice from the window opening exploded, "Here, Lilly Sue, you forgot their poke sallet."

A middle-aged woman, sort of short and squashed down, gushed through the kitchen door and set a large bowl of greens in front of us.

"Just now made it," she said.

We thanked her.

Suddenly something arrested her attention. It may have been the weather report, the menacing threat of flooding. However, she said nothing.

"A muscle spasm," I thought, for she stood erect, her head and neck molded into a question mark doubly punctuated by the front of her upper torso.

"The salad looks delicious," Vi said.

"Not salad, Honey; *sallet*," was the response.

I could sense what Vi was feeling. She didn't mind her naked ignorance showing, but did not want the woman to feel offended that we didn't know that there is something significant, even special, maybe divine, that divides a sallet from a salad.

"Do you do the cooking here?" I asked.

"Oh yes," she responded proudly. "Been here three years, ever since my husband got kilt. He always said I was a good cooker."

"I agree with him," I said. "We're Jim and Vi Hilliard, new in Arkansas."

Quick as a wink, she pulled up a chair, a bit close for our comfort. "Yeah, I knew you wuz."

"You're quite observant," I said, complimentarily.

"Yeah, I guess I am," she admitted. "Are you a preacher?"

This rather surprised me as I beamed, "Why yes, how did you know?"

When she said, "I could tell by your wife," my high beam clicked onto dim. Evidently she thought this identification entitled her to the privilege of a mesmerizing discourse to bring some relief from the intruding thunder and lightning. She referred to her "Armageddon," her struggle between human and spirit, which she somehow alluded to as a struggle between God and Satan.

"I know the real me is in here," she said, beating her chest--not quite high enough. "But how can I get me out of myself?"

My mind wanted to investigate that intriguing thought, but my stomach was more interested in the catfish.

"You can't do it yourself?" I asked, marveling at how easily the greasy green beans slid down my throat.

"No, it ain't no 'do it yourself' job," she replied.

"Have you ever been to a counselor to help you figure it out?"

"I been to God," she answered cautiously, not sure if God qualified as a counselor.

I considered her reply as I looked at the poke sallet.

"Yes," she said, making a stab at the opportunity to continue, "I go to church Sundays and prayer meetings Wednesday nights. I sing in the choir, whenever it sings, and sometimes I teach Sunday School. But I still can't get me out of myself."

I thought, "Heavenly days, what is this all about?!"

What I said was, "Maybe it isn't you that's in there. Maybe you've skipped out like the Prodigal Son, and no telling where you're roaming around."

She was silent. I wondered if I had offended her.

Just then the door burst open and a gust of wind puffed in a teenager. He was a Native American. Everybody looked toward him but paid no attention except the young upside down heart on the stool. His face was friendly as he nodded recognition, but he made no other movement, nor did he speak. The Indian boy closed the door easily and sat at a table in the corner. He laid a .22 rifle across the table with no more regard than if it had been a toothpick.

"What do *you* want, Nation?" asked the waitress from behind the counter, emphasizing the "you" with a slur-tone.

"Coke," was the mild reply. He sat quite still looking out the window, though one sensed he knew every movement each person in the room made, and probably why they made it.

Several minutes passed before the waitress moved to get the Coke. Then in slow motion she took it over, set it on the table belligerently and took his dollar bill.

"Brother Jake over there thinks I'm too outward sinful." The cook motioned to the two men on the stools. "Do you think I am?" she asked.

I waited a moment, sensing that her question deserved more serious attention than I was giving it. Then I replied, "I've been listening to those other persons in you assert themselves, but so far I haven't heard from you, so I don't know what you're like."

She seemed eager to respond, "But these are all me! I'm pretty forward, all right; and greedy, foolish, boastful, proud and...and...even maybe a little lusty, you might say."

Silence...as if she had shocked me.

"Go on," I invited, thinking I might as well be listening to this as to the thunder outside. I had an urge to push the green beans aside, but resisted lest she take it as a gesture to include her.

"All right," she continued as if bracing herself for something like a flash flood that would wash away all of her sin. "All right," she repeated and took the plunge. "I'm all of those things and yet I still want to walk with God. I want to be like Jesus, but Brother Jake says I can't do that until I confess all my sins and get rid of them. Well, I've confessed them a million times."

There was a short silence.

Then with a hollow tone in her throat she said, "Well, not 'zactly for sure, you understand, but I can't get rid of them."

I was sure she was not boasting or teasing. Possibly the lightning of the impending storm outside had charged her need for confession inside.

"Is Brother Jake your pastor?" I asked.

"Oh hell no--I mean he used to be, but now I go over to the Church-a-Christ. Brother Jake has his own church in Dogwood, but it don't amount to much," she said nodding in the direction of the straight arrow and reversed heart sitting at the counter.

"So you're all of those things you've mentioned." It was a statement with a question hovering over it.

"I surely am," she replied in a way that left me dangling, thinking she was even more, and might want to talk about it, God forbid.

At this point my knife and fork slipped on the lubricated beans and a piece of catfish flopped over onto the table. Without batting an eye, her reflex muscles responded as she quickly picked it up and put it back on my plate. I didn't dare look at Vi.

"Which one of these 'yous' do you want to dominate you?" I asked, wondering how Vi was rating my poker-face.

"I want only Jesus to rule my life." It sounded like she was quoting something straight out of the Bible, but I wasn't sure.

"Then why do you hire all those others to do what you want Jesus to do?"

"Hire them! Hell, I don't hire them; they just come in without me asking."

"I think you hire them, and like a lot of Christians, you pay plenty for them to come in and guard you against Jesus taking over."

The silence was unsettling.

"I have to go now," she said suddenly, looking toward the door as an old gentleman entered.

Later, when I went to pay the bill, she was at the cash register. I looked for candy in the old-time glass counter, but saw only Tums.

"No candy?" I asked.

"Only them," she replied.

"Maybe I better take one," I said, trying to muffle the truth of the matter.

Suddenly I belched.

"Make it two," I added.

Turning, I saw the Indian boy get up to leave.

"Here, Nation, come get your change," the waitress called from the other end of the counter. The boy walked over and picked up his change from the counter, then left as quietly as he had come. His movements made me think of Caine in the Kung Fu TV series.

"You orta meet Brother Jake here," the cook said as she handed my change to me. The two men swiveled on their stools. "This here's Brother Jake," she said pointing to the arrow. "I don't know what your name is...they're going to live in New Autumn," she said all of this in one breath to us.

"Jim and Vi Hilliard," I said, shaking the arrow's hand, which felt strangely like a fish hook.

"Jacob Balaam here," the man said, "pastor of the Dogwood Community Church."

I acknowledged the introduction, mentioning that I had just retired from the United Methodist ministry.

"We're un-denominational," he added as if he had not completed the previous statement about his church. Then with tape-like precision, he began attesting to the time and circumstances which the Lord Jesus Christ had saved him.

"Is this your son?" I interrupted, motioning to the upside down heart.

"Yeah, that's Joey," he mumbled without looking at him.

"Joey, he won't let hisself be saved," he added as I turned to Joey sitting on the stool beyond him. When I did that, an amazing sensation came over me; I saw the boy's soul through his face! He was like silent thunder confirming unseen lightning. In him I saw fear and triumph, pain and perception. I saw precision. There was tender masculinity in this over-weight youngster who was on the threshold of manhood; perhaps sainthood, too, I thought. Joey stuttered a bit as he acknowledged the introduction. He gripped my hand firmly, almost appealingly. He was indeed, I thought then and so often later, a heart that was upside down. I also wondered later, "How can the Arrow shoot so often at the Heart and always miss?"

"You folks headed for New Autumn?" Brother Jake asked, interrupting my silent appraisal.

"Yes, we're retiring there," I replied. "How far is it from here?"

"Four miles as the crow flies, six and a half from Dogwood if you walk it by the trail, eighteen and three-quarters if you drive it from here," were his exact statistics. Bull's eye! Black and white!

"We'll be driving, I guess," I said.

"Watch crossing them low-water bridges," he said as if he were in the pulpit. "They're mighty treacherous in floody weather. Like the wiles of Satan, mighty treacherous."

With that he slid off the stool. Joey followed.

"Flossy, you put that on my tab," he said to the cook as they went out the door. Their 1976 Ford pickup hobbled over toward the highway, coughed and belched black smoke as it rattled out of view, though by no means out of sound.

The storm had rolled out as quickly as it had thundered in. We left the Knot Hole and drove on, our eyes greedily grabbing onto the awe and wonder of the scenery. The sun burst out as we were crossing the river on a little ferry near a hamlet aptly named Dogwood because here the dogwood blossoms dominated the hills and dales. We were almost there, our retirement home, our threshold to new horizons!

By these horizons the old Biblical Abraham went out not knowing whither. "Westward ho!" our nation's pioneering cry. By it Vi and I departed the shores of Gitche Gumee to that ol' rockin' chair down in the Arkansas Ozarks for maximum pulsation at minimum effort.

Perhaps it was the mystery of the unknown that caused us to choose this location among the many we had considered. There was something about this particular area that seemed to fulfill our retirement desire for a brand new "Everything."

Here, two sub-cultures have come face to face with each other; i.e., Arkansas mountain people who seem to be in perpetual retirement, and Yankee "move-ins"[3] like ourselves, newly translocated into that hopeful bliss.

The beginnings of our retirement location had their roots in previous years as we searched areas from Maine to Florida, the Blue Ridge Mountains to the Arizona desert lands, where we might spend our tottering years. Old friends sometimes tempted us to remain in the previous parish settings, but the Unknown beckoned to us as it must have done to the pioneers of old.

Then something quite unexpectedly happened last winter while we were passing through Arkansas on our way home from vacationing in Arizona. Well, it wasn't exactly accidental, as the Ozarks had tempted us during previous passages through their beauty. It happened at a routine potty stop at an Arkansas Information Center. I had come out of the men's room, and faithful to the ritual of our gender, was waiting for Vi to appear. As I glanced alternately from my watch to the rest room door, my eye suddenly fell upon a little brochure on the counter. It began teasing me with its slogan, "Add New Autumn Leaves to Your Book of Life."

When at last Vi came out of the "Womens," I showed the brochure to her. It began to twitch our minds like a cat's tail before it pounces. We asked at the desk, "Where is this New Autumn located?" It was a two-hour drive.

We went.

The Realtor drove us through the exquisite village center, with its quaint little shops, past the bank, branch post office, grocery store, hair dresser, and weekly newspaper office. All of them were designed to create an atmosphere of relaxation along the little stream that fed into nearby Spring River. The maintenance of the buildings and grounds invited the visitor to come and stay. The Realtor pointed out the town houses holding on to each other up and down the hillsides, the waterfall and village park where, he said, "Children take their grandpas to fish and get wet." There was a recreational center where the older people could play bingo with gusto, and a miniature golf course for the very "advanced" golfers, unless they preferred to sit at coffee klatches. Here and there various churches snuggled against the hillsides, peaceful and serene among the trees and rock formations.

---

[3]Outsiders who migrate into Arkansas.

We passed the native stone service station, crossed over the low-water bridge, turned left and drove along the little stream. Over another low water bridge "that floods over when it rains a sprinkle or two," the Realtor said. Then he pulled into an open space near a beach where the little stream eventually joins the Mississippi River. An old-fashion swimming pool punctuated the river at this point. A sign, "No Diving from Bridge," garnished the scene.

Continuing his low-key sales pitch, our guide pointed out the hard-packed sawdust nature trail winding up through the trees and brush.

"This main trail makes a mile loop from here," he said, "but you can go farther along the river, up over the rim of Soaring Bluff, through Greasy Bottom Swamp, to the village of Dogwood, about six miles."

"Wouldn't it be nice to live here, near the trail," Vi said.

Right there, I'm sure, the price of the house went up, for the Realtor could contain himself no longer. "Your house is the the one made of native stone, up there from the trail, about five hundred yards. See?"

We saw.

It was magnificent! Not the house--the dream. We bought both. Come and visit us; we'd love to share them with you.

Chapter 3

Brother Jake

They say Brother Jake has been preaching in Dogwood forever. His wife doesn't look that old, but maybe he was there before they were married. He is hell fire and brimstone from A to Z; a foxy ol' coot who loves 'possum and turnip greens almost as well as pulpit pounding which focuses more on the "wily ways of Satan" than the loving grace of God. I guess it has been only in the past decade that he has changed his theme of condemnation from "them revenooers" to "them evolootioners." However, from what they say, he has never altered the thunder of his pulpit noise.

Brother Jake does not attach himself to any denomination. No doubt there are reasons for this. He just seems to do his own thing. He loves to preach, and given the opportunity, he will do so anywhere, any time. In the pulpit, his "Now in conclusions" are part of the body of his sermon.

"Better'n no preacher a'tall," someone said. However, the tone of their voice indicated there was some question attached to the truth of the matter.

"I like him," said another, "he's a good excuse for not going to church."

The village of Dogwood boasts of eighty-three registered voters with just about that many unregistered. Brother Jake is unregistered, his overt witness to the separation of church and state. A dozen people belong to his church; some attend off and on. I'm not sure just how he makes his living otherwise, but the grapevine tells its tales.

Brother Jake inherited his eighty-acre farm from his parents. The pittance paid by the church, if any, would hardly buy seed corn. The few beef cattle that graze contentedly on his acreage pay little more attention to his prophecies than the Dogwood residents. He is a good hunter, so poaching supplements the larder.

Vi and I attended his church last Sunday. There were three others besides Brother Jake, Joey, Mrs. Balaam and Ol' Blue. Ol' Blue is the preacher's blue tick coon-hound which kept us blessedly distracted by tapping his tail on the floor as Brother Jake preached. The tapping became more vigorous each time Brother Jake's fist hit the pulpit. Then during the sermon when the acrid fumes of hellfire became a little much, Ol' Blue got up, sauntered over to the edge of the front pew and staked it out for his own.

Nobody ever uses that pew anyway.

The location of Balaams' small cottage is about half-way between Soaring Bluff and Greasy Bottom Swamp, just off the hiking trail which leads to Dogwood. It's the typical little mountain dwelling with a porch protecting its two front doors. Why the builders blessed these small mountain dwellings with two front doors nobody seems to know. Perhaps there were multi-reasons, the least of which would be to provide rapid access to starlight potty convenience. Balaams' driveway comes toward the house from one direction, and leaves somewhere else; left to right, east to west, up or down, depending on where you happen to be standing, and how you look at it. Mrs. Balaam, whom everybody calls Sari Jane, says it reminds her of her husband. Along with their 1976 Ford pickup, are two old cars in the yard--one that won't run and one that might. In the front yard, to the left of the path, a cedar tree grows from a decaying stump. On the other side, some kind of prickly vine claws and scratches at a scrub oak.

When you approach the house, you will notice how the large rocking chair, made from twisted willow branches, dominates the porch. It is located up front center, positioned like a throne in the judgment hall of a medieval castle. Alongside the rocker lies an old blanket which should have been retired some years ago. Obviously, the blanket provides winter comfort for Ol' Blue, so nobody disturbes it. Lesser conspicuous porch furnishings include a straight-back chair, the proverbial gasoline washing machine and "other items too numerous to mention."

Sari Jane Balaam has two little gardens on the side of their rocky hill. She calls the one her chigger den; the other her petunia patch because, she says, "Petunias are like rocks in Arkansas, the more you pick 'em the more they come." She raises black eyed peas, beans, okra, purple hull peas and turnips. Mostly turnips.

"I ain't no good at raisin' corn," she admits. "The Reverent don't like it too much, anyway."

"Not unlessen it's converted," she adds.

The Balaams purchase their few staple goods at the Dogwood General Mdse. store. The sign painted on the front of the store reads, "Groceries, Feed, Gas, Post Office, Voting, Tax Collecting, and Other Produce." Obviously, from the paint peelings, the "Other Produce" had been added to cover miscellaneous items such as (I found out not long ago) the sale of moonshine in the back room. The county is dry, so the local constable looks upon this practice as a blessing in disguise. He owns the store.

"Besides," he says, "it keeps them bootleggers in tow."

The other day as I came to the Balaam place on my walk, I saw Brother Jake "comforting" himself under an oak tree at the back of his house near the trail. He invited me to sit with him, motioning to a nearby stump. We talked for some time; long enough for him to reach in his pocket and pull out a worn plug of tobacco.

"Here, have a chaw," he said, tossing it to me.

I've no idea how long he had carried it around in his pocket with no protection from either rain or perspiration. The thought of "having a chaw" caused my stomach to sound an alarm. I honored the warning and tried to keep a steady countenance because I knew my host was watching sideways as he spat on a bumble bee bumbling a dandelion near the end of his foot.

I handed the plug back apologetically. "Guess I've never taken a liking to it."

"Joey, he won't touch it, either," he said with ebb tide implications that I was short on real manhood. Again my vibes picked up some hidden import that had to do with Joey.

"Sari Jane, now, she likes it," he continued, "but I cain't afford her none."

Just then Joey came out of the house. The screen door slammed after him.

"Joey, how many times do I have to tell you not to slam that door!" Brother Jake yelled. "You keep trying to scare every deer and quail out of Arkansas!"

He then mumbled to nobody in particular, "He's growin' up to be just like them liberals and evolootioners."

Joey came over and sat on an old stump nearby. He acted as if nothing out of the ordinary had happened. I think he wanted to say something, but he remained silent.

"Joey ain't nothing like my Jakey-Boy," Brother Jake said in a manner that clearly conveyed the state of annoyance which he had toward Joey. "Jakey-Boy was my firstborn, but he died the same day Joey came squalling into this world. He got killed."

Nobody responded.

"A razorback," he continued. His voice became flat, reflective, deep-- painfully reminiscent.

He paused.

"Yessir, that dadburned razorback; biggest I ever did see. He was eleven years old, Jakey-Boy was. Sari Jane's time had come for this here un," he said, motioning toward Joey, "so we was going over to get Harriet--she was the midwife then--and on our way Jakey-Boy and me, we saw the tracks of the biggest hog you ever did see. So I motioned to Jakey-Boy to be quiet, though I didn't have to tell him. He was a born hunter and could track as good as I could even if he was just eleven years old. Yeah, he was already a good hunter, all right. So we trailed this critter through the oaks and soon heard him rootin' and snortin' around, crunchin' them acorns with jowls as big as Joey's ass there and twice as ugly. I took aim but just then a blue jay let out a squawk, and dadburn if that pig didn't come straight toward us. I was scared, just scared as I could be--for Jakey-Boy."

Another pause, accompanied with a shudder.

"Yessir, I was real scared for Jakey-Boy. I shot, but my bullet glanced off that there razorback's head like it was no more'n an acorn falling from the tree."

An awkward moment passed as Brother Jake stared downward into the horror of his experience. Suddenly he returned to the present.

"My bullet bounced off of his head just like that," he repeated, snapping his bony fingers sharply.

The ensuing silence was unnerving, but welcome.

Then Brother Jake took a long, quivering breath and continued, "He got my Jakey-Boy," he reiterated, his glassy stare piercing a deep-set torment.

"Jakey-Boy, my first-born."

Then with pulpit vigor his voice slammed down on the horrible, twisted memory of it all. "That dad burn demon from hell got him!"

His voice trailed off, mumbling, "He got my Jakey-Boy!"

Chapter 4

Christmas Gift

Today is Christmas! The landscape is crystal ice, sparkling in the cold sunlight! There is no sound outside in this pristine world where all is calm, all is bright, except the occasional snap of a tree branch. Whether the sound comes from far or near one cannot tell. In the living room Vi and I, and the fire in the fireplace are sharing each other, all three crackling with excitement. Periodically the fire will spew and sputter to get a word in. It enjoys being with us.

"Do you remember that cedar tree down by the trail last June with the trumpet vine?" Vi asked.

"Spectacular!" I replied. "There we were, walking along in the fragrant life of the new season and suddenly you exclaimed, 'Oh, look, Jim!' I thought you had seen a snake, but as you pointed through the opening among the underbrush, we looked at that tall perfectly shaped cedar with a trumpet vine winding around it all the way to the top. It was a veritable Christmas tree with natural garland."

"And there at the very tip of it, like the Star of Bethlehem, was that big bright orange trumpet blossom pointing toward the mountain top across the river! You could almost hear heaven's angel-chorus caroling, 'Glory to God in the highest!'"

"Let's go look at it now!" Vi said jumping up to get dressed.

"Now, in the ice?" I asked, but it was really an exclamation.

"Sure, come on!"

We half-walked and half-slid down across the lawn to the path, then crunched along on the icy sawdust trail to that magic location. Sure enough, there the tree stood, tall and majestic, its forest greenery sparkling through nature's icy finery. What a contrast from its earlier glory of garland and trumpet which we will see again next spring at resurrection-time.

Our next door neighbors came over awhile ago for a bit of Christmas cheer. She hesitated when she saw the mistletoe hanging from the clapper of the bell above the front door.

"Do you kiss everyone who rings your bell?" she asked guardedly.

"No," I said, "but it lets folks know that a hug and a kiss are acceptable, even likely, at our house."

We discussed the five-foot star I had made from one-by-fours and stood on the front lawn. Vi covered it with foil and edged it with silver garland and twinkling lights. From it we strung strands of wee crystal lights to the gable fascia. We admitted there was something theologically illogical about The Star rising up from the ground with its streamers beaming skyward. It just seems upside down, opposite, backward, or something. Nevertheless, it was the easy way, and our neighbor reasoned that the upward thrusts of beams indicate our reach toward God, "Hoping," she said, "that the angels in heaven are as happy as The Hilliards are in Arkansas."

Wasn't that a nice Christmas gift?

In our back yard, down toward the nature trail, is a growth of flowering quince, sometimes called japonica. It is a large round bush something like a lilac. In the early spring it is covered with beautiful orange blossoms. We think the cold spell in November, followed by sunshine and warm rain, must have sent untimely signals to it--something like they say about the chicken industry turning on midnight lights to spark two-eggs-a-day production--because Vi noticed the tiny buds on the branches in late October. On Advent Sunday she brought some of the twigs inside and incubated them in a vase of warm water. Sure enough, today, Christmas Day, there on the table in the midst of the ceramic Nativity, little leaves and bright orange buds are a-poppin', with the promise of more to come during the Twelve Days of Christmas. They refresh our spirits as we associate each bud with a particular friend. There are many of them, and each is as precious as the next.

Chapter 5

The Nature Trail

We love the nature trail. As the Realtor said, it makes a mile loop from the bridge just downstream from our house. People park their cars nearby along the river bank and hike, jog, streak or limp around the well-packed sawdust pathway. Our lawn slopes down to the trail just before the path starts to weave its way through the growth of vines and flowering wilderness. As you walk, you pass through an assortment of trees, some of which canopy the path. As you are walking through the spring-green hue filtering through the leaves, the full sunlight bursts forth and unexpectedly you bounce down across a ravine. Just past the ravine the trail waltzes you around a little hillock dotted with wild flowers of the season. When you reach the other side of this mini-Mount Olympus, do not be surprised if you see some of the Little People of the Ancient Cherokee Indians coming up from the river which is just beyond. It is best just to pass on without direct notice of these wee folk because if you stop and stare, they will disappear like Irish Leprechauns, and you will wonder if you really saw them. Walking along from this point you begin to play tag with the river as you return to the parking lot.

Along the trail, half-way around at the far end where it first meets the river--right near the habitation of the Little People--a smaller, less traveled trail breaks away and sneaks through the trees and brushes over to Soaring Bluff. From Soaring Bluff, by circumventing Greasy Bottom, this trail ends in Dogwood. A word of caution, though: the extended portion of the trail is a bit like life itself; it gets a little thorny when you try shortcuts.

Amid world difficulties, it is good to have a bit of nature like this at hand. This morning I arose rather early for a couch potato, and took to the trail some time before the sun began to peek up over Summit Mountain across the river. The day promised to be brisk and clear, full of something to discover. It's a day anyone could make into a dream. I could hear the chimes from the United Methodist Church, which sets not in the village center as one might expect, but a half-mile up among the crooks and crannies of the hills and hollows. It is a serene setting, overlooking the valley and dimensional scenery beyond. The church chimes can be heard far and wide, depending on the mood of the day.

This morning they were tone-perfect as I walked along, having taken the hike to let my soul rub elbows with nature. There was a heavy frost decorating the bushes and grasses; billions and trillions of flawless diamonds sparkling the sawdust flakes on the trail as I walked clockwise around the path. Then, in the second round, when I turned and walked counter-clockwise, something magic happened! The sun was at an exact low angle transforming the white-bright crystal-clear diamonds into sparkling *multi-color* prisms. What a phenomenon! It was like a shattered rainbow along life's pathway!

Suddenly from the midst of that wonder, came this silent message: "O Man, gather together your fellowmen and each of you pick up pieces of this wonder, fit them together, and establish my Rainbow Promise of human harmony."

What a message for our day, I thought, as I looked down at all those scattered twinklings which at the moment I perceived as inner linkings of humankind. Something tugged at my soul as I wondered if, indeed, our human-world could be that beautiful.

The church bells continued to echo their hope from hill to hollow, down across the river. Like Christmas tree ornaments, the notes dangled in mid-air among the cedar trees. I thought of the Peanuts comic strip where Schroeder plays his piano and Lucy takes the hanging notes and dangles them hither and yon, or just simply pushes them aside in a melancholy heap. Nevertheless, Schroeder keeps playing.

As I strolled along breathing in this new life and at the same time grievously aware of potential staleness that can hover over retirement, I met an old man shuffling along. He was old. I know he was because his plodding had that metronomic rhythm of resignation rather than resolution. I paused to greet him and discuss the rainbow phenomenon, but his ear-muffs blocked my efforts. He didn't hear. He didn't see. People often don't, you know.

Unlike the shepherds of Bethlehem, he had not noticed this thing that had come to pass.

Suddenly a raven croaked from a nearby tree. I looked up at him just as the sun looked down at me. Evidently this disk of old Ra, once worshipped by Egyptian pharaohs, was jealous that I had marveled at these wonders of rainbow confetti instead of him, their creator, for at once he began to collect the frosty marvels and fade them into simple dewdrops which soon evaporated into the earth from whence they came.

"Nevermore," quoth the raven as he took flight from the tree branch. Nevermore would I experience such a phenomenon--except--except even then the church bells were extending their *raison d'être* beyond themselves. I stopped to listen, and when I did I felt another tug at my soul, again connecting the created to the Creator.

There is no staleness in retirement--unless one invites it.

Chapter 6

Springtime in the Mountains

Many places have beautiful, invigorating seasons, but here in our little Ozark Eden the variety of springtime experiences surpasses all. The prolific species of flowers and birds, the greenness and fresh bouquets in the air are like Christmas-time when all of us are pulled together in heart and mind--perhaps soul, too. I wonder that Jesus wasn't born in the springtime. Surely he is reborn here among God's other splendid creations, and annual re-creations. I am sure for His Second Coming, He will choose this place rather than war-ravaged Jerusalem.

Last week we had an absolutely marvelous time sightseeing in northwestern Arkansas. Eureka Springs is an old Victorian summer home location of pure nostalgic affection among the Ozarks. It is a hodgepodge of gingerbread homes, multiple in size and shape, not only side by side, but sandwiched in from top to bottom, up and down on steep friendly hillsides. Some of these old homes have been converted into bed-and-breakfast places, one named "Arsenic and Old Lace," which is not where we stayed.

The town has now become a tourist attraction with some art galleries, a variety of artisans and musical entertainment. Ripley's *Believe It or Not* has featured several of their oddities, one of which is entering a church through the belfry.

On our way home we had breakfast at The Hillbilly Restaurant. As soon as we walked into the place we had an impulse to say howdy and take off our shoes, put a straw in our mouth and pick up a mountain dulcimer. The freckle faced waitress in blue bib overalls and battered straw hat took our order--"Hillbilly Special" for me, toast and coffee for Vi. The "Special" came on a tub-size platter: three fried eggs, a slab of hickory smoked ham, fried potatoes, bowl of white gravy, a fresh biscuit weighing close to a pound, all garnished with fruit. My stomach began to groan as soon as the platter clunked onto the table. Soon a very huge man, belt size sixty-six I suspect, came by patting his stomach and said, "If you need a bigger belly, we've got 'em."

Good grief!

The waitress tied paper bibs around our necks, and said loudly to all the breakfasters in the room, "If this man eats all this he can lick any hillbilly on the mountain!"

Vi nibbled; I ate. The people-atmosphere was congenial, jolly and full of clowning. It felt family-reunion-like.

After eating almost all of the whole serving (well, not quite), I stood up and roared like a rutting buffalo to the whole dining room, "I ate it all, and am ready to butt up against any hillbilly in the Ozarks!"

A young he-man from across the room stood up and said, "I'll take you on, Old Man."

"Any hillbilly but you," I replied quickly, "because you're my friend."

They laughed, of course, and I, unable to relinquish the spotlight-moment, added, "And because you're my friend, you can pay my check."

He started toward me, Refrigerator caliber, and grinning broadly as he approached, and with a theatrical flourish, took my check and said, "I will pay your check. And because you're my friend--you may pay mine."

I stood dumbfounded as he went back to his table of six athletic huskies, picked up their one check and handed it to me with a second flourish. Not being one to argue with power, I took it with a flourish (a rather weak one, no doubt). When I looked at it, I "unflourished," for not one of them ordered toast and coffee as Vi had done.

"Let's go," Vi said. I interpreted that to mean, "Let's get to H out of here!"

We did.

I would probably be foolish like that more often were it not for our fixed income--and Vi.

The next day was Sunday. We attended the little church in Pea Ridge. The minister had a three-year-old son who, from the Amen corner yelled, "Hi Daddy," just as Daddy started to pray. I guess the Reverend had to ignore it as he did, but I would have caved in. Real fathers must be a lot stronger in the face of sudden confrontation than we "would-be-ones."

In the afternoon we visited the Pea Ridge Military Reserve which is the location of the first major Civil War battle in Arkansas, March 7-8, 1862. Here, because of miscalculations among leaders and insufficient supplies, the Yankees defeated the Confederates. At first, Arkansas had not been eager to enter the War. A vote to secede from the Union had failed a couple of years earlier. After the War began Arkansas was among the last of the eleven states to secede.

On this Sunday when we visited the Reserve, the place was buzzing with Union foot soldiers and cavalry, the remains of those who had staged a re-enactment of the battle on Saturday. When some Yankee scouts picked up on my Okie-Arkie accent, they sought to arrest me as a Confederate spy. My Arkansas drivers license only whetted their design. They let me go, however, when they found out I am married to a genuine Upper Michigan Finn.

Chapter 7

Moonbeams and Turkey Buzzards

Late last evening Vi and I walked down to the river. The moon, full and sturdy, watched us as we sauntered along softly to the center of the low-water bridge. There we stopped, transfixed by those grand twilight shadowings which have the power to infuse all things unto themselves.

Then, would you believe it: as we stood there in the middle of the bridge, the moon suddenly dropped into the water! Without splash, it lay there in the stream, rippling and wringing, wrenching and wrestling and warping, anchored to that moment in time and place. We looked at it, utterly astounded! That heavenly body, so close!

Watching from the bridge, Vi colloquialized one of her instant Haiku poems:

> Straining shifting moon
> Holding yourself together
> The world is like that.

Suddenly a night bird swooped by, and when we glanced up at it, our golden disk immediately returned to its sovereign throne above the night. Its beams reached down and wrapped us in its glow. Upstream the fireflies resumed their ballet, punctuating the warm darkness as far down river as our visual transgression would permit. In that splendor of silence, night began to pull its blanket over all visible things. We knew it would. Even so, in New Autumn, night is beautiful.

Slowly, reluctantly, we turned homeward. Of course we looked back--several times--and watched the wild honeysuckle and trumpet vines wave in silhouette, their fragrance complimenting the delicate view. Then, they, too, vanished as we eased our way through the fresh summer night bouquet, up the pathway from the river to our house.

You simply must come visit us--in the summertime when the moon is full, and the fireflies stir the imagination.

Vi has been altering some trousers for me. They looked magnificent in the catalog pictures, accenting those sleek young muscle-models who revealed naught of common mid-saggings such as mine. So Vi, bless her, adjusted them the best she could to fit what definitely is not Playboy fantasy.

Anyway, I wore them this morning when we walked down to the village center and picked up the mail. We strolled along, hand in hand, past the waterfall in Fish Creek Park. There we sat on a big rock and read the mail. It took six days for a letter to reach us from friends in California. Does that mean that California is in the slow lane of Arkansas? Or is it that Arkansas has finally been drawn into a fast lane?

On our way home we crossed the low-water bridge spanning the river. Then we left the roadway and walked down through a meadow along the river bank. It is a nice little path, on the opposite side of the river from the nature trail parking area. The warm sun touched our backs. Birds twittered to us as we lingered along. We came upon some large rocks jutting out into the stream with jolly little ripplings bumping against them.

"Let's take off our shoes and dangle our feet in the water," Vi said. So there we sat, just as excited as the school of minnows which darted all around counting our twenty toes.

Suddenly Vi pointed toward a turkey buzzard which sat up on a tree limb just across the way.

"Something vaguely familiar about that old bird," she said.

I knew from the tone of her quip that I should have ignored the whole thing, but of course I looked up. There he sat, tottering on his perch, bald head and drooping shoulders. Apparently he took a dim view of Vi's observation because he took flight. As soon as he rose from his perch, he bumped against a tree trunk, then flapped around in a few staggering circles as if he had forgotten which way to go or why he had gotten up in the first place.

"Yes," Vi repeated, "something familiar, all right."

A little portentous, that impersonation. None the less, we rejoiced because life is like that, and we are all pulled together in it. Opportunity is forever at hand, dipping itself into itself, always coming up with something new even if it is no more than the enjoyment of an analyzed caricature of a turkey buzzard.

It is dusk, now. Vi and I are sitting out on the porch, awakened to fresh pulsations as we watch the evening shadows stretch long and friendly across the lawn. We know that tomorrow life will start all over again, and again it will extend itself into new horizons for whosoever will.

Chapter 8

Dogwood Constables

Dogwood is a lonely, lovely location; a little gold star stuck on the shores of White River. Limestone cliffs protect the village to the east, and the rolling river holds it in place to the west. The endless vision of the river stretches southward like a county fair blue ribbon.

I have already mentioned entering Dogwood from the road, but coming into it from the nature trail is a must for everybody, saint and sinner. However, I would give warning to those who are short of wind and leg--or long on ego. The walk is about thirteen miles round trip from New Autumn, strenuous in places. Also the people of Dogwood are not famous for embracing strangers. Dogwoodites are clannish; they're very clannish. They are not snobs; they simply appreciate a respectable distance between themselves and "furiners." They live upwind from the rest of the world and like it that way.

Constable Lou Mercer's father and grandfather were constables in Dogwood before him. In the olden days this was an important position, especially in the isolated pockets of the Ozarks where a stronger hand of the law seldom reached. In the pre-World War One days the constable carried legal authority, not nearly as much as in Medieval days, but enough to make the job worth while. Today, however, it is simply a printed word on the election ballot which lends to the plausibility of assumed responsibilities. The Ozark voter seldom questions this segment of law and order, even though the winning candidate often exaggerates its consignment. The simple name, "constable," snuggled in among the names on that awesome voting ballot is impressive to those who identify with the candidate and with the elective system. The position itself is in retirement--no salary, no authority, no clock, no--whatever else those "Retired" bumper stickers say.

The office of Constable carries no recompense unless one has the power to press one's own authority into the position by unchallenged force, and then from that, bleed whatever values might come through it. The Mercer dynasty has worked steadily at the fine art of developing these pseudo responsibilities into this beneficial assumption; i.e., that the people regard whatever the constable does as legal, lawful and hallowed. In Dogwood, even today, by the authority of community consent, he is their protector. This is the position Lou Mercer inherited by "count of vote" from his father, Charlie Mercer, who likewise or otherwise inherited it from his father, Lance Mercer.

The court house archives hold a number of accounts from the old days, some hand written. One of them, dated May 4, 1868, written by Constable Lance, reads as follows:

On my way home after I went over to Copperhead Pass and warned Hecker that the Feds was pushin for stricter enforcement of the moonshine traffic I heard a hog squeal down in the bottom. I knew that it was them Slogum brothers which are hog rustlers, and sure enough I caught them red handed reshaping the brands on them hogs' ears. So I snuck around through some trees and bushes and just as soon as that hog stopped squealing, I said, "Hold it, you Slogums; you're under arrest." Both of them looked up at me and down the hole in the barrel of my rifle and they knew they didn't have a chance, so the one that held his knife, he threw it down and didn't attempt to throw it at me. I hauled them both in, and let the men in town do what they'd been wanting to do for a long time. We hung them hog rustlers, both of 'em, right out there on that big oak in front of this here store[4].

Evidently the "revenooers" did get tougher on the moonshiners because some time back when Lou Mercer was talking about his father, Charlie, he said, "My pa won some local votes and free licker one time by leading some of them arresting officers astray when they were searching out some of his moonshining friends. Smithson was their name; big family of them spread all up through there, and most of them voted, two or three times, at every election. Anyway, Pa led a couple of those no-good revenooers down into that big ravine over on the other side of Saber Mountain where he knew this big she-bear was keeping her young cubs. When that old she-bear came roaring out of the brush, Pa, he "accidentally" stumbled against one of the revenooers just as that good for nothing squeezed the trigger, and that old bear, she let it be known that *she* didn't like revenooers any more than the moonshiners did. They all dashed to the nearest tree, but that big mamma was mad and she wasn't gonna let any of them off that easy, so up the tree she went after them. Lucky for those

---

[4]The original Dogwood General Mdse. store building facilitated the "court" in those days.

guys, the tree stood on the brink of that limestone drop-off at the south end of the ravine, and you know there's that big pool of water down below it. Well, Pa, he and them revenooers, they climbed out on a far-reaching limb and the limb broke and all three of them together dropped down in that pool--a good thirty feet, it is. Man, that was a drop!

"Well, that old mamma bear, she grumbled a bit and then finally backed down the tree and went to her cubs.

"Them revenooers...well, they grumbled some, too, but Pa said they was happier about escaping with their lives than they would have been if they had arrested the moonshiners.

Chapter 9

Joey

Early this morning Vi and I decided to drive to Dogwood, take the ferry across the river and have lunch at the Knot Hole Cafe. When we arrived at Dogwood, we were a half-hour ahead of the car ferry schedule, so we drove up town which means the main street of two and a half blocks.

"Look," Vi said, pointing across the street.

I stopped the car over on the side of the street and watched.

A young lad had just come out of the store with a bag of groceries in his arms and a rifle slung across his shoulder. Two other boys, one a huge young man about sixteen years old, and the younger built something like a short broom straw. They walked up to the boy with the groceries and said something. The boy started to step around them, but again they barricaded his pathway.

"Isn't that the Indian boy we saw at the Knot Hole Cafe when we first came to Arkansas last year?" Vi asked.

"It sure looks like him," I replied.

"What are they doing to him?" Vi wanted to know.

"I don't know. Let's watch."

The Indian lad kept trying to avoid the two, but with no success. Suddenly the small kid dropped to his hands and knees behind the Indian, and the bully shoved him backward with his doubled up fist, saying something about "stinking Indian get out of my way."

The bag of groceries fell to the sidewalk and split. A five pound sack of flour and a plastic bag of macaroni burst open. The lid had come off a small box of .22 shells.

Vi and I got out of the car and as we walked over to help the lad recover his merchandise, Brother Jake pulled up and parked his pickup at the curb nearby. He and Joey watched as we approached the three boys.

I heard Joey ask his father, "Shouldn't we help Nation?"

"We ain't going to help no Redskin, you know that," replied Brother Jake. "They don't deserve protection from us God fearing soldiers of the cross."

The boys did not see Vi and me approaching them. The larger boy kicked the sack of macaroni and scattered its contents.

"I dare you to pull that gun on me," he said to Nation who was replacing the rifle strap over his shoulder.

"Yeah, you just try it," said his smaller companion.

"It'll be the end of him if he ever does," added the older one, again jabbing the Indian boy in the chest with his fist.

Then the younger boy saw us approaching and signaled the older one. They turned on their heels and went into the store. The larger one looked back and under his breath snarled, "I'll get you next time." The younger one turned with a grin and said, "Yeah, we'll get you, Nation."

Without a word, I began to help pick up the macaroni while the boy who was called Nation picked up his .22 shells. Vi, seeing the predicament, quickly went into the store and came out with a couple of new paper bags.

When Brother Jake disappeared into the store, Joey came over. The Indian boy began scooping up the flour with his hands the best he could, awkwardly putting it in one of the bags Vi held for him. Joey and I retrieved the other items.

"I'm sorry, Nation. Rudy's a big bully," Joey said apologetically.

"Yeah," Nation replied.

Then, to all of us he said, "Thank you," and with no evidence of emotion, calmly went his way.

"Who is Rudy?" I asked.

"Oh, just a guy around town. His dad owns this store, and is also the constable. Rudy likes to pick fights, and Nation would fight if there wasn't any other choice. He'd get mobbed here in town if he did."

"We saw Nation at the Knot Hole Cafe when we first came to Arkansas," I said. "You and your father were there. He seems like a nice, quiet boy."

"He is. He's my friend," replied Joey.

"What are you and your father doing today?" I asked to make conversation with Joey.

"Papa's going fishing as soon as he gets some tobacco in the store. He's going down river, so I'll walk back home."

"Don't you go fishing with him?"

"Naw, he says I scare the fish."

"Why don't you come with us?" Vi invited. "We're just driving around today."

"Yes," I added, "we'll have lunch at the Knot Hole Cafe and then we could drop you off at your home on our way back to New Autumn."

"Excellent idea," Vi said enthusiastically. "I'll buy lunch for you boys."

"How about it, Joey?" I urged. "Come along."

He hesitated, then said shyly, "We--we'd have to wait till Papa leaves."

We understood.

"Meet us down at the ferry," I said as we started for the car.

Later he came down with the ferry operator who said he had been "huntin' time in the store." I suppose that was his way of saying he would have killed some time if he could have found it.

We drove the car aboard the little conveyance which tugged at the cable stretching across the river. Then with a little "toot-toot" from the whistle, we chug-a-lugged across the water, Joey in Seventh Heaven as he entered into this unexpected holiday.

The ferry-man was a talkative guy, short and jolly with a squeaky voice.

"It looks like I'll be out of a job here in a couple of years," he said.

"How's that?" I asked.

"Because they're talking about putting a bridge across the river."

"Where will the bridge be located?"

"Right over there where that knoll is," he said, pointing to a little rise along the bank.

Then making the most of his interested audience, he said, "Some years back, during the flood of--I've forgotten what year--the cable broke and the ferry boat was washed down river. There is a law in Arkansas, or at least there was at that time, that says whatever is washed up on shore from the river becomes the property of the landowner. So this ferry--this very one," he emphasized, "broke loose from her cables and was washed downstream on this farmer's property."

He left the story dangling as he stepped over to adjust a gadget on the engine.

"What happened?" I asked.

"Oh, I had to pump the throttle because the engine was choking up," he replied.

"I mean when the ferry was washed up on the farmer's land," I said.

"Oh," he said and then paused as if I should have known what happened without having to be told. "Why, Ol' Cy, he sold it back to the government."

"Yes sir," he said as his means of livelihood jolted against the bank, "that bridge is going to change this whole area."

We arrived at the cafe soon after eleven o'clock. Lilly Sue, as usual, was standing at the counter by the coffee urn, looking at a newspaper, puffing more smoke from her cigarette than the river ferry had exhaled from its smokestack. She paid no attention to us until we settled in a booth and the cook called to her through the pass-through window, "Hey, Lilly Sue, there's somebody else come in."

With a sigh, spawned from a mixture of resentment and resignation because of the interruption, she closed the newspaper and brutalized her cigarette stub in the ash tray on the counter. Then, without looking our way, she grunted, and came toward us.

"Be nice," Vi said under her breath.

"The menu's up yonder," she said nodding her head sideways toward the old sign above the see-through hole into the kitchen. It was the same as last year: "today's special 2.50."

"What would you like, Joey?" I asked.

Without looking up he asked, "Could I have the special? The hamburgers here aren't much to brag about."

"I'll have the special, too," Vi said quickly, interrupting the questions I was almost asking about the hamburgers. My wife has that talent-- knowing when I'm going to inhale and what I'm going to exhale.

"So will I," I replied resignedly.

"Three specials," Lilly Sue called out as she walked by the see-through window to get our water.

When she returned, I simply couldn't resist asking, "By the way, Lilly Sue, what *is* today's special?"

Without blinking an eye or checking the menu, she replied, "Two-fifty plus tax. The tip ain't included."

"Well," I said in a Lilly Sue monotone, "at least the price hasn't gone up, but the tip just went . . . ."

Vi's under-the-table aim hit on target. I flinched and made some sort of guttural sound that must have sounded like a muffled sneeze to Joey because he looked over and said, "Bless you."

Vi was unable to camouflage her victory.

There were several people in the restaurant. We had chosen the window booth where Vi and I sat on our first visit there. The two ducks we saw last year were outside under the tree, only this time the mother apparently had discovered the folly of trying to hatch rocks (there were plenty of rocks around anyway), so she was prevailing upon the drake to help with the household chore of building a nest. However, he was more interested in chasing a grasshopper which kept teasing him by hopping just beyond his waddle.

A middle aged couple sat in one of the booths against the wall opposite us. They were Afro-American. Three men of local native character sat at a table in the center of the room. Two women, apparently wives of the men, were talking at the end of the table near us. One of them was breast-feeding an infant.

"I'm plumb dead," she said to her friend.

"You're perkier than me," replied her friend. "My twelve year old ain't been home for two days."

"You don't suppose he's lost up in the hills?" inquired the other with no great interest.

"No," replied the other. "No, Ol' Tiger's with him. They know their way around and neither one of them knows how to get lost. It's just that Sam had some trouble at school, so wanted to take a few days off. That seventh grade teacher they've got is something else. He tries to make them learn even if they don't want to. Everybody thinks he's a queer."

"Yeah," replied the other. "I've heard about him. They oughta tie him up and let the skeeters bite him."

"That'd be too good for him," was the response.

One of the men's voices rose above the others, saying, "Cy, my young shoats are getting drunk on your corn squeezin's."

"Well, that's all right, Cal," replied Cy, "corn squeezin's is good for them."

"It ain't that," returned Cal, "but you know that ol' breedin' boar of mine is nasty as they come to begin with, and when he gets some corn squeezin's in him he gets nastier."

"Just like you, Cal," cackled one of the women.

Cal paid no attention. By now, he was telling the other men about "that ol' pew" outside the front door of their church. The Weight Watchers had met at the Church of Christ the other day when he went in "to tell the preacher off." It seemed that some of those "female weighties" had come out and smoked cigarettes as they sat next to each other on the pew.

"You shoulda seen the scallops they left on that dusty old pew," he exclaimed with a guffaw.

I must have laughed a bit, too, because Joey glanced up at me.

Vi, turning her head from the view outside the window, asked, "What's so funny?"

I never did tell her.

I was uneasy about the way Cal kept watching the black couple at the table over by the wall. His two male friends also glanced that way occasionally, but the women paid no attention.

"Joey," I said abruptly, "tell us something about yourself."

"There isn't much of anything about me to tell," came the reply.

"Do you like school?"

"I like school, but...."

He did not finish the sentence because Cal's voice rose abruptly from a low mumble to a volume increase loud enough for the black couple to hear. There could be no mistake in the tone of Cal's voice; it was seasoned with peppered animosity toward the couple, who had just gotten up from the table. They were well dressed. The lady moved toward the door while her husband went to the end of the counter where the cash register was located.

I am not sure that a red flag will distemper a bull as they say, but I am sure that the sight of those two black persons eating in the cafe triggered a reaction within Cal that caused him to strike out verbally with a phobic urge.

"Let me tell you something about niggers," Cal was saying to his friend who had not even mentioned the subject. "Back in the slave days they had brains enough to do some things, but these days they don't know nothin'. And they're too lazy to work, and they ain't got no souls like us white people."

All of this was abrupt, disconnected, but its message was clear and deliberate as Cal glanced at the black man who was paying his check at the end of the counter. The man made no response to the abuse, which incensed Cal all the more, or at least gave him an opening to courage.

"Yessiree," he continued with an air of smug confidence, "what they need is brains and souls, and somebody to make them do what they're supposed to do--and eat where they're suppose to eat."

"Some of them ball players make lots of money," said Cy who was clearly uneasy at Cal's sudden change of mood, for Cal's body was muscular-big.

"Yeah," replied Cal, "and the government ought to do something about that, but them nigger-lovin' Washingtoners just lets them keep going."

"Some of 'em on TV is smart," joined in the third man who had been silent until now. He had joined Cy's effort to check Cal's troublesome mood.

"Naw," Cal said, "they're told what to say. And they try to say it like a white man but they cain't do it."

"They talk Yankee, anyway," he added.

The black man transacted his payment and returned his wallet to his front pants pocket. He turned and faced Cal, though not looking directly as if to threaten or challenge, but quietly standing and listening, taking in the whole room.

With complete ease and understanding, he began to walk toward Cal's table. As he moved, he took out his pocket knife and slowly opened the blade.

"Sir," he said, "they call you Cal. My name, also, is Cal. You're younger than I am so when you were born your parents took my name and gave it to you. It's a good name. It's an intimate thing that you and I have in common."

He took the knife and drew the blade lightly across the top of his forefinger, saying boldly, confidently, yet with no condemnation, "We Cals have another thing in common. It's life-giving blood. You can see that mine is pure and red, just like yours. Your blood could save my life, or mine might save yours one of these days. Who knows?"

He paused just long enough for a drop of blood to fall on the unused paper napkin beside Cal's plate.

Slowly he closed the blade and returned the knife to his pocket. His wife smiled at him as he opened the door for her. I noted with wonder how easily he managed that difficult old antique door that caused me so much push and grunt. I thought of some of those huskies that twirl the Wheel of Fortune as if by their little finger, while most of the contestants expose their red-faced efforts. These were instant mental flashes. My attention immediately returned to Cal who sat without sound or movement.

"Who the hell was that?" he suddenly exclaimed, stretching his neck toward the window, watching the couple walk to their car.

"Do you know who they were?" I asked Joey.

"Yes. It was Dr. and Mrs. Johnston. He's the County Commissioner on Education, or something like that. He visited our classroom just before school let out last week and told us about Mrs. Sanderson."

I was so proud of Joey. He said it just loud enough for Cal and his friends to hear him.

"Who is Mrs. Sanderson?" Vi asked.

"She's a school teacher but she can't work any more because she has to be in a wheel chair all time. She and her husband were in an automobile accident when they were coming to Arkansas from Minnesota to teach at New Autumn. Dr. Johnston said she would help any of us in school who needed tutoring during the summer to catch up on any studies, and it wouldn't cost anything. She would do it free."

"What does her husband do?" I asked.

"Oh, don't you know?"

He seemed surprised that I did not know who Mrs. Sanderson's husband was.

"He's our football coach, and he also our seventh grade teacher."

Then Joey leaned over and said confidentially, just loud enough for the folks at Cal's table to hear, "But he ain't no queer."

Chapter 10

Chigger-Boo!

The maintenance crew came along the trail this week and mowed down the jack-in-the-pulpit Vi had discovered. She was furious. Early this spring she had espied the little Bible thumper under a sycamore tree, and had adopted it as her very own spiritual advisor. No doubt about it, there was something special about that little loner, brave and solitary in his dubious mission. When I asked Vi what his mission was, she replied, "Why, preaching retribution to the chiggers, of course." Then she added, "Sinful little creatures, those chiggers."

"A nuisance and annoying," I said, "but sinful? How?"

"Why, they're sneaky. They appropriate parts of your anatomy with no shame or apology."

Well, this called for careful consideration. The Golden Rule passed in review: "Do unto chiggers as you would have them do unto you." That didn't make much sense because if we would have the chiggers leave us alone, then in turn we must leave them alone.

"No way can you leave a chigger alone," Vi argued, "not when they bite right. Besides, it would be unChristian not to attack those base little sinners at least with the conventional weapons of iodine, Clorox, flaming gopher matches, and appropriate incantations."

She had a point, so the Golden Rule was out.

"Pray for your enemies." Good--until you try it. It had no effect on those little subjects of Satan's lower realm.

"I know," I exclaimed at last! "We'll apply mind over matter! Make yourself bigger than the chigger! Keep saying to yourself, Vi: 'I'll be jiggered if I'll be chiggered.'"

So far it hasn't worked. I know it hasn't, because just now Vi began to scratch her thigh.

I began to hum a tune. It had no purpose—no rhyme or reason—until she asked, "What are you humming? I've never heard such senseless bombination in my life."

My senses picked up.

"Oh, it's just a diggy little ditty. I call it, 'Oh, to Be a Chigger.' It goes like this:

>Two little chiggers on Vi's left thigh
>Two little chiggers will try and try
>One'll get scratched and the other will sigh
>Two little chiggers just itchin' for Vi."

Vi reached for the rolling pin; I the back door.

Chapter 11

Soaring Bluff

For years they have been "fixin'" to pave the graveled road from New Autumn to Dogwood. It will be a shame if they ever do. The little road is narrow but it's awfully comfortable. Sometime when you're driving on it, watch how it nudges the trees as it wiggles and waggles, and tangles its way along the edge of the valleys. You can tell that the hills have graciously accepted this little interloper by the way they let it caress them. I think that's because when it first came to them it did not puncture and scrape their sides like modern excavations do. This little cow-trail turnpike just gently snuggled in among the hills and stroked their curves and patted their tummies. Everything has been loving harmony between them ever since.

Notice, too, how this tiny two-way artery slows up and lingers a bit when it passes Brother Jake Balaam's place. After that, though, momentum increases on a downhill ease to a rather careless grade around Greasy Bottom, all the way to the very spot where the Dogwood ferry boat climbs up on the bank of the White River.

This road between New Autumn and Dogwood does not parallel the nature trail, but a couple of times the two come within a stone's throw of each other. The road is approximately seventeen miles while the extended nature trail is half that distance. A motorist can see the front of Brother Jake Balaam's house from the road, while a hiker can see the back of it from the trail.

The Balaams have a mule which, when not resisting Sari Jane's garden plowing, stands in front of the sagging house and watches the Fords go by. Vi is infatuated with the amiable old fellow. Every time we pass by, it looks up and winks or twitches its tail, depending on the visible extremity. Vi returns the courtesy with a blessing.

There are a few dwellings down through the hollows of this area, but you do not notice them because you're too busy window-shopping the grand views of varied dimensions, especially when the road begins the steep, very steep, downgrade past the beautiful parkway of trees and vines before it reaches the Dogwood ferry. People do not use the road in inclement weather; i.e., if there is a skiff of snow, or a bit of ice, or even heavy rain. Dogwood residents "just wait it out," grateful that there will be no intrusion of outsiders. However, if you want *the* scenic drive in Arkansas, take this one. I know of only one place that will top this cinematic thrill and that is atop Soaring Bluff along the nature trail that starts near our house.

You may reach Soaring Bluff by walking the trail, or by driving and parking your car near that huge bolder where the little cow-poke trail swerves around the mountain near the old Bailey farm. Nobody lives there any more; the house and barn are all gone; nothing remains except in the early springtime the bed of jonquils mark it as an old houseplace. After you park your car, you walk across a small pasture past a pond, and then enter a grove of cedars. There, through the trees down across a little ravine you enter a veritable Garden of Eden minus the fig trees. Keep your clothes on because a fig leaf would afford no protection from the mosquitoes which thrive there. They are fierce, big enough to fly away with a dozen fig leaves, or they would just as soon tear the britches right off of you. A little way from the ravine you come upon the Nature Trail which extends from New Autumn to Dogwood. You join this trail and walk for a few hundred feet through the trees and vines arching above you.

Quite abruptly, you step out onto an unblemished clearing! The view catches you totally unprepared. There on the brink of a three hundred foot limestone cliff a spell-binding vista literally holds you unto itself. You may even hear Homer's Sirens of old competing for your terrestrial mortality. Someone described it as the "Come forth" call which Lazarus heard in his tomb. Regardless of these sensations, one thing is sure: something of yourself will be absorbed, and you will like it.

As these emotions react within you, an unbelievable array of dimensions, one after another, move into sight and feeling. Never could the hues, colors, shapes and designs be matched, even on an Arkansas patchwork quilt.

They say part of the infamous Cherokee Trail of Tears of 1838 went through this area when the United States government forced the last of the Cherokee Indians in the East to abandon their homes and move by wagon and foot to the Oklahoma Territory.

There is a legend, a myth that may be true, about a Cherokee Indian child who saw his parents mistreated and killed during the Trail of Tears. I suspect the legend sprang from Nation's ancestors. In the little boy's search for his parents, he wandered into the mountains and nobody ever heard of him again--except, even yet on nights when the moon is full, one might hear his mournful sobbings calling to his parents. They say he crawled into a nearby cave where a she-bear had just given birth to her cubs while hibernating, and she included the boy-child among her little warm fuzzies.

A variation of the legend tells about timber wolves, when they heard the wailing of the child, sought him out because his cry sounded much like their mournful wail to the moon when they were organizing for a hunt. They comforted and nourished him. Years ago, bounty hunters exterminated the wolves in the area, but the child's cry remains. At dusk the sound changes to a young brave's voice calling for vengeance, a vengeance that would release his parents from their confinement to the nether world. This, then, would permit them to enter into the Happy Hunting Grounds.

I remember the first time I stepped out on the brink of Grand Canyon I gasped and suddenly stepped backward to escape the sensation of falling off into that great abyss. It is the opposite on Soaring Bluff where the force pulls you forward with a powerful urge to step beyond into some mysterious longing. It is a living thing. The emotions of the moment cause the scene to burst into unbelievable micro-macro dimensions of hues, colors, shapes and designs. Then the accompanying scenes in the distance begin to snuggle in close; so close that the treetopped mountains beyond peek at you like the bearded heads of the Seven Dwarfs from their blanketed feather bed. Then the dimensions, far and near, begin to mix with one another like the rich, intense lights of Aurora Borealis across the clear skies over Lake Superior on a crisp October night. Soon, quietly and comfortably, they begin to fade back into the horizons. Your burdens will want to go with them.

Let them.

Sometimes a fresh milky haze covers the depths, and you see the sharp ridges standing in military formation like dominoes ready to tap each other on the shoulder. And you are one of them, ready to be tapped.

At other times the world before you is clearly unclothed. Like your soul, it is unblemished. You look at it and know that God sees it with you. Watch closely--don't glance away, or you will miss God as He nods His head and again breathes those sacred words, "It is good."

You then know that you are His creation.

One summer day during a series of rain squalls, a rainbow stretched from nowhere over to somewhere. Its beginning and ending were less definable than its glory. It confirmed a re-creation of that which is holy. It was God's timeless signal, clearly recognizable.

Another time, standing there, I thought of a visit I had at a Catholic nuns' convent. Of course there was no men's room at hand, so the Sisters directed me to a bathroom at the edge of the private sector of the nunnery. No problem getting there, but in my hasty retreat, after quickly and quietly returning the toilet seat to its original position, I made a wrong turn and found myself among the immaculate sleeping cubicles of light blue and ivory. Panic struck hard! Some horrible sense of guilt and desecration engulfed me. Frantically, I got to Hail out of there!

Atop Soaring Bluff you may be profaning something you don't understand, but it is forgiving and you want to become part of it.

Last week when Vi and I were hiking the extended trail, we met Joey at Soaring Bluff. Together we stood there, looking out across the distances and listening to the silences.

Joey broke the trance, saying, "This is what holds the world together. When I come up here it puts me together, too."

"You don't seem like one who falls apart very easily," I said.

"My pa says I was born in pieces and he's never been able to put me together right," was his reply.

"Fathers sometimes jest about things like that."

"Sometimes," he said, and for once I heard what he said.

I looked at him.

"Are you serious, Joey?" I asked.

When our eyes met there was a union of rare understanding, a trust that needed no explanation. Any attempt at analyzing it would be like building sand castles at high tide. I shall never forget that moment. It contained no age barriers, no inhibitions, no shadows of doubt, no embarrassment. It held what a great Man once said, "Truth will make you free." It caused me to think that if I had a son, I would not waste much time pounding into him the virtues and vices of things that are right and wrong. I would develop a rapport of understanding and acceptance because with that kind of relationship, all of the other good things of life would most surely fall into place.

"You mean your father is not jesting when he says things like that?" I suggested.

"No, he's honest." Joey said. "He's honest in saying what he thinks. He tells all about sin, but I would like to know more about the other, what sin is not. Papa and I just don't think along the same lines, I guess."

"About anything in particular?" asked.

"Mostly about the Bible, I guess," was his reply. "I think the Bible is like a road map. It doesn't matter whether it's something God gave to us or something we developed ourselves. Either way it's a good guide. If we only follow directions it gives, we will do one of two things: we will either jump from one guidepost to another and never reach our destination, or we will wind up smack dab in front of Jesus, which may be just about where we were when we started. Most people simply move along here and there with the Bible, sort of smug-like. We say we believe it because we are taught to say that, and people would think we're not Christian if we didn't. People can't believe the Bible because they know so little of what it says. Nothing in the world has been misinterpreted and blasphemed more than the Bible. And the worst offenders come from those who claim to be led by the Spirit when interpreting it. Maybe I'm one of them."

Here Joey hesitated and looked a bit embarrassed. Or maybe he was surprised at himself. I was.

"Go on, Joey," I urged.

"It seems to me," he continued in a way that reminded me of that little pink drummer bunny on TV, "that if we Christians ever reach the goal which the Bible points to, it will have to be with Jesus Himself rather than spending a lifetime following directions that point toward Him, but never reaching Him. Every Tom, Dick and Harry tells us what Christianity is, and now we've become like those computers at school that need defragging. People's minds get all cluttered up with bits and pieces of sideline issues. They're like Ol' Blue when he chooses a down-hill scent because it's easier to chase. Our denominational doctrines are taught as gospel truth and they make us believe we are walking with Jesus when actually they're tying us in with certain people's interpretations of Scripture rather than to Jesus Himself. So we hobble along like the blind leading the blind."

"Gee whiz," I thought to myself, "this kid is talking to me as if he were my mentor!"

Which, indeed, he was. I felt refreshed, spiritually rejuvinated.

Joey continued, "You interpret a passage of Scripture one way, Papa another, and Nation's great grandmother yet another way, and all the kids at school have their shot at it. When you apply that to a billion other interpretations, then there's bound to be a lot of derailing from The Way, isn't there? That's where a lot of holier than thou prejudices are born and raised."

"It is true that Jesus said He was The Way, but I always thought Scripture acknowledged this," I said.

It was a weak defense, and I knew it.

"It does, and that's my point" came the immediate reply, "Scripture doesn't make any demands on us. That's why we love it and claim to stick to it so defensively. We can make it do what we want, even to the point of thinking it saves us. We can take favored parts of it and ignore unfavored portions. We can do just about anything we want to with Scripture. No one can do that with Jesus. Everybody likes us when we say we stick to the Bible. Nobody likes us when we stick with Jesus."

The kid was dead serious!

His battery hadn't run down yet, for he continued: "All the same, most Christians seem to believe their main goal is to get to heaven, as if heaven were simply a matter of escaping hell."

"What is heaven?" I asked.

"Some of the Bible writers describe it as streets of gold and all that. I never saw it that way. It's got to be something at hand, and there ain't much gold at hand around here. The only way I can think of heaven is like St. Paul said, 'Being at one with Christ,' and Christ was crucified and then resurrected. That's what I think heaven on earth is."

I paused before responding. I paused a long time.

"Do you think Paul was in heaven here on earth?"

"Yes."

"But Paul had his problems, his 'thorn in his flesh', just like we lesser Christians."

"There are no lesser Christians," responded Joey. "At least I don't see how someone can be not as good a Christian as another. You hear people say that, but good is no criteria for Christianity. One person may live a better, more honest life than another, but a Christian is a Christian just as God is God. It's like when we classify God as Holy. If we can do that, then we can also classify Him as something less than holy, even unholy. We can determine what Scripture is or is not--at least that was done at the Council of Trent when the books of today's Bible were voted on and determined. But we cannot determine what Christianity is. Christ has done that."

"Where do you get ideas like this, Joey!" I exclaimed rather than asked.

He quoted Jesus from Scripture: "You, a teacher of God, and do not understand these things?"

As I stood there dumbfounded, I thought, "I'm glad I never had a Joey in my parish."

Now, however, I wish he had been. Perhaps he always was and I knew it not.

Chapter 12

Anatomy of a Dishwasher
and Other Kitchen Appliances

Doing dishes with Vi is always a sunshine event. Let me tell you about it. First, this integral datum: she is left handed; I am not. This is important.

It's important, because recently she designed and furnished the new kitchen for our house. She had the cabinets and appliances installed according to her specifications. She did not include an automatic dish washer because she's afraid of the thing--she might get caught inside without an umbrella.

The garbage disposal is on the left-hand division of the sink, which means that while washing dishes she works left to right. This means, in turn, that her left arm reaches over her right as she puts the washed dishes in the rinse portion of the sink on the right. So far, so good. However...

When she washes the dishes and takes them out of the rinse water with her right hand and places them on the drain board, the sharp ends of the forks and knives are pointing the other way. By "the other way," I mean the opposite of another way, the right way as opposed to the left way. That is to say, when she places them on the drain board they face the left instead of the right way which is the wrong way. Round dishes, like plates, make no difference; that is, if they lean southward on the drain board. However, you take pointed objects like forks, knives, spoons...and butcher knives, ugh! When she puts them on the drain board they point left.

Now watch me try this: with the drying towel in my right hand, I reach to pick up those forks and knives--and butcher knives--which are pointing leftward. I must pick them up with my left hand, and it must be by their handles so they will point outward, not inward toward my stomach. Watch now: in order to get a handle on those weapons, I'm turning and squirming left, right, sideways, trying it forward, then backward. Soon they are jostled into a tangled mess. A very dangerous mess. So I back off and restructure my strategy. I turn around and try to back up toward them, but no help; they don't tolerate sneaks.

I've even tried to change the towel to my left hand so I could utilize my right for this feat. This worked well for a flickering moment--until I started drying that pack of arsenal with my left hand.

I don't know how they do it, these lefties, these south paws.

The circus doesn't end there. Placing said weapons in the drawer so they will lie in a left-handed position is almost as clownish as retrieving them. Ours is one of those plastic containers that has organized compartments which go sideways rather than some other way. Vi plants those doggone knives and things in the drawer as if she were preparing bayonets with the weapons pointing rightward. So now, I'd like you to try this: open the drawer, reach for the knives with your right hand. Yes, do be careful. Pick them up by the handles. Yes, of course, the blades point toward your innards. Take them over to the table anyway. Now try placing them on the table--properly!

There is no use to keep trying. But don't quit, either! I'll tell you why. Doing dishes with Vi is always a sunshine event because....

...Well, remember when you were young and you became bored to death in that "nothing to do" syndrome? Then your best friend came along and said, "Let's do something!" It didn't matter what you did, but the prospect triggered exciting possibilities. Boredom vanished. Dullness became bright, sunshiny.

Left-handed things become right with Vi.

It's Saturday morning before Labor Day. Vi just came in and said the refrigerator motor has been running for over an hour and she doesn't think it is doing its thing. Appliances of household necessities often start their Saturdays by not doing their thing. So Vi urges Mr. Fix-it here to give it a try because Arkansas repairmen are renowned for being easy going and laid back, which means they are unpredictable except on holidays and weekends when they are very predictable...and untouchable. So on this Saturday before Labor Day with a determination that to try and fail is better, I went at it, not too sure that a flashlight, screwdriver, pliers, hammer and wrecking bar would stop the motor. My efforts paid off, because soon after lunch, amid numerous grunts and mumblings, wrenching and body contortions, something within that maze of mystery went sssss. Then the motor stopped, which was the goal of my endeavors.

Chauvinistically I reported my success to Vi. She said nothing, but her expression was voluptuous. I didn't interpret it. The thing about it was that while the motor stopped, neither did it start. Not in the first hour, nor the third, nor later. It didn't do a frigid thing.

About sundown I became aware of a series of noises in the kitchen. Suddenly, a loud BANG! punctuated them. The refrigerator protested with a forceful "ssssss."

Another kick!! Wham!! Kick! And then, "Prrrrr."

"There!" I heard Vi exclaim, and I knew right then that that refrigerator was destined to purr.

Since Vi gave it those fix-kicks, it hasn't missed a P in its Prrr.

Chapter 13

Randy

His name is Randy. I learned that during the children's sermon early in the church service. I learned a lot more about Randy as the hymns droned on and the sermon kept flickering until I thought it would never go out.

We were driving around seeing the sights in Southern Arkansas, and had stopped at a small church, I've forgotten just where now, for Sunday morning worship. The outside sign attracted our attention: "Learning at 9:30; Preaching at 11:00." It was almost eleven, so we parked. This would have been a mistake had it not been for Randy.

Randy was a six-year-old who sat ahead of us with his parents. Well, he sort-of sat with them. Six-year-olds are entitled to their own stake in life, I suppose, and Randy was making the most of his "entitles." Like a pro, he fudged here and there, willfully infringing on the rights of others by intention, not happenstance. The traits of evidential design had found permanent lodging in this active young mind.

As I said, he sat in front of us, not in the first pew ahead, thank God, but the second. However, nobody was sitting in the pew between us. The usher had center-pewed Vi and me but we moved down toward the end so we could see between the heads in front of us and get a better view of what would be going on between the preacher and organist. I was a bit uneasy about moving to that end of the pew because it gave Randy and me perfect eye contact. I can communicate quite well with my eyes but Randy is better. Our approval, disapproval, praise, and appraisal, all had eye-talk. Randy received and transmitted perfectly with eye-com.

Randy's mother sat next to him; not close, but a respectable distance. She was cautious, and I don't think very trusting. His father sat next to her, on the opposite side of where Randy was stationed. I am sure he secretly congratulated himself for thinking ahead and wisely arranging this buffer. As it was, Randy had unto himself the whole four feet end of the pew, his immediate world, which he ruled not by restlessness, for this would invite the invasion of patriarchal force across the boundary line of his mother's lap. No, restlessness was not one of Randy's traits. Intent was.

The choir did not process in. It just sort of lumbered along doing the best it could with what it had. Randy randomly tugged at a robe as they passed his pew, pulling these selected choir members a bit further off-key and tempting them to...well, I'm not sure, but I have a good idea what temptations invaded their minds. However, I am sure that, as they sat front-center during the service, the thought of the return passage through the precarious Straits of Randy stood between them and worship concentration.

Before the pastor uttered a word of invitation to the children to come forward for their time with him, Randy left his pew and immediately staked out his territory on the top step of the chancel. No other kid challenged his four-foot space except a little blond girl who, when Randy defended his area, objected with adequate microphone volume. "Well, I don't see why I can't sit there!"

He had the answer to all the questions the pastor asked and some responses to questions not even voiced. Before the pastor knew it, Randy had taken over the "kiddies' sermon."

"You know what?" he asked the pastor.

Reluctantly the pastor asked, "What, Randy?"

"Susan's dog had six puppies yesterday and my dog, Jeffey, he's their daddy."

Proud as punch, this little godfather.

Randy did not join the other tots for Children's Church after their time with the pastor. I'm glad he didn't. Let me explain.

During the sermon I followed Randy's gaze to the ceiling fan located toward the chancel. As its blades turned lazily, we watched a wasp flying around the area, apparently wanting to land on a particular blade. However, every time he came in for the landing, the blade he had his eye on disappeared and another came around and knocked him into kingdom come. Randy made no objection to my joining his intriguing discovery which was going on in the upper region of God's House. Together we watched the wasp make another circle around the ceiling area only to come down and repeat the miscalculation. It reminded me of the preacher's sermon coming in to make a point but never quite landing it.

This common interest made us friends, Randy and me. It was a secret between us--just the two of us. It never occurred to me to call it off. Afterwards I wondered if God saw it as an attraction or distraction. That made me wonder if it was Christian or not. Jesus paid a lot of attention to the little children, but under different circumstances and probably in a different setting.

Finally I decided it wasn't all that worshipful so I tried to focus upon the pulpit. However, in order for my eyes to line up with the pulpit, they had to focus just above Randy's four-foot domain. This included his functions--or malfunctions, as the case may be.

This time he was standing on the floor, his flexible little back leaning against the seat of his pew. I noticed that his head and hands were floundering this way and that, his body language directing my attention toward the light-colored wall on the right hand side of the pulpit. There clearly on the wall, a spotlight from the left of the pulpit made a shadow-video of the pastor's every movement as he preached--just a pitch off-key from hellfire and brimstone. Nobody but my new friend noticed these shadow-movements. And nobody but he could have mimicked the movements so profoundly. I nudged Vi and pointed to both the shadow-movements and Randy's, but when Randy saw me include Vi, he immediately recoiled onto his pew.

I had betrayed him. Girls were not privy to these private adventures of "men only." It would be a few years before he would include any girl in his body maneuverings.

The pastor announced the closing hymn, and the choir began to recess single file down the aisle singing, "Only Trust Him." Suddenly, from the corner of my eye, I thought I saw the first chorister falter slightly at Randy's location. Then another, and the next. I peeked over and saw a hymnal on the floor, moving slowly, steadily out into the aisle. I looked at my hero. His eyes were upon me. They were communicating this message: "Stranger Friend, do you not perceive that this nefarious business going on in the House of God is derived from some foreign source?"

My return eye-com answered: "Bosom Friend, I have known you all my life, so do not call me stranger. I perceive that this nefarious business going on in the House of God is an inside job, namely you."

Each of us understood, and we were pleased for two reasons; i.e., the communications verified the accuracy of eye-com, and they expressed no judgment.

Friendship was restored.

Such is the way of children. Such was the way with Randy and me. I felt privileged, for here again, I was the only one in that whole crowd of big people to share Randy's inner-most self. The choristers could not see what was going on because they were too intent upon watching the words and music in their hymnals as they proceeded down the aisle. No other member of the congregation shared this moment of the Kingdom because their attention was upon getting ready to leave, dropping their hymnals loudly, carelessly, into the hymnal racks.

I never spoke to Randy; not one word. While we were singing the last stanza of the hymn, Randy's father whisked his family out the side door, so I had no opportunity to speak with my friend. Perhaps that is well, because often talk can spoil a good relationship.

I suppose I will never see Randy again. Not until I start to shave tomorrow morning.

Chapter 14

New Orleans

Vi and I are home from a marvelous four-day bus trip to New Orleans, Natchez, Vicksburg...fresh shrimp, ante-bellums, Civil War. Promenading New Orleans' river front, dinner in French Quarters at the Two Sisters Court, sinuously exploring Bourbon Street till past bedtime-- way past for Vi and me. At night, for several blocks, barricades keep cars off this street. Revelers are able, then, to walk all over to enjoy the attractions on the sidewalk and out in the middle of the street. All along the way, people sing and dance and play. Everybody has a grand time brazenly participating in their homespun sins or cautiously guarding their closeted fantasies. One businessman was barking the main feature of his establishment: "Topless, bottomless. No cover charge!"

Suddenly a man jostled Vi, dislodging the shoulder strap of her purse. He was a sailor, his sails fully spread three sheets to the wind. He had simply miscalculated the jib of the curb. His glasses fell off onto the pavement, breaking one of the lens. He picked them up and put them on, and through the shattered lens, said, "Ah, at lasht. I shzee the world azsh it ish!"

What a discovery! These sailors have it made, I'll tell you--especially on Bourbon Street!

The next morning we took one of those little buggy rides around the French Quarters with a driver who told us about the houses, eateries, and all. What history! What extraordinary ways of preserving both tradition and facilities, though a preacher might do more than just wink at some of these preservations.

During the day in New Orleans, a guide boarded our bus and took us all over the city, showing the main attractions including their huge city park. We stopped and leisurely walked through a cemetery with the guide explaining the family tombs where the body of the deceased must remain for at least a year to deteriorate in the warm humid underground before they are permitted to place another body in the same crypt. Their practice of interring above the ground is necessary because the underground sea level is so near the surface--just a few feet, depending on which curb you are standing on. We visited the "most modern aquarium in the world" where we walked through a transparent tunnel and observed the fish swimming overhead, under and all around, and where, in the bottom of each urnal in the men's rest room, was a bull's eye.

After dark we sat along the river bank and listened to the haunting singing of a young man who would spend the night sleeping on a park bench. He was singing "Danny Boy," his voice rippling across the wide river, then quivering back to shore where we sat. It tingled the spine. We regretted leaving.

The next day on to Natchez where we toured some ante-bellum mansions. One where the sixth generation still lives. The elderly owner and family mingled among us most congenially. Vi and I wondered, though did not mention it, just how comfortable it is to live under those huge twelve-foot high ceilings with only a little fireplace for heat. When we were viewing one of the larger bedrooms, I asked a hostess, "When was the last time this bedroom was used?"

She answered very primly, "Why the Master slept here last night; he sleeps here every night."

"Oh," I breathed, expressing my surprise that the social elite slept in their own bedrooms.

"They live here," she added.

It didn't matter that she failed to interpret my "oh."

Whether the rooms are comfortable or not, I'm sure the Porche convertible and Mercedes Benz parked in the driveway were.

Then a half-day tour of Vicksburg Civil War battle grounds with a little 70 year old lady as our guide. She was bright as a confederate bullet with twice the sting. She proudly pointed out a Methodist church where, as an infant, she slept under a pew, and now as a great grandmother, she "still sleeps in the same pew."

On our tour bus there was a middle age couple whose names were Millie and Willie. Frequently when someone mentioned having been somewhere or done something, Millie would say, "Oh, we've been there and done that." In the afternoon on the trip home, a couple of ladies in front of us were talking "women talk," something about going through menopause. Millie suddenly turned and said, "Oh, we've been there and done that."

The bus rolled on.

Chapter 15

Tweeker -Tweet

The tiny Trick or Treaters came first, perfect little vanguards for the seasoned army which would come after dark. Parents, usually the mother, brought them, these wee ones. She stood in the shadows while the little tots reached skyward for the doorbell. Our first guests were next door neighbors, two and four years old Dick and Jane, of all names.

"Mrs. Hilliard, I bet you can't guess who I am," Jane said as soon as Vi opened the door. Her costume made her look more like a little witch than she really was, even when she picked all the jonquils in our planter last spring.

Before we could respond, she peeled off her wicked-looking mask and said, "See!"

"Why, you're Jane!" Vi exclaimed.

"Yep," she said, satisfied that the revelation would entitle her to an extra portion of treats.

It did.

In the meantime, Dick had kept his silence, rather unusual, we thought.

"Go ahead, Dick," prompted Jane. "Tell them what you're supposed to."

Dick stood still--stage-fright still.

"Tell them," Jane repeated, "like Mamma told you to."

Clearly Jane was becoming impatient, perhaps eager to get on her way to the next source of treats. A little nudge warned Dick he better speak now or forever hold his peace. Then, with the determination one needs to jump off the diving board for the first time, his shrill little voice squeaked loud and clear: "Tweeker Tweet."

His bravery earned a triple portion of "tweets."

Then with Jane's firm, "Come on," she grabbed him by his cowboy shirt and away they galloped across the lawn to the next house. Their mother, not able to keep up, cautioned, "Be careful, you kids," and trailed along wondering just how much liberty to give her children in this given circumstance.

We watched. Wouldn't you have?

The loot next door must have been more rewarding than ours. Or maybe it was more difficult to get, because the kids stayed with those folks longer than they did with us. I didn't say anything to Vi, but I wondered if she harbored the same tinge of jealousy that I did.

Then, as we were about to close the door, out they bounded, up the driveway where they ran into the street from behind some shrubbery.

The mother screamed, the car tires screeched, both of the children disappeared.

Vi and I rushed forward.

The mother picked up Dick who had fallen on the side of the street. We rushed past her to the front of the car where we saw an amazing thing. On the curb were Jane and a high school girl, Tracy Caldwell, both wrapped tightly in Jane's witch's garb with only Tracy's head and feet sticking out. When we pieced together the scenario, we learned that Tracy had just come out of the opposite driveway on her bicycle and saw the car and the danger. With reflex action, she turned her bicycle, grabbed Jane's black cloak. This sudden unbalanced action jerked Tracy from her bicycle. Her body bumped against Jane just enough for both of them to avoid the car. They toppled over, rolling down into the drain ditch, wrapped safely together in the witch's garb.

The mother came running up with Dick. A Band-Aid would take care of his injury.

The neighbors pitched in and bought Tracy a new bike.

Chapter 16

Pecans for Sale

October autumn has given way to November's nipping moods. In the olden days, here in the Ozarks, it would be hog killing time. Today it is hog cheering time at the University of Arkansas football stadium. At our house, the harvest moon has just retired from its night-time labors. During the night on my way to the bathroom I saw its beams resting on the carpet , but when I came in this morning they had silently disappeared as Santa Claus did when I was a kid and sneaked downstairs on the night of nights. Now, however, the sunshine has come down from the hills and is grazing on the lawn. It is wary, for the thick moving clouds want dominance, and the weather man favored them in his morning report.

The buzzards will soon start rousing themselves from their night's lodging on the tree limbs, stretching their wings and one by one rising skyward from their rookery down across the river. This is a morning ritual for hundreds of them after their nightly roosting. By the time the last one is airborne Vi, sitting in front of the blazing fireplace, will finish some sewing. I will return to the third chapter of Michener's *The Novel*, which my one-cell brain finds a little bit left handed. It is, however, a diversion from Louis L'Amour's westerns wherein I slip so very easily into the role of a Sackett hero.

This retirement rocking chair is heavenly! It rolls and rocks and glides at every whim. It never talks back when spoken to; slumbers comfortably when you sleep. All is well in our little world of few concerns. Today there are no decisions to make; and hopefully none tomorrow. Each day takes care of its own twenty-four hours. House doodlings and yard putterings wait patiently. Life like this makes Christian living difficult.

Ho! What's that? Something is moving in the underbrush down toward the river! It's a deer, springing high, arching over the tangled remains of the thick lavender vetch. Quickly it turns onto the trail coming up this way. It's slowing down, stopping, standing, stomping. Motionless now, like one of those ceramic lawn statues. Suddenly it bounds up between our neighbor's house and ours. Across the cul-de-sac it goes!

Time, like the deer, moves swiftly. The last leaf on the naked sycamore tree is flitting and twisting in the wind, trying to release itself. Oh! There! It just pulled itself loose, and like a ghost it is gliding across the lawn, sometimes gusting and swirling and swaying. Quickly it must find its winter lodging, or it will get caught up in the lawn mower mulcher.

Down on the trail the morning hikers, muffled in multi-colored jackets, step briskly into the wind. Brave souls. Yesterday afternoon the temperature was above 70 degrees; within an hour an Alberta Clipper forced it down to 50.

Last Monday Vi and I drove farther than usual back into the hill roads. The burnished oaks covered the Ozarks with sunrise colors. They seem to warm the air, making it fresh and clean and clear. Between the hills and into the valleys we drove, twisting and turning until Vi asked, "Are you sure you can get us out of here?"

"Don't worry," I responded, trying not to let my voice reflect my own doubt because, quite frankly, I wasn't too sure when or how we would get back on a comfortable homeward road. Evidently I still respond to Vi's questions with that courting pompous know-it-all, can-do-it-all chauvinistic spell women cast upon men. I'm not sure what this says about manhood, but it continues to make me feel like "I've got it." Women do pecular things to men--at least Vi does to me.

"Trust me," I continued in response to her dilemma. Then I wondered how many times she has heard me say that--often under similar dubious circumstances.

Back in there somewhere off Copperhead Pass we came upon an old log cabin, its small front porch facing a valley ravine. A rough homemade cardboard sign read, "Pecans for sale." The printer had inverted the "s" and "n", and the red paint had run down giving the effect of fresh blood dripping. It took nerve, but we stopped. Not a soul around, unless barnyard chickens scratching in the front yard have souls. With hesitation, before I lost courage, I stepped up to the door and knocked. In the waiting silence I turned and shrugged my shoulders at Vi, who sat stifling in the car, windows rolled up, doors locked, motioning for me to retreat while I could.

Just then a voice inside asked, "Whatta you want?"

"Have you pecans for sale?"

A mild grunt--sigh. Then slowly, weakly, "Reckon so," came the voice, feeble and guttural.

Then silence.

"How many?" the voice finally asked. For some dumb reason I began to calculate how many pecans we wanted; how many it would take to fill a bag. What size of bag?

Suddenly Vi hissed from the car, "Jim!"

I turned and saw a man come around the corner of the house. He was dark, a young man with straight long black hair. "A foreigner!" The thought, which jumped from my mind so quickly, later embarrassed me that I would think such a thought. However, he was as startled as I, seeing me on his porch, just standing there wondering how many pecans would go into some kind of a bag.

"Oh, you're...you're...." I had started to say "that Indian kid," but caught myself just in time to finish the recognition with, "You're Joey's friend."

"Yes," was all he said.

"We saw your sign about pecans," I began to explain as he leaned his rifle against the house and threw two dead squirrels on the porch.

"I have some," he replied. "How many do you want?"

Here we go again, I thought, then asked, "How many does it take to fill a bag?"

He sort of cocked his head, then asked, "What size of the bag?"

I chuckled a bit of tension away and responded, "Oh, a sack full I guess, or something like that."

"A sack full?"

"Yes," I replied. "You know, a garbage bag."

I had in mind those little carry-out grocery bags. Evidently he thought of those thirty-three gallon garbage bags, I don't know.

"They are inside" he said, noncommittingly.

I was not sure he remembered me, so I introduced myself, mentioning having seen him at the Knot Hole Cafe last year when he came in for a Coke.

"Yes," he said. "I remember seeing you there and in Dogwood one day. Joey says you are a minister. My name is Nation Skreigh."

We entered a room rather large for such a small cabin. It contained a bed, wood heating stove, two straight-back chairs and a dresser whose flaked varnish would arrest the attention of any antique dealer.

"This is Great Grandmother," he explained as we passed by the bed in which a frail old lady lay, withered with life. "She is not well," he added as we passed through a door into a little kitchen with a small table and two chairs, a cupboard, cook stove and wood box. He had stored the pecans in a stave barrel in the woodshed attached to the kitchen.

"I do not have anything to put your pecans in," he said apologetically.

"I have something in the car," I replied and went to the car for the Texas litter bag which Vi keeps tucked half-way under her floor mat. It was not an oversized bag as one might expect from an oversized state. "Don't Mess with Texas" was printed on it--rather boldly, I thought. When I passed back through the living room, the great grandmother began to cough and retch strenuously. Nation went to her. I followed him to her bed.

"Your great grandmother is very ill," I said.

"Yes."

"Shouldn't we get her to a doctor?"

"She will not go."

"I have the car right here and she needs a doctor. We could take her now."

"No!" exclaimed the great grandmother between seizures of coughing and a bit of vomit.

"Is there anything I can do?" I asked. "Otherwise I will step outside and let you take care of her."

"She will be all right in a minute," Nation replied. "Then I will get the pecans for you. I need to sell them."

I gave him the bag and stepped out on the porch. Soon he joined me.

"Your great grandmother is resting better?" I asked.

"Yes. She has spells."

"It's beautiful up here," I said looking over across the hollow to the hills beyond.

"We like it. Great Grandmother will not leave. She is afraid she will never get back if she leaves."

So here and thus these two Cherokee Indians live, remnants of the Trail of Tears a hundred and fifty years ago.

On the way home I recalled the instant label I put on Nation when he suddenly appeared at the porch: a foreigner. "He is Native American," I said aloud. "If anybody is the foreigner, it is I."

Chapter 17

To the Icy Rescue

Our sensations of Christmas here in New Autumn--in the South--are somewhat disconcerting. Of course we did not expect eight-foot snow drifts, but the ice did little to condition us for this holy season. The crystallined landscape, trees and earth, caused our pastor to cancel the worship service last Sunday and also last night's Christmas Eve service. Before dark last evening I scraped the ice from the driveway and straightened the branches of the little Christmas tree Vi had placed on the lawn. They were drooping with ice causing the entire tree to tilt. At nine o'clock we watched a televised Mass, and then opened our presents. The calm, placid evening contrasted greatly with all other Christmas Eves we have had together when we were caught up in the excitement of preparing and conducting three or four church candlelight services.

By midnight we were well on our way toward that long winter's nap, "Mamma in her kerchief and I in my cap," when suddenly Vi woke me up.

"Wh-what's the matter?" I muttered from under the blankets.

"Listen!" she whispered.

Immediately I heard a *"thwamp"* on the roof. Then another.

"What in the world!" I exclaimed, scrambling out from under the covers.

"Reindeer!" Vi was confident.

"Reindeer don't come this far south," I reasoned. However, there are times when you do not reason with Vi.

"Thwamp." Again!

"Thwamp," I mimicked.

"No, no" Vi responded. "You're not hearing it right. There is a difference in a *thwamp* that sounds like a *thwamp* and one that sounds like a stomp."

I am hardly capable of understanding such profound wisdom.

"Let's go see him!" she said, jumping out of bed.

Quickly we donned shoes without socks, cloaks and coats. Stealthily we tip-toed through the house to the front door, careful to make no sound, motioning to each other for quietness, for by now I, too, had become a believer. Slowly we opened the front door and stepped outside into the cold night air. Our spying spree was interruped by the winter wonderland scene before us! Light frosty crystals were floating in the air; millions of them, each accentuated by the corner street light. The multi-colored lights on the little Christmas tree on the lawn created a rainbow halo round about.

Suddenly *thwamp*! Vi was right--it did have a stomp in it!

Our attention flashed roof-ward just in time to see....

Well, we both admit that the bright moon may have blurred our vision, and our concentration was interrupted when an ice-covered black walnut fell on the roof with just a plain thwamp, but we did see and we did hear it, plain as could be: "...AWAY! And to all a good-night!"

An airplane, you say? Were you there?

Vi and I hugged each other and turned to the little Christmas tree on the lawn. In amazement we watched as the fine ice crystals falling from the sky captured the multi-colored lights casting a halo-effect so like the beauty seen by the shepherds on that hillside two thousand years ago when the glory of the Lord shone round about them.

Now, we do not know if anyone will believe this, but there before our very eyes that modest little tree virtually came alive. At least Vi declares it did because all of a sudden its branches began to wave, and there in the stillness of the night a heavenly glow warmed our hearts. At first we thought the wind was stirring, but no, it was the Spirit of the Lord. Then, as if Someone were leading us by our hands, we moved closer. There, dancing around the Tree singing Christmas carols, were all our friends, past and present!

Yes, of course we joined them!

Well, folks, all that happened last night, Christmas Eve. A dream you say? Perhaps so, but how-come this morning both Vi and I told each other the same thing about that "dream?"

During this ice crisis, HOSPICE has arranged with the owners of several four-wheeled vehicles to respond to emergencies. Early this afternoon our pastor received an urgent call from one of our church members for prescribed medicine from the drug store.

"Oh, Reverend," said the voice, "we didn't get the prescription filled Friday, and then this ice came again, and you know what will happen if Homer doesn't get his medicine. Could you have his prescription filled at the drug store and get it here to him? I'm awfully sorry, but......"

Our pastor contacted the druggist. Since all of the four-wheelers were on errands, he set out on this, his private mission of mercy. On the way, his car slid off the road into a ravine. He called me from a nearby house and wondered if I dared take the chance to come and relay the medicine from where he was to Homer who urgently needed it.

A couple of years ago in Colorado we acquired a pair of tire chains, thinking we could use them as we passed through the Rocky Mountains. However, we had never had them on the car.

"I wonder if they should go on the front wheels or the rear ones," I mused as Vi stood by shivering in the garage.

"I think they're suppose to go on the back wheels," she replied.

"But this car has front wheel drive," I responded.

"Then probably they should go on the front wheels," Vi rationalized.

"I guess we'll have to get the jack and do each wheel at a time," I said, jiggling my keys for the trunk.

"Wouldn't it be easier just to line them up behind each wheel and back up, then lap them over the top?" Vi asked. "I'll tell you when to stop," she added.

The actual task was much easier than our mental images had trumped up. That is often the way it is, isn't it? Our minds photograph film that is never developed. Yet, I wonder how truck drivers manage to install those things along the road, especially during a mountain snow storm.

So off I went, over hill and dale, as if Reindeer Rudolph were guiding my sleigh. The medicine arrived on schedule. "Just in time," said Homer's wife.

Then I returned to give aid to our pastor. I showed off my new grip on the world by pulling him out of the ravine and escorting him home.

Right now a fire is blazing in the fireplace, the flames prancing like Blitzen and Dancer, and Vi and I are sitting in front of it, real cozy-like, still talking about what happened last night and reviewing with love and appreciation the Christmas cards we have received.

"The true gift of Christmas is the Gift that has already been given." This quotation came from the televised service last night. Christ has a way of entering our lives all new again. So do our friends.

Chapter 18

Debate the Alternatives

Where Do Cardinals Come From?

It is mid-summer, afternoon, and from the gazebo I see two robins splashing in the little birdbath about thirty feet away under the sycamore trees. Bluebirds like to splash in it, too. One time Vi saw five of them having a whale of a time together in their private little hot tub.

A pair of cardinals reared three babies in their nest in a Rose of Sharon tree just outside the kitchen window. Vi says the mamma cardinal hatches them while the papa feeds her. Then she goes off to build a second nest while he takes care of the babies in the first nest.

"Good Catholic Cardinals," I said, "with that kind of propagation."

Vi tells me that Catholic Cardinals don't propagate.

The Skunker and the Skunkee:

Skunked again last night! Playing rummikub with Vi and losing has its rewards: the bad feeling of losing is more stirring, more tingling, than the warm, snug feeling of winning. So I keep returning for more, like Charley Brown returning to the football Lucy holds for him every football season. He kicks and she jerks the ball away. This sends him into a flip-flop, not unlike the tailspin I go into with my chauvinistic expression of humility for getting "beat by a girl!"

Doctor's Appointment:

This morning I went to the local clinic for an annual checkup and to have a tick bite analyzed for there have been reports of Lyme disease.

"Are you allergic to penicillin or anything?" asked the doctor.

"Only doctor bills," I replied.

He smiled, replying, "I can give you a booster if you think it's necessary."

"No, I guess not," I said, "they knock me out the way they are."

When the nurse came in, she was brandishing the syringe and asked, "Do you want the penicillin in the arm or in the hip?"

"Are you going to give it to me?" I asked.

"Yes, of course," she replied, throwing a puzzled look.

"Then I'll have it in the hip," I said with overtones of a sensuous smirk.

"Roll up your sleeve, Buster!" she replied with one overtone while she jabbed with another.

I asked the doctor if there is anything that can keep me from going to sleep when I read in the evenings--and mornings, and afternoons.

"What do you read?" he asked.

I drew from my pocket a copy of a pulp western I had brought along to read while waiting for him to keep his appointment with me.

He looked at the material and said, "No wonder you go to sleep reading."

When I checked out, the nurse said, "All your tests have turned out fine, Jim."

"Then I'm a perfect specimen," I responded.

"If you say so," she said, "but consider how that term is used in a doctor's office."

Chapter 19

Bouncing Around the Rockies
(Summer vacation)

To the West! Caravans of covered wagons, tracked by rubber tired four wheelers capable of withstanding the furnace hot winds whipping through radiated air conditioners. Over the Wide Western Plains, riding point with the great cattle drives of Texas Longhorns now replaced with Herefords confined to stockyards seen for miles on end along four-lane expressways. Stretching across the Panhandle, saddle sores from bucket seats. Time out for a quick view and hike down Palo Duro Canyon, twenty-five miles south of Amarillo where some of Louis L'Amour's heroes showed their stuff. Some renegade Plains Indians did, too.

Onward, onward! The call of the Rocky Mountain heights. An afternoon stop at Colorado Springs' Garden of the Gods. Head 'em up and move 'em out at 7:30 a.m., campfire and jerky replaced with coffee and donuts in the motel lobby. Fording rivers, daring the horrendous craggy depths of Dante's gorges, invading the kingdom of eagles in the soaring heights of lingering snow fields. Getting lost in the Rockies by taking a side trip on Quandary Road. Things began to shape up considerably when we came to Selma's bar which featured "Killer Red."

Beautiful Estes Park, gateway to the scenic heights of the Rocky Mountain National Park which we video taped and video taped...and video taped.

A rodeo in the rain at Steamboat Springs, Colorado, where, during breakfast the next morning at the table next to ours, a rodeo cowboy sprinkled his eggs with pepper until he sneezed. "There, that's enough," he muttered to himself.

On to the magnificent Dinosaur National Monument where one may view and touch the bones and skeletons of these ancient beasts. Exceptional, also, are the museum and gardens in Vernal, Utah.

Up across the state line into Evanston, Wyoming, where a little Volkswagen sported the big letters BURP for its license plate. "Hot Beer and Poor Service" was a feature in one roadside stand, and "Happy

Junker" at a nearby used car lot. A lingering visit at Fort Bridger where we purchased horehound candy and priced buffalo hides at the old sutler's store. The Indian blankets at Jim Bridger's stockade had prices higher than our budget could reach.

Back, then, to the Utah canyons whose grandeur must hold God's angels in awe--and frighten the Devil's. Utah, built of mountainous splendor guarding the fertile valleys of alfalfa hay. Hark! The exciting demonstration at Promontory where the two railroads met with the transcontinental connection of the expanding East with the frontier West-- "from sea to shining sea!" Behold the two train engines, replicas of the originals, huffing and puffing down the tracks toward each other, their smokestacks belching coal-black pollutants, their bells a-ringin' the tintinnabulation of Poe's famous poem, and whistles toot-tootin' as they met at the exact spot where the Golden Spike had been driven into the final tie on May 10, 1869. What a feat then! What a sight now!

A tour of Salt Lake City's Mormon Tabernacle, and a couple of nights with friends, Dottie and Wendell. Wendell is the epitome of Western cowboy caricature. He and I sat out under the shade tree and talked the afternoon away while Vi and Dottie went shopping for something they never bought.

In Arches National Park, Utah, a couple was standing by their bicycles as we walked by. Suddenly she snarled at him, "It's too damned hot to bike. My fat won't take it!" His response seemed to echo the thunder clouds coming in from the darkened West. Later on in the afternoon following a little rain squall, all was forgiven by a beautiful rainbow, its perfect heavenly arch joining one of the imperfect earthly arches.

Time now, to boomerang homeward. Back through Colorado; a short visit with friends where we made ice cream, topped with fresh Colorado peaches! Then into Kansas, meandering like the Arkansas River along the Santa Fe Trail, a route marked with historical sites where Indian treaties were signed with difficulty, broken with ease. The townspeople re-enact the treaty-signing at Medicine Lodge every five years. Today, however, instead of the White Man trading beads of dubious value to the Red Man, the Red Man now sells them back to the White Tourist at a profitable gain.

Homeward-ho! But first, overnight in Dodge City's Boot Hill Bed & Breakfast where the silenced six-guns prod the Sandman to his task.

Overnight in Joplin, Missouri, and then on to a lunch stop at the Mountain Goat Restaurant where Vi finished reading C. S. Lewis' *Mere Christianity*, to me. Something in the book made us reflect that we are not Christ's hands and feet at all. He is ours. Lewis' theological interpretations challenge us to attack the shoddy, bullying Christianity found in so many phases of our great religion.

Right now it is so good to be home, laid back, retired in Arkansas where we will probably never rise to the fervor of saving the world from shoddy thinking, much less living. We are simply enjoying each twenty-four hours, beginning with sunrises.

Chapter 20

Persimmon Pudding

There is a bumper crop of persimmons along the nature trail this year. One particular tree, whose reproductive appendages overhang the trail, has already wasted much of its fruit on the ground. Even so, an abundance of fresh specimens still dangle, not yet severed from their umbilical cords.

Vi and I were walking the trail last evening, and as I looked forward and upward, I perceived a couple of persimmons which looked outrageously suspicious. Now, I am not prone to hearing voices *per se*, but I am sure I heard the ripest one say to the other, "Here comes Jim-boy. Last night he squashed the juice out of my cousin, Lydia, lying helplessly there on the ground."

"What are you going to do about it?" asked his dangling companion.

"Watch!"

No sooner had he spoken that word when *kah-plosh!* right on my bold, bald head. Right on top!

It was a *very* ripe persimmon. Fat.

Vi questioned the conversation of this episode, but one thing she did not deny: the brutal mess anointing my crown.

Just then a couple of ladies walked by, and with no offer of sympathy, hanky or compassion, they passed on, one saying to the other, "Did you see what I saw?" As their voices drifted out of hearing range, I thought one said something about "...his brains."

Vi has decided not to make persimmon pudding this year.

The week before Christmas, the small fry presented their Children's Christmas Program in the form of a junior cantata--very junior, but oh, so grown-up! Joseph and Mary had to stand up front during the 30 minute presentation. Joseph did very well until about half-time when he began to yawn openly, uninhibited by all those Christian eyes upon him. A rumble of chucklings throughout the congregation punctuated that scene of pure innocence.

About that time the up-lifted arms of the angel, who stood over the Birth scene, began to droop. However, she flexed them frequently--that is, until the silver garland of her sleeve caught the corner of the cradle and flipped the Baby Jesus from the manger. Suddenly there was with the angel a multitude of the heavenly host of winged cherubs in the little choir praising God and singing, "Glory to God." Meanwhile, someone quickly retrieved Baby Jesus and returned him to his place of fame. He made no outcry, though one could scarcely ignore the sudden gasps of worldly anxiety from those of us who had eyes to see.

Chapter 21

Tithing

Vi and I spent the week-end driving along the Mississippi River down through the delta region of Arkansas. When we stopped at a village church at eleven o'clock, we were late--just in time for the "Tithes and Offerings."

Today is the annual Stewardship Sunday in our United Methodist Church. Most congregations understand that it is a disciplinary obligation for the minister to talk about money on this one day of the year. Usually he or she will call upon Scriptural references of ten per cent[5]. However, the sermon from this pulpit was not the usual appeal to meet financial obligations. It was about...well, the minister said tithing is like marriage. She said you don't *make* a marriage as if it were an angel food cake you can dump into the garbage if it fails. You don't even work at marriage; you don't give to it, you don't save it. What you do is *be* the marriage. You are it for better or worse. When you *are* the marriage, you do not destroy it; that would be suicide. One protects oneself.

"When you *tithe*," she continued, "you do not give. You do not give your tithe to God, or to the church, or to any other objective. You do not give your tithe toward any cause or purpose. Tithing is not a gift, and it is not a sacrifice. When you give or when you sacrifice, you sever yourself from the subject. You do not sever tithing from yourself. Tithing is the fulfillment of giving. Therefore, it is a joy, a treasure laid up in heaven. And you, yourself, enter because you *are* your tithing.

"Like marriage, tithing is very personal. It is like loving parents extending themselves in their children, and in turn the children become the hopes and desires, and the extension, of the parents themselves.

"Using the ten per cent gauge for tithing is trumpery because it is formula-giving; it counts the cost. It concentrates on the amount rather than the tithe. Look at the widow who extended her entire self in her last

---

[5]Deuteronomy 14:22, et.al.

penny.   That extension, not the penny, was her real livelihood.   In contrast, look at the Pharisee who gave his ten percent-plus gifts."

She ended her discourse saying, "Christ tithes when one takes Holy Communion."

I would liked to have talked to her more about this matter, especially about Christ's Tithing, but her parishioners, rather than simply filing out the door with formal handshakes, literally enveloped her in their love and enthusiasm.

"I wonder which one of them captured her for Sunday dinner," Vi mused as we drove on down the levy.

Chapter 22

The First Friends of Jesus

Our Church School Superintendent asked me to write a story for the little ones, to be read during the Christmas season. Worthy or not, I have opted to share it with you:

The Little Town of Bethlehem was crowded. The government had commanded all the people in the land to come and register. There was much activity in the streets. Many people were watching the parade that was coming down the street where the inn was located.

Some of the forest trees had come to see the excitement. They loved the beautiful uniforms and shining instruments of the band because truly it was a sight to see.

One little drummer boy, much smaller than the other band members, was far behind. His short legs just could not keep up with the march no matter how fast he beat his little drum.

The people laughed and the forest trees smirked. All except the one who was called Skinny Limbs. The other trees laughed at her because her branches were so spindly. Besides, she had lost all her summer leaves. Skinny Limbs stood near some of the other forest trees on the street near the path that led down to the stable from the inn.

Skinny Limbs saw the little drummer boy trying so hard to keep up with the band. She tried to encourage him by calling out, "Keep trying, Little Drummer Boy!" But no matter how much she tried to encourage him, he just could not go fast enough.

Then the other trees, dressed in their fine forest greenery, with all their jewels of silver and gold tinsel, their dazzling ornaments and sparkling lights, looked at the little tree with the spindly arms.

"I'm glad I don't have an ugly shape like that one," one said.

"Yes, and her clothes!" exclaimed another. "Why she doesn't have a leaf left!"

"My father says her family tree never had much, so how could you expect her to be dressed any better!"

All of this made Skinny Limbs sad. She felt bad when the other trees said things like that. They wouldn't let her join in any forest-tree games.

The parade went by, leaving the little drummer boy far behind.

Suddenly a man and woman came down the path from the inn to the stable door on the side street.

"Why Joseph, this will do very nicely," the woman said.

"But Mary...it's a stable!" The man's voice was apologetic as they made preparations to spend the night there.

Soon the woman exclaimed, "Joseph, I'm going to have the baby very soon...right away!"

And so it came to pass.

The night began to get chilly. Soon the Baby started to cry.

"What shall we do," Joseph exclaimed. "The Baby is chilled and we have no blanket to keep him warm."

Mary held Jesus close to her, but they both shivered.

Before long some shepherds appeared at the stable door. "We have come to see the Babe wrapped in swaddling clothes," they said. "Some angels told us about Him while we were watching our flocks by night."

The shepherds gave Jesus a little lamb, which snuggled close to him in the manger, but neither of them could keep warm, for the night air was cold.

Shortly an amazing thing happened.

"What is this?" asked one of the forest trees.

"Why it's three men coming on camels!"

"They're from foreign countries."

"And they look so rich."

"Look at that star in front of them. It's so beautiful, so bright."

The camels stopped at the stable entrance.

"We have come to see the new-born King," said the riders as they dismounted.

They entered the stable and knelt before Jesus, giving him gold, frankincense and myrrh.

"Is that baby a king?" one of the forest trees asked.

"What kind of a king would be born in a stable?"

"Without even enough clothing to keep Him warm!"

They all laughed.

All except the little tree with the spindly branches.

Suddenly an angel from heaven came down. It took the star that had guided the kings, and placed it on top of Skinny Limbs. All at once the little ragged tree was changed into a beautiful tree with the shining star on top of her head. The little tree reached up and directed the warm glow of the star upon Jesus and the little lamb. Very soon they stopped shivering. Their cheeks became warm and glowing.

Mary and Joseph thanked the little tree. The Little Lord Jesus reached out and blessed Skinny Limbs.

The three Wise Men said, "Little Tree, no longer will they call you Skinny Limbs. From now on you shall be named Christmas Tree!"

Then everyone sang to the tune of "Rudolph the Rednosed Reindeer:"

"Then all the other forest trees, they all shouted out with glee,

Beautiful, beautiful Christmas Tree, you'll go down in history."

The little lamb wagged its tail.

Then came, "Boom! Boom, boom, boom, a rumpa-pa-pa," and everybody looked around. They saw the little drummer boy coming down the path that led from the inn to the stable. He marched right up to the stable and beat his little drum for Jesus. And Jesus smiled at him.

Then the three Wise Men stepped forward and said, "Jesus, truly You are our King. You're the King of kings, and Lord of lords!"

What a happy time it was for everyone in the Little Town of Bethlehem that first Christmas night when Jesus was born to Mary and Joseph!

Before long, the Baby Jesus became sleepy. One by one His guests took their leave. The three Wise Men, having given their gifts, mounted their camels, and with good-byes fit for royalty they departed into the night to return to their own countries.

After the wise men left, the shepherds took one last peek at the Little Lord Jesus asleep on the hay. They congratulated Joseph and Mary for such a fine strong Baby, saying someday they hoped He, too, would become a good shepherd.

"You may keep the little lamb," they told Jesus as they left to return to watching their flocks by night.

The cows laid down and began to doze. The little donkey which Mary road was more tired than he thought because his ears began to droop and his eye lids became heavy with sleep. The little lamb snuggled closer to Jesus, and with a twitch of its tail said, "Good night," and began to dream about still waters in green pastures and its mother's warm milk mixed with chocolate.

The stable mice, in very squeeky voices said, "Good night, Baby Jesus," and dashed off to their little bedrooms in the wall of the stable where their mother tucked them in one by one.

Christmas Tree asked Mary, "Should I turn off my star?"

Mary thought the light should be left on. "Besides," she said, "Its glow will keep Jesus warm through the night."

The Little Drummer Boy was the last to leave. He just couldn't keep his eyes off of Baby Jesus. He wanted to be like this little friend, but wasn't sure what Jesus was like.

"Should I play my drum for Him again?" he asked Joseph.

Joseph looked at Mary.

Mary smiled and said, "I think not right now, for you see the Baby has gone to sleep and you would not want to awaken Him, would you?"

Then Mary began to sing a song, "The Little Lord Jesus Asleep On the Hay."

The little Drummer Boy tapped his foot lightly to keep time with the tune. Soon he, too, went to sleep on a pile of hay next to Jesus.

As the Wise men journeyed into the night, they spoke of many things which wise men think. Who could this Child be? What did all this mean?

"I see Him growing up to be a Man who will bring prosperity to His people," said Casper, whose gift of gold represented substance of need like food, clothing and shelter. "No longer will people hunger and thirst, for He will be the bread of life, the living water."

"Yes," said Melchior who had given the frankincense which represented the inner treasure of man's thought and influence. "Also, Jesus will give us something very special; something beyond the mere physical needs of the body. He will change our way of thinking as well as living. Life will be beautiful with Him."

Balthazzar, the wisest of the three, expressed agreement with the insight of the other two. "However," he added, "I am persuaded that this Baby Jesus will grow up to be the King of kings and Lord of lords, for He will deliver His people from the bondage of their sins. I am sure," he continued with conviction, "That He is the Savior of the world."

Then he began to sing a song, one that the other two had never heard before: Joy to the world, the Lord is come;

Let earth receive her King;
Let every heart prepare him room
And heaven and nature sing.

Then his voice trailed off into silence as he began to peer intensely through the semi-darkness of the night.

"Ho, what's this!?" he exclaimed, for there in the trail before them was a child...and with him a lamb.

The child was crying. He appeared to be lost. The little lamb was crying, too for it was dark, and they were alone, and he was afraid of wolves.

"What's the matter, Child?" asked Melchoir. "Who are you? Are you lost? Where did you come from?"

The boy had gone with his shepherd-father to tend the flocks by night. He said an angel appeared unto them on the hillside and told his father to go into Bethlehem to see a Baby that had been born. He said there was beautiful music in the sky and lots of angels were singing. The father asked the boy to stay with the sheep while he took this little lamb's twin for a present to the Baby in Bethlehem. While the boy was watching the sheep, the little lamb, who missed his twin brother, started across the hills in search of him. He became lost. The little boy went to find the lost lamb, but when he found it, he, too, became lost, and could not find his way back to the fold. He did not know which way to turn, nor how far to go.

The wise men put their heads together, as wise men do, to decide what action should be taken.

Suddenly the boy looked heavenward and saw a bright star coming toward him! "Look," he exclaimed, "it's a star. Maybe it will show me the way!"

Casper gasped. "Indeed it is," he said, "though to me, instead of a star, it appears to be a young lad who has grown in favor with God and man."

Then he turned to the little boy who was lost, and said, "I perceive, young friend, that He has come to show you the way you should grow up."

Melchoir stood in amazement. "I see the star, too!" he was almost in tears. "But He is like unto a great teacher to me. A teacher with such knowledge and kindness that the whole world will see His light, and God in heaven will be glorified."

By this time the star was very close. Balthazzar slowly knelt in great reverence. He knew the star was from heaven because he, with his two companions, had followed it for many weeks.

"The star is like unto the myrrh I gave to the newborn King who was wrapped in swaddling clothes back in Bethlehem. He is a gift to the world, no doubt; a Prince of Peace; perhaps God Himself."

"Glory be to God in the highest!" exclaimed the three wise men, as wise men should.

"And on earth peace, goodwill to us all," added the little boy holding his lamb close to his breast. The little lamb wagged its tail.

Suddenly, to the astonishment of them all, including the little lamb, the Star spoke. It was a simple statement.

"Come, follow me," it said.

Then it began to move away.

With a happy heart, trusting the Star completely, the little boy and his lamb with its waggery tail began to follow. There was great joy when the Star took them back to the hillside where the other sheep slept.

Just then the boy's father came running up the hillside.

"Son," he said breathlessly, "Wait until I tell you what happened!"

"But Daddy," said the boy just as excitedly, "let me tell you what has happened!"

The boy and his father spent the rest of the night telling each other what they had seen and heard. All the sheep woke up and gathered round about and listened carefully. There were no wolves around to frighten them. Or if there were, they just laid down by the lambs and listened, too.

The Wise Men, also, gathered around and listened.

At daybreak, the father shepherd said, "Son, we must to now and tell your mother and little sisters about these things that have come to pass."

So they gathered their flock together and left the shepherds' hill.

At the same time, the three Wise Men mounted their camels and departed to their own countries, wiser than ever before.

Chapter 23

Maybelle Sutherland

Nelda Triangle and Maybelle Sutherland would never be taken for twins. They do not think, talk, look or act alike. They were born together so just got into the habit of living together, I guess. That's about all they have in common, though. Nelda clerks at the Dogwood Mdse.. Store. She is short and wiry, always ready to defend her point of view.

Maybelle is not exactly the opposite of Nelda, but almost. Years ago when Nelda married Lon Triangle, it was only natural that Maybelle should live with them. It turned out that Lon liked Maybelle more than his wife. Some eyebrowed speculations made their rounds when Nelda and Maybelle took a couple of months off to visit relatives in Georgia, and returned with newborn Lonnie.

"We thought sure as shootin' he would be a girl, and we wanted her to burst into this world in the same house where we were born, as was our mother and Grandma Snyder," was the explanation from Nelda.

That was twenty-seven years or so ago.

No doubt Maybelle would be more beautiful today had her facial muscles been set at different tensions up through the years. She and Nelda had attended Brother Jake's church until Lonnie was born. When they built the Methodist church in New Autumn, Maybelle started going there. Nelda switched from Brother Jake's church to the Church of Christ in Dogwood.

One day while Vi attended her church circle's luncheon, I drove up to the Knot Hole Cafe for a sandwich. The booth where Vi and I always sit was occupied by a couple of ladies, so I sat at a nearby table.

One of the ladies said to the other, "I don't understand Maybelle at all."

"She'll put a hex on you," replied the lady's friend. "That's what happened to Joey Balaam, you know. You remember when he was a little kid and Brother Jake had that baptism down at the river? You remember that, don't you?"

"Naw," replied the other, "I don't go to no baptisms."

"Well, it happened anyway. Musta been before you came to Dogwood. It wasn't exactly a baptism, not to begin with. It was the day when Brother Jake married Lonnie Triangle to Sylvia Baker. Trio--they called him that--he was a wild one. Poor kid, never did know for sure which one was his mother. But he was always real popular with the other kids at school. When he got into high school they began to call him Trio, not because his name was Triangle, but because he always had three girls on the string at the same time. If one of them ditched him, right away he got another to take her place. Never had more or less than three. After he got married, nobody ever did know what happened. He just disappeared one day.

"Him and Rachael Slocum was suppose to-a got married on that Saturday, but when him and some of the boys got drunk that Friday night at their bachelors' party, they all decided to go coon huntin'. Right there in the middle of the night, about midnight I guess it was, they all grabbed their guns and took to the hills--forgot all about the wedding. When Rachael found out about it the next morning, she was so mad she got the other two girls of Trio's and when he came home they was waiting for him. They sobered him up good and proper, and then derned if the four of them didn't have another big party instead of a wedding right then and there on Saturday right in the middle of the day! Well, Rachael didn't want to marry him any more, but the other two did, so Ol' Trio, he took a broom straw and broke it, one long and one short, and he held the straws himself for the draw. It was Sylvia Baker; she won him. They decided to get married Sunday morning in church. Well, the whole town thought this called for a celebration so we all got into the spirit of that wedding, I'll tell you. Only time that church was ever full, not to count all those other people standing outside a-whoopin' and hollerin' as Brother Jake preached. He got so wound up preaching about how you're suppose to have sex only when you're married, he went way out of bounds with it.

Finally Brother Jake got them married, and we sang 'Revive Us Again,' and then everybody went down to the river, down by that grove of elm trees and, man, what a celebration that was! Dinner on the ground and white lightening bubbling like water from that flowing well over at Wilson Springs. They tied a rope to one of the branches that hung out over the river and the kids, every one of them got theirselves dunked a dozen times swinging out over the water. One kid almost drowned, he did. After dinner Brother Jake got to preaching all over again, and derned if he didn't get Maybelle converted. They said she had to get baptized right away, so when Brother Jake done it, she rose up out of the water shouting glory to Gawd and everybody began clapping their hands and yelling Amen. Then all at once Maybelle froze, frigid as a statue, her clothes wet and clinging to her like bark on a sycamore tree. Everybody got silent all of a sudden because they saw that she was staring at little Joey Balaam who was playing with them other kids, you know, Rudy Meyers and Rose Ann Hill and them. And then Joey began to cry and toddled off to his mother. Just then Brother Jake fell into the water. Some said he had washed up a little too close to Maybelle, others said he musta slipped off the rock he was standing on, and some said he was too drunk even to be standing on the promises of God much less the rock of ages. Nobody knew for sure what happened, but Joey never was right after that."

"What did Maybelle do?" asked the friend.

"She finally began to limber up a bit and shake like a leaf. Nelda--they said it was the tenderest thing they ever saw a human do--she went down into the water with her shoes and clothes all on, and put her arm around Maybelle and took her home. It was real touching--tenderest thing I ever saw done."

"I guess that ended the picnic?"

"Aw, no; let me tell you. Ol' Trio and his cronies, they came down and hoisted Brother Jake on their shoulders and got him to preaching again, third time that day! Brother Jake even tried to get Trio saved, but Ol' Trio, he turned the tables and began to preach to Brother Jake and had him on his knees before the throne of God, weeping and wailing for his shortcomings of not being forceful enough to subdue the wiles of Satan."

"Do you really think Maybelle put a hex on Joey?"

"Aw, no; she ain't got the guts. Still you wonder why Joey acts like he does. Maybe it's true; I don't know."

"What did Maybelle do then?"

"After Nelda took her home, she never went out much any more. She joined up with them Methodists down at New Autumn."

When she mentioned "Methodists and New Autumn," I look looked at my watch. It was almost two o'clock! Vi's circle meeting would be over by the time I could return to New Autumn, so hurriedly I paid my bill and left this live, on-stage talk show, wondering how much of it, if any, could be true.

Nelda's hours at the store are from eight to four. Every morning she and Maybelle walk the mile and half across the valley from their house to the store. Nelda has a cup of coffee and donut at the store while Maybelle returns home and prepares her serving of oatmeal and whole wheat toast.

One morning on her way home after accompanying Nelda to the store, Maybelle stopped and watched an armadillo burrow into the ground near some 'possum grape vines. Then she turned and stepped over onto a flat rock lying in a little mini-cove isolated from the flowing stream. She stood still, looking down at her reflection in the water. Here, the water was calm, mirror-still, but deep enough to create a tiny swell which periodically took her reflection and warped it into unrecognizable contortions. Maybelle watched spellbound as the reflection began to carry her image away into oblivion. Hypnotically her mind followed. Beyond the confines of her body she seemed to see Lonnie, a cuddly baby, crying for attention.

"Lonnie," she exclaimed reaching out. She had never called him Trio, even though he insisted upon it when he entered high school.

When she reached out for him, her arms folded around emptiness, for the swell had returned her reflection to its original image. Maybelle felt disconcerted, but the fantasy was renewed when the swell again began to contort reality into another hypnotic impairment.

This time Lonnie, a lad of twelve, bathing himself without help now, began asking questions about sex which Nelda encouraged but Maybelle hushed. When she blocked one of the questions which Lonnie had asked, the aberration warped itself back into place and Maybelle's true image was restored at her feet.

No sooner, however, had this been done when the reflection began to anesthetize Maybelle's reality a third time, greatly relieving her pain. Now she watched proudly as Lonnie received his high school diploma. He turned to her with his winning grin, then suddenly the grin turned to bewilderment as his eyes turned to Nelda. Then again, as suddenly as her image disappeared, it re-appeared. Maybelle was looking at herself.

The still water surrounding the flat rock once more warped her image and dragged her into the state of oblivion. The wedding service in Brother Jake's church had just begun and she and Nelda were there. Suddenly there was a boisterous commotion at the door and Lonnie entered with three girls, all obviously in a state of high revelry. Ol' Blue began barking and for once Brother Jake had nothing to say.

Soon order was restored and Brother Jake stood Lonnie and the three girls facing him, their backs to the congregation.

"First we'll sing a hymn," Brother Jake announced. "What hymn would you like sung at this-here wedding of yours, Trio?"

Lonnie looked around befuddled. Then quickly with a glint in his eyes, he reached out and pulled his three companions in close and said, "Let's all sing 'Bringing in the Sheaves.' That's what I want sung at this wedding."

So they did. Lonnie turned around and lead the singing with gusto.

"Now, Trio, turn around and face me," Brother Jake continued, clearing his throat as if he were a mayor about to make a political speech. "We're ready to begin.   We're here in the sight of God and these witnesses...."

Brother Jake broke off the sentence and asked, "Who are your witnesses, Trio?"

Lonnie turned around to the congregation and said loudly, yet invitingly, "Why, all these folks are gonna witness this wedding--ain't you?"

They did.

Brother Jake accepted this as an official sufficiency, and thereby continued with the ceremony.

"All right, then, we've gathered here in the sight of God and these witnesses to join together Trio, that is Lonnie Triangle, and...."

Again his voice trailed off into quandary.

"Who you marrying, Trio?" he asked.

The congregation wondered, too.

Spontaneously, as a volcano errupting, Sylvia Baker spoke up, "Me. I won him fair and square."

Her two friends confirmed the feat as if it were an Olympian gold medal.

Maybelle was crying when the water returned her reflection. However, it gave her little time for this indulgence because yet again the warp took her to Lonnie.

Except this time he was not there.

She stood looking at herself at the bottom of her feet, and wondered if, indeed, Lonnie had ever been. Sometimes his existence matched some of her other dreams which often could not be differentiated from reality. Again, Maybelle thought of terminating both the reality and unreality of her life.

"The water is deeper downstream," she mused.

Ten minutes later as she walked out into the deeper water her mind and soul seemed at ease. There was no real thought of suicide--just a few steps toward tranquility. The water reached her waist, then her shoulders--her neck, chin, and suddenly she stepped into a hole and the water entombed her.

Instinctively, her reflexes began to splash the water.

Brother Jake, who had been fishing beyond a growth of reeds, looked up from his bobber, but could see nothing. Cautiously he drew in his line and walked through the reeds to get a better look.

"A bear!" he thought with alarm, and began to back away, yet keeping his eye toward the commotion.

Maybelle's sanity had returned as she thrashed the water. First a whimper escaped her breath, then a cry for help as her arms and head emerged. When Brother Jake realized what was happening, he dropped his fishing pole and waded out into the water to help. By the time he and Maybelle finished struggling, both were dragging each other up on shore where they lay reviving from the spent energies.

Rudy and Tag came upon them.

Before Brother Jake could reach Dogwood to tell how he had saved Maybelle Sutherland from drowning, the gossip had hit the wind like maple leaves in a November thunder storm. Old gossipings were revived, how Maybelle had "slithered" up to Brother Jake "when she was wet with baptism," and how she cast a spell on Joey, and how tramps were always welcome at her house.

However, in all the days ahead, no one had the will nor courage to let it reach the ears of Nelda, and thereby, Maybelle was oblivious of the flooding defamation.

Rudy quickly awakened to his new-found power. If his self-ego could be heightened to this point by casting ill will toward one person, what might happen when he tried this nefarious sport on others?!!

Chapter 24

Retirement at Labor

Our Literacy Council met this morning. There were the usual eighteen, most of whom were retired school teachers. None of us could remotely estimate how many "meetings" we had attended in our lifetime. Inwardly I smiled with appreciation as I looked at our lolling chair-worn bodies. From the noisy metal folding chairs below, our upper torsos extended over onto the table-tops above. It reminded me of my friend's dairy barn in southern Wisconsin when the milk cows lined up facing each other in their stanchions. Likewise, this morning we lined ourselves up along our tables, facing each other, prepared at this milking to yield from our fluid expertise what nourishment we could for the benefit of humankind.

I had not wanted to go to the meeting. There were too many of those insatiable "Honey-do" jobs at home which tend to suck up my time like goldfish gasping for water.

"I have three new prospective students," our president said. This brought me out of my nebulous thoughts which had escaped the stanchions, and had begun milling around a Labor Day sermon which I was to deliver next Sunday in the absence of our pastor.

"One is a young lady referred to us by the Women's Shelter in Case City," our president continued. "She left her husband and is striking out on her own. Another is a high school dropout with an eleven month old child. She has ambitions for a G.E.D. The third is a local Indian boy who lives out in the hills from Dogwood."

Immediately my ears perked up, something like Vi's mule-friend over near Balaams.

"What is the boy's name?" I asked.

"Let's see here," the president said shuffling through the file. "Nation Skreigh. Seems he had a friend call and submit his name to us the other day. My mother took the information over the phone. He lives near Dogwood according to what Mother thought he said. It doesn't look like he...."

"May I have him?" I asked, as she continued to shuffle the papers.

"Of course, Jim," she said, gratefully handing the file to me.

After lunch I set out for Nation's cabin with the literacy material and my old portable typewriter. A couple of miles out, I stopped by the river bank and began to work on the Labor Day sermon. There, in the middle of a thousand square miles of mountain forest, I began to formulate a religious rationale for working. As I sat on my little canvas stool with the typewriter positioned on the tree-stump desk, I gazed through the tree branches, down the valley which fanned out from either side of the river. Its billions of leaves appeared as a giant green blanket, each leaf hanging and dangling and strangling and struggling--working to reach the sunlight upon which it depended for life.

Below the little knoll upon which I had perched myself, Spring River flowed, wide and shallow, swimming in itself. It was a little bit nervous along the edges as it carved apologetically into the embankments. One could tell from its determination and steady work that it would survive another million years.

To my left were the remains of an old concrete bridge, jutting half-way out into the river, a crumbling testimony of men earning their living on this WPA project a half century ago.

My eyes wandered to the miniature cove along the bank where a fish suddenly jumped from the still waters, busy at his daily task of keeping alive.

"The creative work of God," I exclaimed under my breath. "How infinite, and what a challenge for us human beings to fit our modern, technical, *unnatural* work into this marvelous scheme of nature."

I doubted that would be a good statement to include in a sermon, so I directed my thoughts toward other possibilities that might correlate the work of God with the work of man.

Just then a noise from behind caused me to jerk around in a strained position, senses alert. I thought it might be a bear coming to investigate the 'possom grapes over by a clump of pine trees behind me. Goose pimpling noises always seem to come from behind. It turned out to be a little chipmunk which scampered over some dry leaves at the base of a tree. It darted here and there among some rocks and weeds. Closer and closer it came by quick, cautious sprints. I'm sure it wanted to make friends but safety advised care as it investigated this human being at work. After all, it, too, had its work to do.

There I sat, watching the stillness and the movement of those things which stirred my thinking apparatus: the swishing swirling stream before me, the soft coolness of wind--sometimes the fury of it. I thought about the silent falling snows of Michigan's cold winters, and the equally silent sun rays of Arizona's hot summers. What a variety of life, sound and color to aid the toil of man! "O God, what is man that you are mindful of him," came the cry of the Biblical Psalmist. I began to concentrate on what life might truly be in relation to energy, strength, industry, existence, thought, movement, even consciousness.

Suddenly a roar, pop, bang, dr-dr-r-r-r snatched my thoughts away from all that meditational rapture. An old logging truck was coasting downhill in low gear.

"Now there's sound and movement and life for you," I reflected. "Man earning his daily bread by the sweat of his...carburetor."

I thoroughly enjoyed those moments, sitting in the bosom of that vast wilderness watching the "goings-on" of nature. It may be that our relationship with one another is our relationship with God, and somehow God's creation of nature pulls it all together. God's work and our work may have a closer kinship than we suppose.

Surely there is benefit when we harmonize our pullings and pushings, our shovings and shiftings into a natural order of creating. I was about to plunge into the symphony of God's orchestration of work and nature when I looked upstream and saw Nation coming along the river bank with his gun and fishing pole.

I saw him only a moment before he waved to me.

"Hello, Nation," I called as he came up. "Any luck, or are you just getting ready to try it?"

"Looking for supper," he said.

"There's a big fat chipmunk around here somewhere."

"I would rather have a big fat bear," he replied.

"Not me," I said, hoping nothing in my voice revealed the cowardliness I exercised few minutes ago when I thought a chipmunk might be a bear.

"How is your great grandmother doing?" I asked.

"She has been pretty perky lately; walking around in the house. Each day she says she hopes to get out on the porch tomorrow," he said as he walked up to where I was sitting. "What are you doing?"

"I'm getting a sermon ready for Sunday," I replied. "Our pastor will be away and I'm filling in for him. Trying to make some sense out of our earning bread by the sweat of our brow, as the Bible says. I should be over talking with your great grandmother, squeezing a sermon out of her wisdom."

"She might help you, all right, but not me," Nation said with an embarrassed grin. "Work is not one of my biggies."

"You're at work now, aren't you, looking for supper?"

"Yeah, I guess so, but I would like to find a job, but nobody will hire me."

"You can't find a job?" I asked, inviting him to talk further about the matter if he wished.

"No."

"How come?"

"Because I'm Indian," he said.

"How does it feel, Nation--how do *you* feel deep inside about being an Indian?"

He hesitated, then said, "Well, deep down in I'm proud of it, but nobody else is."

"That's what you were created to be, so would you say God is a failure?"

"No, that ain't it."

"Then would you say the Great Spirit failed in his creation of us who are not Indian?"

"No, I do not think that."

"Sounds like I'm prodding, doesn't it?"

"A little bit, I guess," he admitted.

"Of course you know we're not talking about failure of what is created, don't you?" I said.

"I guess not."

"What is it, then--that we're talking about?" I asked bluntly.

With little reflection, he said, "Me, I guess."

"Well, yes," I replied, "we were talking about what I'm doing out here, what God has done in His creation, and and what you're going to have for supper. Is it OK if the three of us--you, God and I--find out more about you?"

"I would be glad if someone figured me out, because I cannot do it myself," he responded with an burst of gratitude.

"Let's work on that, Nation, as we go along getting better acquainted. Right now I have something else to talk to you about. I'm a teacher for the Literacy Program. Did you contact them about learning to read?"

"Yes, Joey said he would call them. I want to learn to read."

"I am one of their tutors. Would you like for me to be your teacher and get you started in the program, or would you prefer someone else to teach you?"

He looked up, surprised; apparently pleased.

"Would you teach me?"

There in his own familiar surroundings I showed him the material, explained the procedure and set up a weekly schedule. His interest accelerated when I suggested that tracking down the meaning of letters and words and sentences was like tracking an animal in the woods. He opted to meet at his home rather than in some designated classroom setting.

He was ready to learn to read.

Chapter 25

Pig Out-ing

We see in the local weekly newspaper that the annual Ozark Hog Roundup is scheduled the first week in November. In the olden days the mountain people grouped together and rounded up their hogs for branding, somewhat like the western cattlemen did their herds In the spring, before letting the hogs out into the wilds to fend for themselves, the owners would make certain cuts or marks on the animals' ears or elsewhere. This branded them for identification. By late fall when the weather turned cool, the hogs would be fat on acorns, roots, fruits and other nutrients they had foraged from the mountain forest. Then, during this season of approaching winter, the owners executed their roundup from which each family identified and culled out their own animals for market or home use.

Today, like rodeos, there are local sham-roundups at various times throughout the area. However, I'm not sure I want to do any razorback "rounduping," even though they say it's only a festive occasion. Who can predict what branding might take place, once they get a Move-in Yankee back there in them hollars!

Chapter 26

Great Grandmother Skreigh

Today is Wednesday before Thanksgiving Day. Last night long after midnight, Joey called and said that Nation thought his great grandmother was about to die.

"I just came from there and am calling from home, but Dad doesn't know it. Nation didn't want him to. He wonders if you can go out there because there is something she wants to tell you. I think it is real important."

It took me an hour to get there, preacher-driving. Nation met me on the porch, holding a kerosene lamp, and apologized for asking me to do this. He was sure his great grandmother would not live through the night.

"She wants to see you," he said. Then added, "She has heard the Owl."

He looked to see if I understood. I did not, but said nothing.

Inside, Nation said, "Great Grandmother, Reverend Hilliard is here."

She did not respond.

"May I offer a prayer?" I asked, and Nation nodded his head.

I recited the Lord's Prayer and then prayed, "Lord God of us all, please let Your daughter respond according to her desire. Nevertheless, Your will be done."

Silence. The stillness of the moment held us closely. Suddenly Nation whispered, "Lord?" He said it as if he were addressing someone definitely present. I glanced around the room. As I did so, there came over me the same sort of sensation that the shepherds must have felt on that first Christmas night when the "Glory of the Lord shone round about them."

"Lord!" Nation exclaimed.

Then the phenomenon passed.

As soon as it did, Mrs. Skreigh said in a low distinct voice, "Reverend Hilliard, you are here."

"Yes." Nation and I both said it at the same time.

Her energy revived.

"At sundown," she said, "I heard The Screech of the Owl (she pronounced "screech" as the Scottish "skreigh"). Perhaps you know what that means?"

"I have not told him," Nation said.

"Our tribe's totem has always been the Owl," she continued "Every few generations its screech is heard by one of us in a way that is not heard with mortal ears. We do not explain it; we simply tell of it. I never thought that I would hear it, but I did, at sunset this evening. Nation will hear it, too, someday."

She stopped to breathe and rest for a moment. Then she went on, "I think it might be like the Christian baptism of the Holy Spirit, but I don't know because I have heard so many different versions of that. There is no mistake about this, though; it is the message of the Great Spirit, direct, clear, blessed. The prophets would have called it the Word of God.

"But I did not ask you to come all the way out here at night to talk about that. I will be leaving this world on the morning sunrise. I would ask that you, only you and your wife and Nation, and Joey if Nation wants him, to attend to my burial here on our little piece of land. Nation knows all about it. You will do it?"

"Daughter of the Great Spirit," I said as though in some kind of trance. "I am unfamiliar with your burial customs, but to answer your question, in the name of Jesus Christ I will do as you ask as well as I can."

"Nation said you would understand."

During the short silence that prevailed, I perceived that God came to the Hebrews on their side of the globe in communicative ways they understood. Likewise He comes to us, now on our side of the globe.

"Strange indeed, and mysterious are the ways of the Great One," Mrs. Skreigh said as though she had shared the revelation. "Generations ago, back East, when the White Man came to our land, we incorporated his Christian ways into our ancient traditions. That was not difficult because both seemed to be rooted in the same source. Now of your own accord, at my burial, you will incorporate some of our Cherokee traditions into your Christian ways, and you will not be afraid."

She held her poise for a moment. I thought that was a strange thing to say, but made no response.

She relaxed. I thought she had gone, but then she stirred.

"What a wonderful world this is after all," she said.

Nation was silent. I looked at him, instead of seeing sad tears, his countenance was like St. Stephen's must have been at the Jews' rock-throwing contest. Surely the "Spirit of the Lord was upon him."

"There is another thing, if you please," Great Grandmother continued. "There is a paper, a document, sewn in my mattress here, just under my heart (she smiled). Nation, as soon as I am buried, you will get it and show it to Reverend Hilliard."

Nation did not respond. There were no questions; none seemed necessary. He had learned to trust this grand old lady who in ancient days in her own society would have been called "Beloved."

Then, with surprising firmness, she extended her frail little hand, first to me, then to Nation.

We waited comfortably. It began to get light.

I looked up at Nation and followed his wide-eyed gaze. He was not looking at his great grandmother, but out the window. He was looking at an owl sitting on a branch. Quite frankly, this startled me; it was a bit unsettling. Then my eyes caught the rim of the sun showing the top of its arch over the edge of the mountain beyond the valley. I glanced down at our Beloved Woman, then instantly my eyes shifted back to where the owl had been on the branch.

It was not there.

Nation leaned down, closed his great grandmother's eyes. "She has gone--gone with the Owl," he said.

A peaceful silence embraced us.

"She heard the Owl," Nation said with a soft exclamation that contained more meaning than I could comprehend.

After a moment I asked, "Do you want me to help you with the funeral arrangements?"

"We will bury her here," was his reply.

"I'm not sure what the regulations are, but you'll need to get a death certificate, and other matters taken care of."

"Nobody will know," he said as his eyes questioned toward me.

I waited a moment, then replied, "I would tell no one about it, Nation, but for my part I'll need to go according to the laws."

He nodded.

"Well, OK," I said, going toward the door. "Let's go into town and see what all needs to be done."

I could see that he did not want to leave his great grandmother. I supposed he needed to perform some sort of ritual of mourning or something. I did not know.

"I'll tell you what," I suggested. "You stay here while I go home and make a few calls to find out what all must be done."

This pleased him and he seemed not the least bit apprehensive to be there alone with death, which he probably interpreted as life.

At home I called my funeral director friend who told me that a doctor or coroner would have to verify the death.

"Or, a HOSPICE nurse could sign the certificate," he said.

"Great!" I replied, "Because I'm on the HOSPICE Board of Directors and can get Susan Farwell to take care of it."

At noon I drove out and picked up Nation. He and I went into town where we raced from one place to another as each office sent us to the next. We spent more time than we could afford at the Health Department determining the requirements for burial on private land. After getting virtually no verbal information, we went through the sheaves of paper they had handed us. Finally we laid them all aside, including the "Application for Location or Extension of Boundaries for Cemeteries," and opted to proceed as necessary and say as little as possible to anyone.

"Anyway," Nation reasoned, "my family has been lying out there in their graves longer than these papers have been lying around here."

Nation declined the suggestion that he fill out forms for $250 burial assistance for low income families, which they said he was eligible to receive.

After completing the requirements and learning that there were no restrictions for caskets or time limits for holding the body before burial, we started homeward. It was late.

On the way home, we were silent until Nation said, "She wanted real bad to be buried out there beside Great Grandfather. I will dig the grave and maybe we could do it tomorrow?"

"I will get someone to help you dig the grave," I offered.

"No, we do it this way."

"You and Joey?" I asked.

"No."

Silence.

Then I supposed that by "we" he meant his family, the ones lying in that hallowed ground, their family cemetery.

However, I asked, "Nation, who do you mean by 'we'"?

"Us," was his only reply.

Then he repeated, "She wanted real bad to be buried out there beside Great Grandfather. I will dig the grave and maybe we could do it tomorrow?"

"What time did you have in mind?"

I felt like a child. Not Nation, though. He handled his responsibilities with the air of a Washington Senator, but with much greater haste and efficiency.

"I will get to work at it right away," he said. "It will be ready by sunrise."

I was puzzled. "You mean you'll dig the grave tonight?...so it will be ready by sunrise?"

"Yes."

"But it's going to be dark in another hour."

"The moon will be up, full."

My mind flashed this teenager, suddenly a young man now, alone, digging a grave in the silhouette of the big, brisk, round November moon.

"It'll take all night to dig the grave and there are other things to be done," I said, protesting. Then I added, "Can't you wait until tomorrow and get some help?"

"Will you be here at sun-up? I will have it ready by then."

"Sun-up?"

"Yes," he said, "it will be like a continuation. I mean she died just as the sun came up. I thought it would be a good thing if we buried her at the same time so everything would continue along and she wouldn't have to wait for anything."

I marveled at this thought which revealed a great faith. My mind recalled the words of Jesus to the man next to him on the cross, "Today you will see me in paradise." No delay. So like Jesus.

I said, "Well, OK; I'll be here at sun-up. Is there anything special that I should know about your tradition that would be helpful?"

"You'll do it right," he said.

"You seem to know more about it than I," was my reply.

"I will do what I do, the way I do it. You will, too."

I needed that vote of confidence.

He insisted that I drop him off at a shortcut trail to his cabin, which I did. Then I drove on home. It was almost dark.

Vi was beside herself when I told her all of this.

"Hard to believe," she muttered, and I agreed.

After thinking through on it, she suddenly exploded.

"Why, that kid can't be out there all alone with his dead great grandmother!"

"He isn't as much a kid as you might think," I said.

"He's hardly fifteen years old," she reasoned, pacing back and forth in front of me a couple of times. "Out there alone with his dead great grandmother--digging her grave!"

Then she punctuated the imagery: "Without supper!"

In the same breath, she picked up the telephone and ordered three take-out dinners from the local diner. "We'll pick them up in ten minutes," she said firmly, hung up the phone and dashed to the bathroom, telling me to change into my old clothes. Then, before I had time to buckle my belt, we were out the door headed for Copperhead Pass.

There was a lamp burning in Nation's cabin when we arrived. I stopped the car and turned off the headlights, got out and called, "Nation, it's Reverend Hilliard."

He came around the side of the house carrying his rifle, just like the time when we bought the pecans.

"Oh, hello," he said, "I am glad it is you."

"Were you expecting someone else?" I asked giving recognition to the rifle.

"Uh...no," he replied, recoiling a bit. "No, no one at all."

"But I am glad you came," he added with implications of great relief.

"Mrs. Hilliard thought you might like some supper," I said, "so she brought some for all three of us."

"Do you want to come in?" he asked.

"Why don't we eat out here on the steps," Vi said quickly. "There's plenty of light through the window."

So there the three of us sat on the rickety porch steps, the full moon not quite showing, but the lamplight through the window was enough to reflect our styrofoam take-out containers nestling the restaurant's gristed catfish and hush puppies. There was something warm and right about our camaraderie as the soft glow of the lamp came to us through the window, bringing with it that eternal extension of Great Grandmother Skreigh. Nobody knows her except Nation, I thought. Only Nation and God. Yet here in death she was warming our souls--she "who is dead and yet lives" was sending the signal that there is "light in darkness."

Vi was the first to speak of it. "I feel very warm and secure here, now," she said. "It makes me wonder if there is such a thing as death, after all."

Nation, more than I, understood what she was saying. The four of us were strangely at peace in that setting which normally would have brought on unpredictable trauma.

"The whole world ought to be like this," I said. "I don't understand it, but somehow I don't need to understand."

"I'm glad you brought me," Vi said.

"It was you who brought me," I reminded her.

Then I told Nation about Vi's reaction when I arrived home. He looked up at her with a smile on his lips and eyes that expressed gratitude. He said nothing.

"Nation, how do you relate God to this?" I asked.

"You mean to Great Grandmother's death?"

"Well, that, too, but do you feel the presence of God here tonight?"

"Joey would know how to answer you better than I," he replied, "because my thinking about religious things is like my great grandmother's. Joey's is different from mine--but they are not like his father's."

"I would like to know more about how your thinking is like your great grandmother's, and how Joey's is unlike his father's," I said.

With some hesitation he replied, "Joey has disagreements with his father."

"You mean about the Bible?"

"And other things."

"Yes, I guess so," I replied, "but didn't you and your great grandmother have disagreements?"

He looked away and shuffled his foot as if he didn't know how to answer.

Then he said, "I guess I never thought about disagreeing with my great grandmother. She was always free to think and free to do. She let me be that way, too, so we never thought of it as disagreement but simply accepted each other as we are. Joey and his father are always in conflict about what his father thinks is right or wrong. Great Grandmother was not that way. She and harmony were pretty much together."

"Tell me more, Nation--about her and harmony."

"Well, she thought that the Great Spirit was not as much interested in our social taboos as most Christians seem to think. She did not confuse traditional taboos with religious sins like Brother Jake does."

"That's interesting," I mused.

"Well," he continued, "it's like Brother Jake always talks about these things which he calls sins. Don't do this and don't do that. Great Grandmother lived more in harmony with the surrounding natures that God not only created in us, but created us in. She used to say, 'Nation, it is good to go out in the woods and live in the midst of what the Great One has created because you are one of those creations. Remember, Nation,' she said, 'wherever you are and whatever you do, and whoever you are with, remember that you are God's creation and you are either helping Him develop or destroy that creation.' So I just grew up not thinking any other way. And I remember her saying, 'It is good to know that the Great One never created anything that does not harmonize with Himself and everything He created.'"

"Your great grandmother distinguished between the nature of God and the nature He created?" Vi asked.

"Yes."

"I think she did not confuse traditional taboos with religious sin like Brother Jake does," he said. "She thought there is more harmony in the nature of human beings and animals than most folks admit."

"What do you mean?" I asked.

"She did not see how doing natural things could be sinful. They might be offensive to the social order, but not sinful if they are in harmony with the way the Great Spirit created us."

"What about killing?" Vi asked. "Killing seems to be natural for animals and for some people."

"Is it natural?" Nation responded. "Is that God's creation, or is that something some animals and people have learned since creation? I cannot think that killing of any kind is the creation of God."

Nothing was said for a moment. It seemed superfluous to get into the issues of war, sex and self defense.

Then Nation continued, "My great grandmother told me that saying naughty words is offensive but not sinful unless we used them offensively. Social restrictions are good for order, but the violation of them is not necessarily blasphemous toward God. In this, Great Grandmother figured there is a difference between sin against one another and sin against God. She said Jesus pointed this up when He got after the Pharisees for paying so much attention to Moses' law like Brother Jake does, but neglecting God's law."

"How do _you_ see all of this?" I asked.

"Well," he replied, "social laws are important, of course, but I think we should pay more attention to God's laws. If we did that, then the social laws would pretty much take care of themselves. But when we give most of our attention to the social laws, we do like Jesus said, neglect God's laws. That is what my great grandmother thought, but when she talked about it, people did not like it; I guess they did not understand."

"What are God's laws?" Vi asked.

"To love, do justice, have mercy, show kindness," Nation replied, showing no surprise that we might not know that.

Then he added, "But here, again, we turn even _those_ laws inward toward ourselves instead of toward God."

"Are you saying that there is a difference between human love, justice, mercy, kindness, and God's love, justice, mercy and kindness?" Vi asked.

"Yes," was Nation's reply. "Human love, justice, mercy and kindness seem to vary, depending on circumstances, but God's love, justice, mercy and kindness are constant and do not vary."

"Would you explain?"

"If I were God I could do that," Nation said with a smile. "I would explain it by giving those things to you. When I try to explain, I must do so with human language and in human terms, and through human understandings and experiences. When I do this, it becomes confined to those things. You could say it falls from grace. So about all I can do is strive for it and let God do the rest."

"How might He do it?" Vi asked.

"Through a burning bush, a strange warmed feeling, or..."

He stopped.

"Or? An owl?" I offered.

"Whatever or however He chooses. The *way* He does it is incidental. The fact that He does it is the important thing."

"Did Christ enter into your great grandmother's theology?" I asked.

"What does theology mean?"

"Her religion, her understanding of God."

"Oh, yes, sure. But not like Brother Jake says. One time she said, 'Christ and Brother Jake are different.'"

"Sounds like she knew both of them."

"She knew Christ better. I do not know if anybody knows Brother Jake. Joey says he does not. Not very good anyway. Maybe Mrs. Balaam does."

He turned and looked in through the window and saw his great grandmother's body lying on the bed. Then he looked out across the valley where the moon was just showing itself between two mountain peaks across the valley.

"It's better to live in harmony," he said as he laid his "dinner plate" aside, picked up his shovel and walked down the hill to an open area bordered by a few wild cedar trees. He located a stake which had been driven into the ground. There he turned over a shovel full of earth. From that point he took two and a half measured strides east and turned over the second shovel full. Then one stride south where he marked with another dig. Following that, another two and a half strides west with a fourth turnover of dirt. Then finally back to his original marking. With a stick he drew lines between the markings and began to dig along them. He dug neither slow nor fast, but at a steady pace such as a horse might take on a long journey. The metallic sound of the spade hitting the rocks made me think of what it must sound like when Sari Jane Balaam works in her garden.

"Aren't you going to help him?" Vi asked.

"When he gets tired, and that won't take long."

However, I underestimated his endurance, because he worked steadily for over an hour. We could tell he was having some difficulties, though, so Vi took a flashlight from the car and we walked down.

"Looks like I've hit a big rock," he said breathing heavily. The moon reflected the perspiration on his back. "I've dug around it but it keeps getting bigger."

The exposed part of the rock was large, the top just a few inches below the ground level.

"That will be difficult to move," I suggested. "Why don't you move the grave farther over and avoid it?"

"No!" he replied sharply. "Great Grandmother wants to be here."

With that he began to dig deeper around the boulder, encountering more and more rocks of lesser challenge, but the grave digging remained within the exact dimensions he had prescribed. The poor kid was wearing himself out, though his determination was far from diminishing. I offered to help but he was resolved to his task, so Vi and I returned to the porch steps.

"Should we go in and straighten up the house or anything?" Vi asked.

"No, we better just stay here for now."

Nation evidently was making little headway, so after another hour we walked down. He had dug less than a foot over all. It is said that Arkansans do not know how to dig in the ground; they only know how to stir up rocks, and there may be some truth in that. However, this monster of a rock was too big and heavy to lift out of the grave.

"Maybe we could dig with a steep down-grade on the opposite side of it," I suggested, "and then roll it over out of the way."

"That's where Great Grandfather is," was Nation's reply as he kept tugging and sweating and grunting.

Then he stopped. Wiping the perspiration from his face with his dirty hands, he said, "You had a good idea, but we will have to roll it across this grave to the other side so we will not disturb Great Grandfather."

He stepped over and began hacking away on the opposite side of his grave dimensions.

"I will dig out here on this other side," he said, "and then loosen that boulder and roll it down over the bottom of the grave."

"Good thinking, Nation," I responded, "but here, let me dig out from where you've marked the dimension."

Gratefully he handed the shovel to me, and I banged away at the rocks and dirt, careful not to dig within the grave dimensions for I realized that he must be the one to dig the actual grave. After some perspiring and grunting on my part, I dug a portion alongside the grave large enough and deep enough to hold the boulder. Then we loosened it and wedged it across into the lower hole.

Nation picked up the shovel and proceeded with his task.

"Is there anything Mrs. Hilliard and I can do?" I asked.

He stopped and looked at me.

"I didn't know how to fix her hair or anything," he said. "She used to keep it braided, but after she got too sick she couldn't. She has a dress to be buried in. I put it on the bed."

"I'll take care of her," said Vi.

We could tell that this lifted a heavy load of concern from his mind. He returned to his digging with renewed energy.

Vi, bless her heart, did the best she could with what little help I offered. Quietly we discussed how she might be laid in the grave--wrapped in a blanket, we supposed. We completed our task and then I walked down to join Nation. The moon was far beyond its zenith; daybreak was only a couple or three hours away.

"Nation, why don't you come up and rest awhile and get a drink of water? Vi would like to know if your great grandmother looks all right."

Quickly he left the shovel and I gave him a hand out of the grave, for quite literally he had dug himself into a hole. When I took his hand, he was trembling from exertion.

"It's easier digging now," he said, "since I got past most of the rocks."

"You're worn out; you better let me help you."

"No, I must do it, he said. "It won't take long now."

We remained outside while he went in to view his great grandmother. When he came back out, his whole countenance was refreshed and at ease. He looked at Vi, and with an emotion of soul-depth sincerity said, "Thank you," and without further ado, returned to his digging.

I called after him, "Nation, if you won't let me help you, Vi and I will go home for a little while. We'll be back as soon as we can. Would you like for us to bring Joey?"

He simply turned and nodded courteously.

When we returned home, Thanksgiving Day was breaking. Vi quickly made coffee and collected some breakfast items. I dialed Balaam's phone number and, wouldn't you know, Brother Jake answered. I told him that Nation and his great grandmother had arranged for me to have her funeral and I would like to speak with Joey to see if he wanted to go with us.

"Joey's in bed," came the curt response. "Besides, I don't want him attending no heathen funeral."

"It would be a good thing for Nation--and Joey, too--if you'd let him come with us," I said, almost pleadingly.

"It's a heathen funeral if that old woman didn't confess Jesus Christ as her personal Savior."

"She believed in Christ."

"Did you ask her the four steps to salvation?"

"Perhaps not," I replied, "but isn't Christ, rather than an examination, the means of Christian salvation?"

"She was the anti-Christ. She profaned the Word of God."

"Will you let Joey come?"

"No, I don't want him to be responsible for another soul in hell."

"Well, good-bye, Brother Jake."

I wanted to cry. As I laid the phone down, my mind screamed at my soul, "Who is right or wrong in this business of Christianity!?"

"How should we dress?" Vi asked.

"I don't know. I think Indians like full dress for special occasions," I replied, wondering myself what to put on.

"I've no idea what clothes he has, what he will wear," Vi said, using good foresight. We decided to wear our best for the occasion, the same we would wear at any funeral.

Daylight had not quite broken when we returned to the cabin. Nation met us at the door, bathed and dressed in a brown sports coat and blue trousers. He held a tie, saying, "I didn't know how to do it." I started to tie it for him, but simply couldn't do so from that forward position which was backward to a mirror. Vi did it for him. Then she went to the little kitchen and began preparing the breakfast we had brought.

Nation said, "Her coffin is in the woodshed. She told me how to make it a long time ago."

We brought it into the living room and placed it alongside the bed. It was a rough, crude thing, but in that moment it was the most beautiful piece of artwork we had ever seen! Carefully we laid her little body into it, making it as comfortable-looking as possible. Nation smoothed her dress and placed her hair braids down the front over her shoulders. "That's the way she used to wear them," he said with gentle satisfaction.

We ate little; there was no time to linger. Reverently, solemnly, we carried our precious charge to the grave site, Nation holding the rope handle on the right side, me the left, Vi balancing the foot of the casket. We placed the casket beside the grave, and I began the short funeral service just as the sun surfaced over the mountain.

"Yahweh-Jehovah, Great Spirit of the ancients," I began, raising my arms skyward, "God of our fathers, God of all creation, Lord of all. We lift our hearts in praise and thanksgiving for Great Grandmother Anna Skreigh, and for Nation. O Lord, God of us all, this one thing we ask: as you shared your love, your compassion and understanding with Great Grandmother Anna, please share that love with Nation, with Vi and me, and with all humankind. Now, with confidence in God the Father, God the Son and God the Holy Spirit, we join Nation as he lays his great grandmother's body into this chosen resting place, but to you, O Great Spirit, whom, in Jesus Christ, she has chosen above all, we commend her spirit, remembering how Jesus said upon the cross, 'Father, into your hands I commend my spirit.' Amen."

The three of us lowered the casket into the grave. That beautiful casket, so crudely created by a boy with such loving care, now holding the body of that gifted creation of Almighty God. Both casket and body would return to the earth from whence they came. What about the love, though--that eternal love which the Creator had added to both the body and the casket when they were created? My soul whispered the answer: love, too, returns to its source of origin.

I read Psalm 23 and together we recited the Lord's Prayer. Then simultaneously we looked skyward, faithfully confident that Great Grandmother Skreigh had entered her new home. We felt sure that, had we been in Paradise, we would have seen her there, but even so, God and His heaven seemed very near. I thought about The Screech of the Owl.

When I looked at Nation, he nodded satisfaction; then reached for the shovel. Vi and I went to the car and drove home in peaceful silence.

At noon when Vi was getting a little lunch ready, Nation appeared at the door with the document from his great grandmother's mattress.

"Come in and have lunch with us, Nation," Vi invited. "It isn't as much as the Indians and Pilgrims had together on that first Thanksgiving Day, and it can't compare with the traditional feast most people have today, but even so, the three of us can be as thankful as anyone."

Nation handed the papers to me.

"What do they say?" I asked.

"I don't know. I can't read. Will you read them to me?"

Of course, how thoughtless of me. That's why his great grandmother wanted me to see it. Reverently I laid the document in the middle of the table and said, "Shall we read it after we eat?"

When we finished lunch, which did not take long, I asked, "Shall I read the papers now?"

He nodded.

I unfolded several sheets of rough aged pulp paper, lined with light blue lines. The sheets had been torn raggedly at the top. There was something very familiar about them, one of those yesteryear flashes. Of course! The paper was from a Big Chief writing tablet such as I had used in the beginning grades of my public education. The tablets had a dark red front cover with a broadside silhouette of an Indian Chief whose head and regalia of feathers were featured in gold dust.

This nostalgia quickened further third grade memories. I smiled as I thought of how the finger signals have changed over the years; i.e., sixty-five years ago to raise your hand with one finger pointing skyward signaled the teacher to give permission to sharpen your pencil. Two fingers extended skyward like a victory sign meant "May I leave the room?" which today would be interpreted, "May I go to the bathroom?"

I began to read the contents written in pencil, possibly one of those old cedar penny pencils capped with that little dab of white eraser which never lasted.

The document was written in excellent penmanship. It was dated November 16, 1907. I read as follows:

> Today, November 16, 1907, this Indian Territory where we were confined in 1838, becomes Oklahoma, the 46th United State. We Cherokees asked that the state be called Sequoya in honor of the member of our tribe who designed the Cherokee syllabary, but they named it Oklahoma, a Creek word meaning "red man."
>
> I write this paper with the hope that it might someday reach the hands of any living kinsmen I might have. My wife died six years ago. The only remaining relative I have who might be living is a grandson whose name is Enoch Skreigh. I do not know if he lives; I have not heard anything about him for many years. It may be important for the well-being of our Cherokee People that this information reach him because members of our family have always been responsible for the Sacred Fire of our Cherokee Nation. I do not know how this tradition began, but when the soldiers killed my father on the Trail of Tears, I fell heir to that responsibility, though I was only eight years old at the time. The people in the section of the caravan with whom my father traveled did not know whether other Fire Keepers existed along the Trail, so when the soldier shot my father, my elders told me to do the best I could with what little knowledge and instruction I had concerning the holy ritual. When I grew into adulthood, I retained the heritage in our locality. I did the best I could, but I know the preparations were sorrowfully incomplete because the Fire lacked the power it had in the olden days. This may be the reason so many of the hardships came to us, like when the Hebrews lost the power of their Ark of the Covenant.

I do not know. My grandson would inherit this venerable position from me if he were here. Perhaps he could rekindle its spiritual significance.

Nevertheless, at each ceremony-time I have faithfully executed the ritual by reviving the Fire on top of the old ashes as reverently and conscientiously as I could. Each season I offered the New Fire to those who still believed in its powers, but fewer and fewer people have had faith in it. For one thing, the younger people do not believe the Great Spirit requires them to cook the first fruits of their crops with the New Fire. I do not know that I do either, any more. The last time I prepare it for that purpose, nobody came for it.

This morning at sunrise I rekindled the Fire for the last time.

Now, with the sun at its zenith, I sit here with tears in my eyes, watching the death of this national sacrosanctity which has been practiced by us since the beginning of our time. Its life is flickering. The Flame will follow the fate of our Nation, the once great and mighty Cherokee Nation, into oblivion. Even if any of the other Fire Carriers have survived and locate these ashes and rekindle the Sacred Flame, it will be for some new purpose. The old is gone.

I say that, because today, November 16, 1907, the new Severalty Act of the United States Government will alter the ownership of this western land our nation owns--this Indian Territory for which our eastern land was exchanged in 1838. This afternoon, the land will no longer be under communal ownership. The officials will divide it into parcels, and then they will deed these parcels of land to individual members of the tribe for personal ownership. This Act will absolve our Nation. Officially, it will transfer us from members of the Cherokee Nation to citizens of the United States of America. If the Cherokee Nation continues to exist at all, it will be in name only, and in the journals of history.

The ambivalence between the two governing factors, Cherokee and American, has often created confusion for us Cherokees, both as a nation and as individuals. I was fortunate, because my foster parents insisted that I finish high school and then they sent me to Normal to become a teacher. Consistently, they taught me to hold no pre-judgments of any kind, but to glean the best from all things, especially from each of these two civilizations. I have done that with some success, and it has helped me to live with the conflicts among my white neighbors as well as my fellow tribesmen, especially the persistent factions between the followers of our Treaty Party people and the Late Immigrants within our tribe.

Another purpose for my writing this document is to record and pass along what I know about a certain thing or two that happened, and perhaps still happens, in our family line. I would like for this information to reach any surviving member of my family.

The first thing I wish to mention is The Screech of the Owl. It is not heard often, but when one of us does hear it, there is always life-change for that person. The Screech does not bring death; it brings Life. Death comes in a variety of forms, but it should never be related to The Screech. It changes whoever hears it from his or her old form of life to another. Sometimes this transformation takes place and the person continues to live on earth. Sometimes not. In any event, The Screech is a gift of Life.

It is also necessary to understand that The Screech comes from our totem, the Owl, but it is not the ordinary sound owls make. I will elaborate upon this when I write about "Ultimatessence" in this treatise.

This phenomenon of The Screech has been in our family from the times of the Ancient Ones. I have never heard it. My mother did, though, because when that soldier shot my father, she ran toward him but did not stop where he had fallen. She ran over that great bluff where I saw her disappear. They say she caught onto my father's departing Spirit. I do not know, but I do remember hearing the ordinary screech of an owl about that same time. When my mother heard The Screech, it was the last time any of us has ever heard it. So we wonder if it followed her to wherever she had gone.

Some years ago here in the Territory my grandson had some serious trouble with another lad in school. The other lad's family was one of those from the old militant Late Immigrant group led by John Ross during the Trail of Tears. This faction was vehemently against selling or trading our eastern land to the Whites in exchange for western land. Our family was in sympathy with the Treaty Party group, led by Major Ridge, to make the trade because they could see no favorable alternative to the federal government's demand that Cherokees be removed from the East. While some of the Treaty Party moved to the western lands with Major Ridge in 1837, most of the nation's population remained in the East, believing that the United States Nation and the Cherokee Nation would work out the difficulties. Some of us who stayed hoped to integrate peacefully into the White society, but others resorted to militant means to settle the differences.

Suddenly without warning one spring day in 1838, the White army and civilian militants began burning and siezing our homes and confiscating our property. Within a day's time they forced families into barricades where they imprisoned us during the summer season with insufficient food, water, clothing or shelter from the sun and rain. In the fall and winter they marched us westward, forcing us over the Trail of Tears to this designated land which they called Indian Territory.

Within a short time Ross' faction gained control of the Cherokee government in this new land. There was bitter animosity between his group and the rest of us which almost led to a civil war between Ross' New Immigrants and Major Ridge's Treaty Party. The animosity exploded when some of Ross' group secretely assassinated Major Ridge and some others by reenacting the old Cherokee Blood Law which called for death to anyone who relinquished Cherokee land by sale or trade to the Whites.

After that, time healed little as wounds upon wounds constantly festered and old revenges gouged deeper as the months turned into years. Our youth became hardened.

One day my grandson, who was in high school, became involved in a fight with one of the Late Immigrant kids, and in the heat of anger he verbally threatened to kill the kid whose name was Kato. Soon thereafter, Kato met with a fatal accident for which my grandson was blamed.

It was after dark when He Who Hears Well came running breathlessly to our house saying that a mob of "Rosses" was getting "lickered up" over on Council Grounds and were talking about revenge.

"Revenge for what?" I asked.

"They think your grandson killed Kato."

"Killed him!" I exclaimed. "I didn't know he was dead."

"He was killed this afternoon," replied He Who Hears Well urgently. "He was out cutting fence posts when a dead tree limb fell on him. They think your grandson did it because of that fight the two boys had last week."

Just then my grandson came in the back door saying, "Grandfather, there is a bunch of people coming."

Quickly we explained the situation to him. By then the mob of a dozen men with torches had burst into our front yard and called out for my grandson. I went to the door and responded, "What do you want with him?"

"He killed Kato today," one of them replied, and before he could finish, others vociferated revenge.

Various ones cried out:

"Yeah, and we are gonna get him tonight."

"He is gonna pay for what he did to Kato ".

"That murderer, we shoulda got him a long time ago along with all you other Treaties!"

"Come on, boys, we're gonna search this place."

"Yeah, he is there somewhere."

With that, they began to force their way into the house, ignoring my protests.

"There he is, I see him," cried one of them.

They stormed the house and seized my grandson, disregarding his protests of not having seen Kato that day.

He Who Hears Well and I could not stop them as they dragged Enoch out the door.

"Let's string him up on that tree over there," someone said.

In the darkness, amid the clumsy, drunken frenzy, He Who Hears Well helped my grandson struggle loose. He dashed around the house. I ran quickly to the barn with him.

"Get Old Gray," I whispered as I grabbed the bridle for the horse. He jumped astride and raced down the lane behind the barn which led to the wooded hills eastward.

That is the last time I saw my grandson, Enoch Skreigh.

Years later we heard that he had married a Cherokee girl over in the Ozark Mountains somewhere in what is now the State of Arkansas. The traveler who brought the information said it was near "The Place of the Calling." That is all we ever heard about him. I sometimes wonder if that is not the place where my mother disappeared over the great bluff somewhere along the Trail of Tears.

There is another thing that seems peculiar to our family bloodline, though I suppose this comes to us from parental teaching rather than some mysterious source. Since neither I nor my deceased wife have any known progeny other than the grandson who fled to Arkansas, I write about these things hoping that, with the development of railroads and automobiles, and the United States postal system, this document will one day reach my grandson or perhaps his children.

The family peculiarity to which I allude is not a religious thing any more than The Screech is. It has to do with Life, a dimension of living. One learns it by the exemplary communications of parents and close relatives rather than by words of instruction. So there will be difficulty in exploring its meaning through writing, and I can hope for little clarity resulting from this effort.

Let me begin by borrowing the Biblical Garden of Eden concept. Adam and Eve lived in complete harmony with God; they were at one with God as Jesus was at one with Him. They were endowed with all the attributes of God, lacking one thing: the knowledge of evil. There was no evil in their hearts, minds, bodies or souls. This means they knew everything except evil. Or perhaps they just did not know how to differentiate between good and evil. Knowledge of the evil of ignorance, crime, hunger, thirst, imprisonment did not exist for them. Free will was unadulterated. There was no evil in thought, power, or nakedness.

Is this not something we all long for? It is living at one with God. I understand that is the way Jesus lived, though being like us He did have knowledge of evil.

Think of it: there would be no struggle for power because everyone would have ultimate power. By the same token, there would be no search for knowledge because every person would possess all knowledge. Is this not a common concept of the Christian's heaven?

The Cherokee name for this phenomenon may be translated loosely as "Ultimatessence."

Ultimatessence re-establishes the attributes that God gave mankind at creation. Jesus the Christ may have been the first person to have been given this gift since Adam and Eve. Jesus indicated that others, perhaps ultimately all humankind, would obtain it.

Therefore, it is conceivable that the possibility of Ultimatessence be within an individual today just as it was in Christ. Periodically it has come to a few people in our ancestral line. Our tradition says The Screech of the Owl always precedes Ultimatessence.

Ultimatessence has no limitations, no impossibilities. Again, however, do not equate it with God. It is the culmination of God's creation, evidently offered as a gift.

Now, after having said that, let me say this about Ultimatessence: when everything possible has been said and written about it, only one thing holds fast and that is that only Ultimatessence itself can clarify itself. Our prevenient concepts, our primordial affiliations with it tell us only what they can.

However, I must reiterate this one thing: when someone in our family hears The Screech of the Owl, it always means an entirely different life for that person; a life perfected in the innermost self. That is Ultimatessence. It may or may not manifest itself while the person continues to live on earth.

I write these things in the hope that these traditions will not end with me as the Sacred Fire just now did. Perhaps this document will reach the hands of my grandson in Arkansas, or his progeny. Again, his name is Enoch Skreigh. They said he married a Cherokee named Anna.

Signed this 16th day of November, 1907, Tahlequah, State of Oklahoma, no longer the Territory of the Indians. The Promised Land, granted to us "forever" by written treaties, is no more.

--Enoch Nation Skreigh.

Chapter 27

Winter in Arizona

Soon after Anna Skreigh's funeral, Vi and I decided to spend part of the winter in Arizona. We arrived at our duplex in Tempe yesterday.

On our way out we drove south of Oklahoma City. On a back road along the Red River we stopped the car and I said to Vi, "This is the very place where Ol' Gus and Call crossed with their herd of cattle enroute to Montana in Larry McMurtry's novel, *Lonesome Dove*."

"How do you know this was 'the very place'"? Vi asked.

"Well, I was there, wasn't I?"

"Of course you weren't there! What are you talking about?"

"Vi, when you read Larry McMurtry, you are there, where his characters are."

At noon we stopped for lunch in Abilene--still in Texas--where a pickup truck came to a jolting halt beside our car. A tall cowboy unfolded himself from the seat. He adjusted his ten-gallon Stetson, hitched up his tailored jeans, examined his high heeled boots, and flashed the polished silver buckle on his wide belt. His shoulders, broad as the western sky, were complimented by each of these movements. There he stood, tall and masculine as he reached up, cocked his hat a bit more and then pulled out a little thread of a lasso from his pocket and snapped it onto a miniature French poodle.

Down the street they cantered.

"Get along little doggie, get along, get along," Vi began to hum.

Farther along in West Texas we experienced a touch of the Old West when we stopped at the Circle Deck Corral. While we were watching the horses mill around inside, a tall lean man stood near the gate. With the keen eye of one who knew horses, he entered the corral and chose the pick of the lot. It was a black mustang, evidently fresh from the wild western plains, yet suited for the rugged sierras. Its head arched royally, its jaws determined. It pranced and reared and pawed the sky with its forelegs.

This was his horse.

The man's hair was just as gray as mine, but the crow-foot wrinkles fanning out from each eye told of struggles won the hard way. With a stout heart and strong hand he took the reins firmly and mounted this chosen steed, the fleetest, the most daring to be found on the Circle Deck range. Bravely, courageously he swung into the saddle. With the strength and vigor of a rodeo bull the mustang surged forward, breaking the sound barrier and cracking the face of the earth with one single bound. Then, with tail high and nostrils flaring, it erupted upward and downward and sideways and roundways.

Through it all, the bronco buster remained steadfast in the saddle as distance fell behind, speed splitting the wind like a shooting star. Perspiration streamed from the man's hands as he held onto the brass carousel pole which protruded from the ceiling down through the shoulders of the black mustang to the floor of the Circle Deck Corral. Behold the wonder as he looked straight ahead with the exhilarated excitement of bygone years when the carnival came to town. Even now he kept a tight rein on the surging fears that never quite made it to the surface--except in his eyes.

And I rode with him.

Trekking along--still in Texas!--we acquired another "Don't Mess with Texas" litter bag. Near the New Mexico border we stopped at a motel where the rooms had washbowl sinks molded in the shape and contour of Texas.

"Isn't this novel," I said, "but wouldn't you hate to clean them?'

Vi replied quick as a wink, "Don't worry about it because they don't get dirty. You don't mess with Texas."

On through New Mexico where, at a service station convenience store, the clerk refused service to a young man because he had no shirt on. An elderly man standing by said, "Here, son," as he quickly unbuttoned his short-sleeved shirt, laid it across the young man's shoulders, who then paid for his Coke, returned the shirt and departed. No generation gap there.

This happened across the street from a Mexican restaurant named "Hot Stuff."

December has been easy on us since we arrived in Arizona. Each day golden sunshine crowns the surrounding mountains and fills the desert valleys. The hiking trails are like garlands draping the foothills and arroyos. Our lives are plumb full of God's glory.

The other day we thought to brighten up the patio with a little pot of flowers. So off to the nursery we went where Vi selected a colorful pansy, a bright yellow one, which she took to the checkout counter. The young man handed her a rather large cardboard box and placed the lonely little plant in it, tilting it a bit so we could get full view of its insignificance in that huge surrounding.

"Would you like to look around some more?" he asked, knowing full well how small, even a tad chintzy, the little plant looked in its huge cardboard environment. I have no doubt he was reading Vi's thought that it would look very lonely on the patio.

Yes, we did just as the young entrepreneur thought we might; we looked around and proceeded to inspect the bounteous selection of flowers in the nursery gardens long enough to half-fill the big box. Back to the check-out man.

"Oh, here's a little gift," he said, placing a tiny cactus in an empty corner of the box. "We have them left over from Christmas," he said coyly. "They're on sale, half-price but you may have this one with our compliments."

His teeth flashed a beautiful smile that included both of us, for customer exclusion was not in his strategy.

"Maybe you'd like to select some companions for this little fellow and create your own cactus planter."

While talking, he transferred the little gift to another empty box which appeared magically from under the counter and pushed it towards us.

The original little pansy was delighted when I signed the receipt of the stunned credit card and let her join her two boxes of companions. Nevertheless, the cactus creation is pretty, all five of them crowded into a rather costly sandstone bowl decorated in a Southwestern motif.

Surely God had foresight to place that young man on some church's finance committee--as chairman.

Near the Phoenix Zoo is Papago Park. Within the park is a series of red rock formations, some quite lofty. One particular formation has a rough trail leading upward some five hundred feet to the base of the rock. From there on the east side of the park one can walk around on a wide ledge through a large hole in the rock. Behold! East has become West as you view the other side of the mountain.

One day Vi and I were taking this adventure. As we walked upward, enjoying the views and fresh air, we overtook a young man, a victim of Down's syndrome, who was working very hard at the rather steep climb.

We encouraged him as we passed by, but he paid no attention to us, so intent was he upon his endeavor.

We reached the top where the steps ended and sat down on the ledge about fifty feet from the hole. From this vantage point we watched our friend. Never once did he lag in his efforts toward the task which was very difficult for him. When he reached our level on the ledge, he looked around and proceeded with determination toward the hole.

Vi and I re-focused our attention on the wild life of both zoo and city which stretched before us.

Suddenly we heard loud, guttural, indiscernible cries from beyond the hole in the wall! The sounds were not necessarily notes of distress, but rather as far as we could tell they were jubilant. Nevertheless, we hurried around through the hole, and there on the ledge from which one could overlook the world in the opposite direction was our friend heralding his achievement to his new-found kingdom, saying over and over, "You did it! You did it!"

When we returned to the base of this mountain-top experience, we met a group of Downeys with their supervisors. Of course we related to them what we had experienced.

"Yes," said one of the supervisors, "he insisted on going on ahead by himself. We encourage them to achieve on their own, and when they do, we exclaim, 'You did it! You did it!'"

Another victory was chalked up for this young achiever!

The other day we visited the home of some Chinese friends who have invented a unique way of getting rid of scorpions around their new desert dwelling. Our friends keep all sorts of pets and animals in and around their house, so the use of scorpion poison was ruled out.

"I know," exclaimed the young matron of the estate. "Scorpions are high on chickens' pecking order. They love to eat scorpions."

So forthwith she puchased a brood of chickens, one of which grew into a prolific layer. Her name is Laydella. Laydella has chosen a Christmas wreath made of straw in which to deposit her daily produce. Our friend had stored the wreath on a shelf located in the carport. The shelf is not sturdy. When the hen hops upon it, it tilts downward toward a bed of abondoned pet rocks huddling in the afternoon sun beside the house.

The hen, hardly more than a broiler, seems to be perfectly satisfied to make her daily contribution and let it roll gently down the plank to its demise on the bed of rocks.

However, our friend has devised (so she says) a means of salvation for these helpless embryos who keep coming out of their shells. First she padded the rocks with an old saddle blanket. This prevented the eggs from cracking up. There on the soft blanket the embryos flock together while the sun rays warm them to a hatching degree. So far, however, she has not heard one peep out of them. That might be because our Chinese friend conditioned Broiler Laydella to produce her output at two o'clock in the afternoon. That is when the sun is at its baking zenith. Then as each egg rolls gently down the plank, it gyrates itself into the perfect egg roll, crisp and fresh from the broiler!

Today Vi patched a little fault in the sofa fabric. She did a fine job; you can hardly notice where the split had been. It was a much better job than the one I did on the garbage dumpster.

Here in Tempe, the city furnishes each dwelling with a huge plastic dumpster for garbage. It is much larger than a full-size barrel. It is large enough to swallow Jonah, even after he had been swallowed. The lid is on hinges, and the wheels make it easy to convey the contraption to the curb. Each week a truck comes, and with automatic arms it reaches out, picks up this huge container, lifts it up and over, dumps the contents into the truck, and returns dumpster to the curb. Ingenious!

This morning while Vi patched the sofa, I began to scrub the dumpster. It needed it! I thought I could lean over, down into the thing and reach the bottom with the scrub brush--almost but not quite. I stretched a bit farther--just a little bit farther and I would be there. The smell was getting to me. Desperately, when I gave one final lunge to take care of the situation, the situation took care of me! In one gulp from that monster, I went in like Jonah into the belly of the whale! There I was, arms, head, body and nose squirming around in that mess with my legs kicking the thin air outside.

No, I wasn't damaged, but I envisioned the truck coming and lifting me into its bosom, and I wasn't quite ready for that kind of trucking. When I yelled for Vi to come to my rescue, it sounded like I was inside one of those super boom boxes.

Then I heard a dog barking and a man's voice coming from outer space saying, "Do you need some help?"

"Of course I need help," I said frantically, "but don't let that dog get my legs!"

"Don't worry," he replied, "your legs are too high for him."

It was our neighbor, Alfred, with his collie. Alfred took the lid off the dumpster and turned it over on its side. Somehow it got away from him and began rolling down the driveway with me rolling around inside like in one of these big cement mixer trucks you see on the road. The dog growled and barked as I came slithering out, and when he recognized that the garbage-can intruder was not some raiding varmint, he began licking me like a mother lion after her baby cub.

We spent much of our Christmas time with some friends, Connie and her daughter, Angela, who live in Angela's large, new house in another section of town. A couple of weeks ago we helped put up her first Christmas tree there. The tree was a wild thing from its sapling youth. Angela had managed to get a government tree-cutting permit, so she and a friend had gone up near Grand Canyon in a pickup and selected this unrestrained twelve foot wilderness wonder. The tree, determined and unruly, created some excitement when her friend's larger one kicked it off the pickup in downtown Prescott. It happened at one of those intersections where they were selling Christmas trees, and I guess the police had to verify that Angela had not stolen her evergreen renegade from the lot when she retrieved it from the curb.

At home the tree was docile enough when we squeezed it through the front double doors into the foyer and drawing room. Then bad news rushed in when Angela's two terriers came barking and tugging at the tree's sawed off trunk. In one frantic, bronco-busting frenzy the tree unsprang and hurtled from the plastic sheet into the middle of the drawing room, spouting pine pitch all over the white carpet. Vi went berserk, Connie rung her hands crying, "Oh dear," but Angela simply sprinkled brown sugar on the pitch and the dogs did the best they could.

We finally got the overgrown sucker upright--somewhat. Then darned if it didn't jackknife right over into the middle of the room again with me flat-faced down under it! Picture it from the lofty cathedral ceiling: Jim under that outer-space varmint calling for mercy, Vi pulling at branches toward the entryway, Angela tugging toward the dining room, and her mother ringing her hands repeating, "Oh dear, oh dear," while the two dogs gave voice to exceeding great joy.

Then the miracle of Christmas! As I looked frantically through those branches and saw the trauma I began to laugh. Suddenly there was with me the mirth of a heavenly host--first Vi, then Angela and Connie, and would you believe, the dogs. We simply lay, stood, stooped and bounced together in joyous transfiguration.

Thus bagan our "season to be jolly."

Earlier in December we had brunch with some friends in Fountain Hills, east of Phoenix. From their patio we could see the city fountain, the world's tallest they say, shooting five hundred and sixty feet straight up in the air.

Our friends told us that two coveys of Gambel quail roost in the cedar trees at the edge of their carport, and sure enough, while we were there a dozen of the birds dropped down from the trees like little sacks of feathers, and helped themselves to the seeds that had been thrown out for them. As they pecked at the seeds, the little top notches on their heads kept time like the rapid bobbing of a midget drum major's plume, only faster. Our friends said that one morning a coyote came hoping for a breakfast of one of them, but they fluttered away just in time. A roadrunner raced by while we were there, and two cactus wrens came and sang to us as we enjoyed our brunch, though we tried to hide our eggs from their view. Later on, two chipmunks appeared, their little snouts close to the patio floor like miniature vacuum cleaners inhaling the remaining seeds.

The community of Chandler, south of Phoenix, was only a spot in the road some years back, a little desert crossroads where refreshment at the hitching rail cafe was coffee so strong they tamped it into the cups. Chandler is different now. Housing developments for a radius of miles have squeezed out the desert cacti and irrigated alfalfa fields. All that was familiar has been changed, except their town Christmas tree. We paid homage to it, that traditional fifty foot high transformation of tumbleweeds. A merry sight indeed. Yes, a fifty-foot high Christmas tree made of tumbleweeds!

God has been gracious to us during 1991. Not even a headache for either of us, though I confess, now that it is Christmas time, that I may have unwittingly or otherwise caused a few headaches.

A real thing happened last week in downtown Tempe. We stopped in at a little sidewalk cafe near Arizona State University. As we were having lunch, right there before our very eyes entered a true Kris Kringle caricature. If he was not a civilian Santa Claus, he should have been. When he sat down, his jolly bigness bumped the table, causing the condiments to clink out a jingle bells tune. This, of course, captured the attention of a small boy sitting with his parents at the next table. It was clear that the boy held some reservations about the true identity of this new neighbor, but he remained hopeful in spite of the disappointing clumsiness. He was not one to chance any erring of identity at this time of the year.

"Are you Santa?" he blurted out with a clear, unrepressed frankness.

All heads turned to the scene.

The parents made feeble jestures to subdue the child, but we who shared the boy's reservations were pleased with their half-hearted discipline.

Then suddenly all attention bounced toward a calamity near the sidewalk. An elderly man had fallen and knocked his chair over. No damage other than dignity accompanied the fall. However, as soon as the eyes of the boy and the jolly old St. Nick caricature met again the boy arose from his table and dashed over to the old couple's table, saying, "My Grandpa's foot hit the card table yesterday when he and Grandma were playing cards, and Grandma said, 'That's what happens when you get old.'"

"That's right, Son," replied the man as his countenance immediately turned from embarrassment to ease and pleasure.

"Are you old?" the boy asked.

"No, Son," came the reply. "I was a moment ago, but right now, thanks to you, I'm not old at all."

"I didn't think so," said the boy.

Then, stepping closer to the old man, he asked, "Can I ask you something?"

"You surely may," said the man.

"I'll have to whisper it," confided the boy.

The man reached down and lifted the boy onto his lap and held his ear close to the boy's face. The boy cupped his hand beside his mouth and whispered something. Both faces, all four eyes, focused directly upon Mr. Kringle sitting near our table. The *tete-a-tete* was serious. It was very serious.

The authority of the grandpa-man was unquestionable as he nodded his affirmation. It was awfully convincing.

Of course, like most kids, Vi and I stopped believing in Santa Claus about the time our public schooling began. Yet, that little boy and old man were quite positive, and obviously they knew what they were talking about. Santa, dressed in civilian clothes, might have been sitting right next to our table. We did not know for sure, but when we looked over at him again, he was pulling out his pocket computer. It had a list of names on it. He was checking it twice.

Vi sat and watched comfortably, but I began to sweat a little.

On Christmas Day Vi and I took the old portable typewriter, the daily newspaper and "Li'l-Oscar-the-Cooler" packed with bread and lunch meat, oranges, water and cookies, and drove ninety miles northward on

Highway 87 up through the Tonto Basin to the bottom of the Mogollon Rim. There we turned off onto a dirt road so insignificant it is not even noted on the map.

About ten miles along this mountain road, a javelina crossed our way. Quickly I stopped the car, grabbed the camcorder and followed the grunting animal into the brush. Sure enough, the camera picked up a good view of him rooting around in the dirt. It gave no notice of my human interest to record him for living room TV viewing. The excitement of the spectacle, as it came to me through the camcorder's view finder, commanded so much of my attention that his companions, who were immediately behind to my left, excaped my attention Alas!. Too late! The sudden grunts and snorts from the auxiliary animals caused me to jump backward with the horrible feeling of attack! A fierce pain seared the calf of my leg! I dropped the camcorder and surged forward toward the car, only to bump into one of those demons as he ran grunting across my pathway.

The outcome? I had backed into a clump of prickly pear cactus whose thorns were as vicious as boar tusks and twice as sharp! The pig I stumbled over was just as frightened as I.

When I reached the car, Vi was hysterical!

"Where's the camcorder?" she asked, laughter bursting out all over. "If only I had had it!"

I'm glad she didn't.

A few more miles through this gorgeous landscaping of picturesque rock formations, fording an occasional streamlet, brought us around a hairpin curve. Just beyond this curve, over a steep ridge, we found a little valley paradise.

"This," we said, "is our reserved dining room where we will have Christmas dinner with our friends."

So there we sat on a huge granite boulder beside a little stream racing through the middle of our private wilderness. We were alone with the beauty of our memories and the surrounding magnificence. There our wanderings on Christmas Day ended like Joseph and Mary when they, too, came to their appointed place. Truly, it does feel like He, whom the Family Circle kids recently identified as the Star of Bethlehem, guided us there.

Last Sunday night we were driving eastward on a rural highway toward the Fort McDowell Indian Reservation Casino. There we faced sixteen-miles of casino traffic on the Beeline Highway, the cars bumper to bumper. These hundreds of headlights were headed homeward from the casino toward the Phoenix metropolis. One pair of headlights was bright, all others dim.

We purchased a bread maker for Christmas. It has just completed its first loaf, so come now, and join us for hot home-made bread dripping with butter, topped with home-made raspberry jam or wild plum jelly. We'd love to have you.

Last week they opened the local rodeo with this prayer: "Lord, Most High God, here we are, cowboys and cowboy fans coming to You with our bumps and thumps in the public arena, and in the private sectors of our lives. Touch, protect, heal, forgive. Join us, please, O God, in our camaraderie that we may share each other's wins and losses, dreams and endeavors, and come to know each other's hearts as You do. Amen."

On the fountain brink at the Fiesta Mall sat a young girl, pretty, accented by her tight, thigh-high skirt. She held a cigarette outward and upward with teacup fingers. Around her stood a gaggle of admirers.
Youths acting like adults have little more quality than adults acting like youths.

One morning, an example of courage and determination found in today's youth unfolded in the pew ahead of us at Central Church, downtown Phoenix. A girl about eighteen came down the aisle just before the service began. She looked around contemplatively as if to make sure that her location for worship harbored no imperfection. Abruptly she stopped at the end of the pew just ahead of us. One could tell by her very countenance that this pew, and none other, was to be her place for worship. She looked down quite pleasantly, steadfastly, at the obese lady sitting at the immediate end of the pew. Until then, nobody, not even the ushers, had challenged that stalwart person for the empty space in the pew beyond her. However, the young lady had made up her mind that this was to be her location for worship. Almost angelically, she quietly accented her determination as she stood, overtly coveting her selected space on this pew.
The heavy lady looked up at the girl, then gestured with a nod out across the display of back-heads in an attempt to call the girl's attention to the pew availability beyond. The girl stood firmly. The plumpness of the lady quivered in protest as she tried to withdraw her bountiful thighs inward so the girl could pass. No way could the young one squeeze through, and they both knew it. However, the young lady did not fret.

She just stood there. Finally the lady grunted as she half-scooted and half-bobbed over just enough for the girl to sit tightly against her or withdraw to another location. Even yet, youth stood her ground, glancing beyond at the length of the unoccupied pew. The portly folds began to make preparations for another surrender. She repeated her efforts. Then, just as the organ crescendoed for the processional hymn, the lady bounced a couple of times and settled down like a double portion of jiggle-jello. The young girl sat quite comfortably at worship beside her pew companion. The two of them talked a bit, prayed and sang together, and listened. The benediction punctuated a new friendship.

A week or so ago we received this letter from Joey Balaam:

January 21, 1990

Dear Bro. Hilliard and Mrs.,

How are you all? I am fine. School is OK, too. I wrote down a lot of things I think about and put them in my trunk and Papa found them and threw them all away. He said I had no business collecting thoughts like that. Things like I don't think the Bible was ever meant to take the place of God. I wrote down a question that said "Do we follow Christ or the Bible?" And I had written that Christianity would give people a good relationship with each other if we wouldn't say we believe things which we don't, and tell others they are wrong because they don't believe like we do. One note said that if we claimed to be saved just to escape hell, then we've missed what Christ is all about. And Papa was real furious when he read where I wrote that the Bible is not God speaking to us, but mostly it was what He spoke to others a long time ago, and I said if we listened today we would understand what Jesus says, because he said, "He who has ears, let him hear."

In another note I wrote that our hearts rule our actions and that's why God pays more attention to what's in our hearts than He does to our actions.

I never saw Papa so angry as when he saw where I wrote that the Bible gives us second hand Christianity because it is a Christianity that was given to those people who wrote the Bible and then they passed it along. I didn't mean no harm when I wrote that. And I said that's why we misunderstand and mistake things because those people who wrote down what the Bible says don't make it as clear as God does when he gives us understanding direct from Himself. I like the Bible, but seems to me when people take it for the word of God it's like taking an echo for the real voice. When I wrote that the parables of Jesus didn't really happen, like the rich man didn't really see and talk with Abraham from hell, Papa hit the ceiling and said the Bible said he did, then he did, and if anyone changes one jot or tittle of the Word of God they will burn in hell. Well, I would never change the Bible, but I wish people would receive first-hand teaching from Jesus today like those people who wrote the Bible did.

And when Papa saw my note that said the Old Testament is Jewish religion, he burned it like a Ku Klux Klanner's cross right there in front of me.

He said no kid of his has a right to think like I do and he ought to send me to the insane asylum. He's cooled down some now but not hardly. He won't let me go anywhere except to church and prayer meeting. And he keeps preaching at me all the time. I guess I am kinda funny but I can't help it. I don't feel like an odd-ball like everybody seems to think I am. I just can't think about Christianity like Papa and others do. I think God loves me and won't let me burn over those flames of hell Papa keeps talking about all the time. What do you think?

What I'm writing for is I know you are my friends and I wonder if you would also be my trunk where I could store my thoughts. I know that sounds crazy, but I don't want to lose them so I need somewhere safe to put them so maybe you could put them in your computer or maybe just remember them. I want to keep them because I think they're from God, and someday I might get you to show them to Mr. Leonard or talk to him about them. He is my friend in Dogwood and I've been talking to him a lot since you all have been away this winter.

I hope you're enjoying Arizona. The weather is not too bad here. Papa is a lot stormier. But he's my father.
Your friend,
Joey.

Joey's trunk! Where he can store his innermost thoughts. Where he can store himself.

"No small thing," Vi said.

Indeed it is no small thing for one human being to be the recipient of another.

We responded to Joey's letter, telling him about our rough trek into Cochise's Stronghold in the Dragoon Mountains in Southern Arizona. Along the way into the Stronghold, we took a snapshot of seven deer splashing across the stream and frolicking in a meadow. We enclosed the picture and a brochure of Cochise folklore and asked him to share them with Nation. Our being there made the history of that great Indian chief come alive for us.

"Yes," we wrote to Joey, "indeed we will be your trunk which you can open and close at any time and store with us whatever you wish. The information you give us will be kept safe and secret.

Last week we visited Boot Hill Cemetery at Tombstone. There a grave marker bears the apology, "Hanged by Mistake." Other epitaphs as novel as the OK Corral pumps life to that old grave yard, but luncheon at one of the restaurants took the Oscar.

Inside the restaurant a sign greeted us: "Seat Yourself." This was easier said than done because when I walked halfway across the room and stepped around the corner of a table to pull Vi's chair out, I bumped into their mirrored wall! In shock and confusion I looked up and saw Vi standing in front of me, trying not to join the restaurant clientele in their hushed mirth.

It took me longer than it should have to realize what had happened, but how was I to know that the table I started around was only a half-table with two chairs, not four? I turned around, and saw Vi standing at another empty table, waiting patiently for me to return to my senses and join her.

Attached to the menu with a paper clip was a little carbon copy square of paper with the hand-written notice: "Special--Buffalo Burgers and Sarsaparilla."

"Wonder what that would do to you," I mused to myself, overheard by Vi.

"Nothing more than otherwise," was her response, wise or otherwise.

A lady and man at a table across the room were talking with each other, she waving her arms profusely. I wondered if they were real or mirrored against the wall, for I surely couldn't tell if they were here or there.

While waiting for our orders, I spotted the sign, "Restrooms" on the wall near the kitchen. I excused myself and went forthwith. The instant I reached to push the rest room door open I thought to look up at the identification to make sure I was entering the proper gender-room because so far things hadn't been going too well for me. Just as I glanced up, behold! the sign that said, "Cowboys," read backward as in a mirror. Naturally I jerked back, not wanting to bump against a reflecting door. I simply did not need any more bumping around in that place. Naturally, I looked around to see if anyone saw me as one does when one slips down on an icy sidewalk on main street up North. Sure enough, everybody in the restaurant had their eyes upon this one-man circus. Oh, how I wished

Vi would come and take me by the hand again, this time down to the OK Corral for a real shoot-out!

I shrugged my shoulders, composed myself, and sheepishly looked up at the backward "Cowboy" sign again, and then over at the wall opposite. Nothing there--nothing except the tables of people watching. Then came the realization! The "Cowboy" sign above the real door had been printed backward to make it appear as if it were mirrored.

Well, golly sakes, by that time I didn't need to go.

The brochure promoted covered wagon rides in the desert, a shoot-out on Main Street that featured Rosey's Cantina, saloons, and, uh..."other live entertainment." All of this, the notice pointed out, was for the rugged cactus-pricked westerners as well as the white-wristwatch[6] snowbirds. Reservations were required, so Thursday morning we stopped to make them.

Mistake No. 1: I went in alone.

An open gate admitted me into the grounds where I was free to walk down Main Street, Old West. Nobody was around, but a sign was at hand which read: "Cactus Red-eye, Recycled Tobacco, Hello Dollies." Nearby was a door upon which was printed, "Information."

Well!

Mistake No. 2: I opened the door for information.

The little room contained a desk, some posters and a stairway. Nobody was present.

"Hello Dolly," I called, my voice wavering somewhere between an Arkansas hog call and what I tried to make sound like a wild west whoop of a seasoned cowboy just off the trail.

Immediately a feminine voice from upstairs called down, "Come on up!"

Hesitation. But not much.

"I'm a cautious man," I called.

"And I'm a bold woman," came the response.

The stairs groaned; and they squeaked. So did my inner soul. "If you had your Bible with you, Jim Hilliard, this wouldn't be happening," came the warning from some benign source. At the same time, I resolved not to back away from the task at hand and stick to it like a man.

"Do you make reservations?" My voice still had that little peculiar pinch to it--and a bit of a quiver.

"Honey, you don't need reservations this early in the day."

---

[6]Pale band around the wrist where watch has prevented sun-tanning.

"I mean dinner."

"Yes, I know. What did you think I meant?"

Darned if I knew, but the steps kept squeaking, cowering under my heavy load. When I reached the top and looked around, a woman came out of one of those doors down the hallway.

She was dressed!

I mean she had clothes on...clothes that were working. I mean she had working clothes on. A regular working dress is what she had on, the kind that regular women work in.

"How many?" she asked pleasantly.

"How many...how many what?" I mumbled.

Honestly, my maverick mind had no brand on what I had come for!

"You came for dinner reservations?" The way she emphasized "dinner" let me know full well that she knew my downfall.

Finally she got out of me what I had come for in the first place, and I stumbled back down the stairs. In the car when Vi asked if I was all right, I mumbled something, I don't remember just what now.

The Tumbleweed Bar is a little neighborhood pub located down the street from our duplex here in Arizona. Our friend, Angela, lived ten years in this duplex before she purchased another dwelling to accommodate her mother who now lives with her. Angela's birthday is next week. Vi and I have been collecting things, some more foolish than others, as gifts for the occasion.

I'm sure Angela has never been in the Tumbleweed Bar, though we tease her a lot about all the time she must have spent there. No, she has never been there, but I have.

I was there this morning.

The bright idea (which turned out to be pretty dim) came to me that a souvenir from The Tumbleweed would be a good thing to include in Angela's birthday Pandora Box. So a couple of hours before noon, I parked the car around back and tiptoed to the door where I cautiously looked around, pushed it open and squeezed inside quick as a wink. There the juke box music was so loud it slammed the door shut. Everybody looked.

Having come in suddenly from the bright sunlight outside, the room seemed exceptionally dark and smoggy, but I made out the forms of five men sitting at the bar. The lady in charge was kind enough to wait until my vision dilated enough to focus upon the dimness before she asked professionally, "May I help you?"

"I just came in for a souvenir," I mumbled.

"That's a new one on me, Friend," she said. "Do you want it lite or regular?"

I had no more idea what she was talking about than she I. That is, I don't think we understood each other. I remember wondering what the men sitting on the bar stools thought. One of them had already snickered in his beer.

"It's for my friend," I said. "She's having a birthday."

"Having a what!?" came the lady's response.

She said it in a way that prompted a few more sounds from the barmen.

You would think to say, "I want a souvenir from the Tumbleweed Bar" would be simple and easy. Sometimes it isn't.

Suddenly it came!--the solution!

"She and her boyfriend used to come in here," I blurted out, immediately marveling at my lying ability.

I was awfully glad the place was dark.

"Oh, I see," the girl said, and I thought she must have cat eyes to see in all the dimness of both my statements and the smoky room.

Then she began her list of suggestions: "How about an ash tray with our name on it. They're only $5.50; the plastic ones. The glass ones you can get for not much more. Or a beer mug here, $12.98. We have T-shirts that say 'Tumbleweed Bar, Come As You Are,' and would you believe they're only $14.50?"

I didn't want to *buy* anything, much less at those intoxicating prices.

"Do you have a book of matches?" I asked. "Or a napkin?"

"Well, Dear," she waved her hands in disbelief. "We used to have matches with our name on them but they got too expensive. And these men here don't care about napkins--just a bar rag sometimes when they spill over."

She was precious, wanting to be so helpful. I couldn't tell her that Angela and her mother both are deathly against smoking, so the ash tray wouldn't do. I didn't want to tell her that, because she kept jumping a cigarette from her lips to her fingers. I thought her two fingers looked like a pair of scissors trying to cut off the bad habit. Or maybe the cigarette was just too hot to stay in one place very long, I don't know. Besides, I could just imagine the guffaws of those men at the bar if I had said I didn't think Angela would drink her tea from a beer mug. Then, too, Angela is too large and wise to wear T-shirts, regardless of the message. At the same time I didn't want to be laughed at again by those men, all of whom had turned, watching shamelessly, slyly interacting among themselves. At the same time, I didn't want this helpful young lady to think of me as a cheapskate, not that I would ever see her again.

Slowly, the brain waves searched for possibilities to appease the dilemma. Maybe it is proper, out West here, to buy a round of drinks.

So in an awkward sort of way I shelled out money for my glass of water and five bug of meers. No, beers of mug.... Whatever.

Anyway, as we sat there, the men and barmaid wanted to know all about my friend, Angela. Seems like one drink called for another, so it took some time for me to tell them all about Angela and her boyfriend. Then I had to take more time than ever to repeat it all. When I left, one of them called out, "Jim, ol' buddy, you tell your angel friend thish here is the besht souvenir she never did got--get."

I didn't tell her anything.

Chapter 28

Nation's Cave

It is now April. Vi and I came home from Arizona a couple of weeks ago. Nation is into his seventh month of the Literacy Program and doing exceptionally well. He liked the teacher who taught him while I was gone.

"Are you sure you didn't know how to read?" I asked. His only difficulty was transposing from cognizance to registered application.

"I dropped out of school," he said, "because even in the second and third grades the kids thought I was some kind of freak. I knew I was not like them, but I didn't know why except they called me a stinkin' Indian. Later my great grandmother did not object to me dropping out of school because she knew how painful it was for me. She said, 'Nation, maybe there is more value in your living in harmony with nature, as our people have always done, than suffering the insults of the kids in school.' I do not think she thought nature learning was more important than book learning, but she knew what was going on. Anyway, I wish I could read better, and then I could learn a lot more things."

"You're not about to discourage me, Nation," I replied, "so don't discourage yourself. You're getting there so fast that before another year is overwith you may be reading better than I."

"I have trouble writing, too," he said. "It is like I have heard you say, that some ideas are clear enough in your head, but you have trouble pulling them out and putting them on paper so they will get the right message across to people who read them."

"What are some of the things you have learned about nature, Nation?" I asked, refocusing the subject of the conversation.

"I never had no one to teach me except Great Grandmother. She told me all she knew about everything, even the ancient ones, and she told me about things that happened when she was a girl, and stories about our tribe in the East, but I had to learn how to find animals and shoot them by myself. She did not like guns."

"What are some of the more interesting things you learned from your great grandmother?"

"She liked the folklore of our nation, but stories about the Trail of Tears is what she talked about most in her later years. I guess it was like the Wilderness Journey in the Old Testament except along the Trail the Whites were driving prisoners instead of God leading escapees. The Jews always talk about their Deliverance; Great Grandmother talked about the Cherokees being forced to submit to the change. Subjugation she called it. Talking about bad things like that was not her normal conversation, but I suppose it was like Southerners not letting go of the Civil War and pre-Civil War days."

"Was your great grandmother resentful?"

"No, she did not resent things, and she was not disgruntled about anything. It is just that a previous existence had been taken away from her people and she would look back and wonder how it would be now if they had not been driven out of their native land. Kinda like looking back to the Garden of Eden, I think. Like I said, Southern Whites do a lot of that kind of looking back, and it seems like they all see themselves as the plantation owners."

A smile cracked his lips, and then he went on, adjusting the subject, "Our people had occupied that land back east for many generations. They believed God gave it to our nation just as strongly as the Hebrews believed that about the Promised Land. But when my great grandmother talked about it, there was no hatred or hard feelings. She just stated facts as she understood them."

"Let's take a walk," I said, "and you tell me about it, will you, Nation? Tell me the way your great grandmother told you, would you mind?"

Nation led me into a ravine at the back of his house. Instead of walking along talking as I had anticipated, he took the lead at a steady pace. At first the path was well defined, but soon it began to fade until there was no visible evidence of any pathway anywhere. He seemed to know where he was going and how to get there. We walked this way for half an hour, weaving in and out among the trees and brush and mountain boulders. Only my stepping on twigs, and brushing against branches broke the silence. It seemed like every time I tried to avoid a noise-maker, I stepped on a louder one. My "book-learning" on this subject from reading Louis L'Amour's westerns about silence on the wilderness trail was OK but I lacked practice.

After a time Nation came to a halt before two large cedar trees standing side by side at the foot of a high caprock. I followed his gaze as it swept the valley below and the mountainside beyond.

"Here."

The one word was the whole sentence. He said it with emphasis, and then brushed between the two trees.

I followed. Then I understood. The two trees protected a secret. Faithfully they stood guard, their sharp sword-like branches drawn to halt intruders. At Nation's word, "Here," they let us pass. Suddenly, as if by magic, Ali Baba's "Open, Sesamé" became real, for immediately before us was an open cave!

We stooped to enter.

The cave was somewhat circular, about fifteen feet in diameter. The ceiling was irregular. There are hundreds of caves and caverns throughout the Ozarks. The sizes vary from the magnificent specimen at Blanchard Springs to this little one-room hide away, Nation's private retreat. You would expect darkness to prevail in a little resort packet like this, but not so, for even after our having come in from the bright afternoon sunlight it was comfortably light. When I mentioned this, Nation explained.

"In the mornings after the sun gets above the tops of those two cedars, it shines in, and in the afternoon it reflects off of those limestone cliffs over there across the ravine," he said, pointing to the source of this phenomenon.

"Do you come here often?" I asked, assuming this was so.

"Yes, it's a good place to come. But I like Soaring Bluff better. There's a se...."

He broke off the sentence in mid-word. His whole body stiffened a bit as if he had said something out of place.

"I have my own secret places," I said, hoping to override his uneasy silence. "Nothing like this or the one you may have at Soaring Bluff because mine are all in my head."

Nation was silent. So was I. I sensed he wanted to say more if I would let him.

He did; he picked up on what I had said.

"Is it true, like Joey told me, that you are his trunk, and he can give you his secret thoughts and they will be kept safe?" he asked.

"Yes," I replied, "that's one of my secret things, and I keep it for Joey. Another one is like sometimes at Soaring Bluff I stand there and wish I could understand what's going on somewhere in the back of my mind. I feel like I could find solutions to some of the human dilemmas if I could clearly interpret the thoughts that stir up my thinking. For example, I think, why must there be prejudices? And then I reason that prejudices don't have to exist. But I can't find any real applicable solutions to eradicate them, even within my thinking."

Then I added, "There are other times when I dream of a place like your cave here where I could come and be still and listen to whatever there is to hear. It's better to have places like this that are real instead of things in my mind which are not real."

Neither of us said anything for a minute.

Then Nation said, "I guess I always thought things in the mind were just as real, and maybe even more so, than things and places in the world. My great grandmother liked this place. She brought me here ever since I can remember, and she would tell me about things--like teachers do in school rooms."

There were two rocks inside his retreat, one large and one small, both relatively flat on top. He motioned for me to sit on the larger one. He took the smaller.

"Great Grandmother always sat there," he said reverently. "This one has always been mine."

I felt a bit uneasy, sitting on this hallowed rock. I thought that Nation surely wasn't expecting me to take his beloved great grandmother's place. Briefly though, and perhaps foolishly, I wondered how it would be to have a grandson like Nation.

We sat for a few moments, comfortable in the silence.

"You can come here any time you want to," he said suddenly.

"No, Nation," I replied. "This is your place. I'll never come here without you."

I sensed that he might have been a bit disappointed.

"Tell me about your great grandmother," I said.

He began his narrative much like his great grandmother must have done hundreds of times.

"In the ancient days our ancestors lived in what is now called the Georgia-Alabama-Tennessee area. More and more white settlers came from the East. Our people adapted easily to their ways, and even incorporated their Christian religion into our ancient customs and beliefs. There were lots of similarities in the two religions, anyway. Our nation prospered with the new civilization of the Whites. There were many benefits for us Indians other than rifles and iron pots.

"Then when the white man began to take more and more of our land, and to impose his government upon our people, 'the natives began to get restless'. There were uprisings and local blood-sheddings now and again when treaties were not kept and when the white government would do nothing about their encroachments upon our lands.

"In December, 1835, the New Echota Treaty offered our whole Cherokee Nation payment for their land and property, including expenses to move everyone to a land west, far across the Mother River. Here, they were told, they would be given land where they could live forever without harassment from the increasing numbers of white settlers. A good number of them accepted the offer and moved west. They became known later as the Old Settlers.

"However, many of our tribesmen chose to stay in the east. Some of them tried to keep our eastern lands by peacefully negotiating agreements with the government, but others chose to fight rather than give up their properties even by peaceful negotiations. They were the ones who caused the "Indian uprisings" mentioned in school history books and stories. Both of these choices were unwise for our people because, in time, matters got worse for everybody. The White government did nothing when our homes, farms, businesses were illegally taken by the Whites. Many of our people were murdered and tortured, and still nothing was done to protect them.

"Then in 1838 the White military suddenly invaded our lands, confiscated our properties, and compelled our people to go west to what was called Indian Territory. A few escaped into the mountains and some of their heirs still live there. My great grandmother's ancestors were in that group. My great grandfather came from descendents of the 1838 drive, The Trail of Tears."

"Not all of them joined the migration, then?" I asked.

Nation sat for a moment without answering. There were vibes in his hesitation that caused me to wonder what I had asked. I thought, "Maybe he places value not only in the communication of _asking_ a question, but also the _way_ a question is asked." I suspected that he appreciated direct facts, but direct questions made him feel uncomfortable.

Such was not the reason for his discomfiture, as I learned immediately when he said, "My great grandmother said words can make meanings clear and bright, or they can cover over meanings and make them dull and hazy and misleading. She said her people learned that from the treaty makings. She thought a word that hardens or softens the fact is not a good word to use. She did not use "migration" to describe the trail where tears were shed."

He looked at me with eyes asking me to understand. I did understand and accepted his correction, feeling wiser, more adult, because it was an adult way of handling an uncomfortable situation. Could this be the standard way of Indian teaching? I felt sure it was the way the old ones taught their children in this enlightening culture.

Nation went on. "Some joined a chief called Major Ridge and they took advantage of the generous offer of the American government and left the next year. My ancestors did not. In 1838 when the forcing began, my great grandmother's foreparents escaped into the mountains rather than be captured by the soldiers who demolished their village in Tennessee. But they captured the family of my ancestor on my father's side and took them to the designated territory west of the Mother River. The father of that family was named Swift Feather because he was skinny and light. They said he ran like a feather in the wind. In town they called him Sailor because the white men said he reminded them of a ship's sail when he ran. His parents made clothes of skins and sold them in their shop in town.

"His wife's name was Lost Petal. Her family lived on a farm. When Swift Feather and Lost Petal were married, they lived on a farm. They had a son and called him Enoch. Enoch Nation Skreigh was his full name.

"In those earlier days the settlers and Cherokees were very friendly towards each other in business matters. Most of the Cherokees thought the representatives in Washington would work out the land treaties to satisfy everybody. They kept hoping to live peacefully and adopt many of the white man's ways. For the most part they all lived much the same, anyway, though there was less and less social interactions with one another as the years went by. Yet, each traded with the other as much as they did with their own kind.

"Like earlier in the day which Swift Feather and Lost Petal and their little boy, Enoch, were captured, some soldiers came to their farm and bought butter and grain and stuff from them. They were friendly and paid for everything as always. Then that evening a while before dusk, a bunch of soldiers came upon them and tied them and took them away. Enoch was eight years old and tried to cling to his father and mother, but they tied him separately. When they looked back they saw their house and barn burning. Swift Feather did not think the Whites would do this to them because he was half white. His father had been a Scotsman by the name of Skreigh who had come from a Scottish settlement not far away. Lost Petal was not a hundred per cent Indian, either. But the soldiers took all three of them like criminals, and herded them, along with many other Indians, into one of their gathering holds, a sort of stockade, where they were kept during the hot summer hardly any shelter from the sun or rain. Then in the fall of the year they were forced by foot, or horse if they had one, to join their tribal relatives in the territory for Indians far to the west.

"During the journey, the caravan was making slower progress than any of them had anticipated. Some of the delay was caused by the weather which was mixed rain and snow on the day Swift Feather was killed. The lack of food made it worse. Game was scarce and the assigned hunters spent more time than necessary gambling and womanizing. Everybody, Indians and soldiers alike, were tired, irritable and quick-tempered. Some were very ill and many were beginning to die.

"One evening in mid-winter they camped beside a little stream that ran into a swampy area in what is now northern Arkansas. We think it was up there between Greasy Swamp and Soaring Bluff. They assigned Swift Feather to the detail to collect fire wood for the camp. A sergeant by the name of Karney guarded the detail. He was one of the camp hunters, and had been making passes at Lost Petal. The soldiers kept the men and women in separate groups along the way, day and night. This was both torture and relief to Swift Feather--torture because he was not able to be with his wife and son, but relief because he knew that they were near him. The greatest pain and humiliation were seeing them suffer and him not able to do anything about it.

"That evening their little boy, Enoch, was watching his father working with the other men gathering wood from a ravine when he saw his mother go to the stream to get some water. She ignored Sergeant Karney when he called to her. This angered the sergeant, so he told a fellow guard to watch "that little doe's buck" (meaning Swift Feather), and then he went down to where Lost Petal was getting the water.

"Enoch saw him attack his mother and heard her scream as Sergeant Karney forced her down the bank in some tall grass. When she screamed, his father bounded toward her, but the guard had a shotgun pointed at his stomach. He knocked it away and dashed toward his wife. In the sudden fracas, the gun discharged and accidentally shot the officer in charge of that section of the caravan.

"Just before Swift Feather reached Lost Petal, another soldier stepped between them with his gun aimed and ready. Sergeant Karney held Lost Petal to the ground and looked up and said to the soldier who was holding her husband at bay, 'I heard a shotgun blast. What happened up there?'

"'I think this here Injun killed Lieutenant Snyder,' replied the soldier, gouging the rifle deeper into Swift Feather's stomach.

"'You did that just so you could see what I was doing here?' Sergeant Karney snarled as he grinned at Swift Feather. 'Why, I'd think you Injuns would know all about this here kind of business without having to come spying on a man privately.'

"Then, getting up he added, 'If Lieutenant Snyder is dead, that puts me in charge of this here outfit, in which case I can finish what I started here any time I want to. But let me tell you something, Injun, you better not interfere again.'

"Immediately Lost Petal jumped up and as she started to run toward her husband, Karney stuck out his foot and tripped her. He and his friend laughed.

"Suddenly, Swift Feather exploded with our ancient Cherokee war cry. The soldier shot him and he fell dead to the ground. Lost Petal continued running toward him. Then without stopping, she rushed on past his body and raced up the hill through some evergreen trees and disappeared. Some people said that she was running toward his spirit rather than his body.

"Some soldiers charged up the ridge after her, but when they came back they said they saw her jump off a high cliff. They swore that when she jumped, she just disappeared, nobody knows where. She was never seen after that. Sergeant Karney took a hunting party and investigated the foot of the cliff and all around, but they didn't find any evidence of her body; no clothing or anything."

"Great Grandmother believes Lost Petal heard The Screech and that she actually did join Swift Feather. Nobody knows for sure."

"What do you think, Nation?" I asked.

"Nobody knows for sure," was his answer.

Then he added, "Great Grandmother believed in The Screech. She thought it always gave a message of deliverance for anyone who heard it, so she longed for it like the Jews have always longed for Elijah or the Christians for Jesus. One time she said, 'Nation, someday you will hear it.' Like I say, nobody knows for sure about these things."

"What happened to young Enoch, Swift Feather's little boy?" I asked.

"A married couple took him in. They were better off than most of the others in the march. They sent him to school and he became a teacher. He's the one who wrote the document you read to me when Great Grandmother died."

"By the way," I said, "it's getting late; we better go. Are you sure you know your way back home?"

He grinned.

Just before we stooped to exit the cave, he stopped and turned around, facing me.

"Sometime I will show you something at Soaring Bluff."

He turned abruptly and we walked past the guards into the early twilight of the evening. The sun had disappeared behind a mountain-top, but it would be twilight for some time yet. Nation led the way back to his cabin, neither rushing nor lagging. Dogwood blossoms glowed through the tree branches. They are always brightest at this time of day. There seemed to be millions of them this evening. They made the forest look like a heavenly cloud, and I was in the midst of it. Yes! That was it! I was walking along on Cloud Nine, savoring this never-to-be-forgotten experience with one of our Native Sons.

Chapter 29

Student Teaching

Vi just came in and said lunch is ready on the gazebo.

"What are we having?" I asked.

"Come and see."

I did. It was lunch meat sandwiches, bright red strawberry jello, iced tea and some rice pudding left over from last night. I love her rice pudding! You would, too, for surely the recipe was chosen for God's own banquet table.

While we were eating, I said to Vi, "I'm apprehensive about that woodpecker. Since the wrens have selected the garage for their personal mansion, this woody-boy seems to think the gazebo is his own private bird feeder."

You'd think a profound statement like that would have bowled Vi over, but she gave no notice.

Suddenly a humming bird zoomed through the gazebo just above our heads. It reminded us of the airplane crop-duster we saw sailing under the telephone lines in the rice fields over toward the Mississippi Delta one day. Just then one of the little humming show-offs appeared two feet from Vi's mouth as she opened up to take a spoonful of jello. It stopped in mid-air and hovered over the strawberry jello on her plate. This startled Vi, of course, and when she jerked her head back the little intruder whirred away.

"Why are you concerned about the woodpecker?" she asked.

"He makes me uneasy the way he keeps sizing up my head."

I'm sure Vi didn't mean it when she mumbled, "He'll never be able to penetrate your head." She's kinder than that.

Then, as if I hadn't caught on, she took another bite of sandwich and added, "I know."

"You know what?" I asked as innocently as I could.

"That that woodpecker won't be able to penetrate your head."

I'll never understand my wife! Why would she say a thing like that?

Before I had a chance to respond to these "penetrations," Vi said, "Oh, look! There's Joey coming up the trail."

"Isn't Joey an amiable, reticent, jolting, oddball, though?" I mused. "But I like talking with him."

"Kinda like talking with God," Vi said.

I wasn't too sure about that, but I let the statement stand.

"He's a misfit," I responded calling to her attention our original graphic perception of him as a heart turned upside down.

"Wasn't Jesus a misfit? His life was something like an upside down heart, too, wasn't it?"

Vi is not one to let well enough alone.

"Come on up, Joey," I called, waving.

He left the trail and started up across the lawn.

Vi went inside the house and brought out another plate and glass of tea.

"Come and sit down and have some lunch with us," she invited as he approached the gazebo.

He started to decline, but I added, "Vi will be mad at you if you don't."

"I wouldn't want her to be mad at me," he said grinning.

"Have a chair," Vi said, pointing toward the empty plate and glass of tea.

After the preliminaries of getting settled into the business of eating were completed, I told Joey about our bird conversation a few minutes ago. No sympathy from him when Vi suggested the woodpecker would never get its beak straightened out if it went for my billiard-ball head.

"What is your mother doing today?" she asked.

"She's getting the garden ready. She thinks it's too early to plant peas, but Papa told her to do it anyway."

"What has your dad been up to this morning?" I asked.

"He's down-river fishing," Joey replied. "He left me at Fish Creek Park this morning with the pickup full of firewood to sell, but nobody seems to want wood this late in the spring."

"If you don't sell it, maybe your dad will use it for a little hellfire preaching," I suggested, but Joey didn't think he needed any extra fuel for that.

"I suppose not," I responded. "When he goes after sins he reminds me of that 'fat broad' character in the B. C. comics who keeps clobbering the snake."

"Yeah," Joey said with a grin and a slow drawl. "I told Mama he goes after sins like that little pink drummer rabbit on television—he never stops."

"What did your mother say?" Vi asked.

"Oh, nothing. She never says much. But she understands."

"Is your load of wood still down at the park?" I asked.

"Yes."

"What if your dad comes back and you're not there?" I asked. "Did you leave a note?"

"No," replied Joey. "He won't be back till almost dark, just before supper time. When he fishes, he stays all day."

"We could use the wood for our fireplace this fall," I said. "When you get ready, go down and bring it up."

"I will have to wait for Papa. I am not allowed to drive," Joey said.

"Well, OK," I said. Then added, "Let's talk. What would you like to talk about?"

He nibbled at his sandwich and then said, "I would like to hear about some of your experiences in your church," he said. "I bet they were a lot different from Papa's."

"We all have basic things that happen," I said, "but the most embarrassing time I had was when I first started out as a pastor in the Upper Peninsula of Michigan. I lived in a village five miles from where the undertaker had his funeral business. One day he telephoned me and said an old miner had died when he fell off a railroad trestle. He was walking home down the railroad track after an evening in the local bar. The man was a loner; few people knew him. The funeral director gave me his name along with the names of the pall bearers he had lined up, none of whom I knew. I scribbled the information on a piece of paper and made the necessary preparations.

"The next day I arrived at the funeral parlor just in time to begin the service. The pall bearers were about the only persons present. They were seated on the front row. I committed the body of Eino Taskila to its final resting place and commended his soul to God. When I did this, there was an immediate reaction from the pall bearers as if something drastic had suddenly happened. Automatically I glanced over at the casket. Everything seemed to be all right, but I felt uneasy, anyway.

"When the service ended, we moved the body from the bier inside to the hearse outside. As soon as the undertaker closed the door of the funeral coach, he turned to me and said, 'That was fine, Reverend, except you got the names mixed up. Eino Taskila is the name of one of the pall bearers. The deceased's name is Eero Tuominen.'

"Ugh! Those Finnish names! How could an Okie like me ever get them straight, even after marrying a Finn!

"Well, there was nothing to do but go over to the car where Eino Taskila and the other five bewildered men sat, those men who so kindly had come to carry What's His Name to his final resting place. They understood. There are times when the unforgivable is forgiven.

"When we arrived at the cemetery, some of the sand from the corner of the grave had fallen down into the pine box which was to receive the casket of...of...whatever his name was.

"'I have a spade in the car,' Eino said, and brought it forthwith.

"When he started to hop down into the grave to shovel out the sand that had caved in, I said, 'Hold on, Friend. Let someone else do that; you've already had one close call today.'

"That brought reconciliation between me and those six pall bearers. After that Eino and I became fishing partners.

"A few years later I moved down-state to another parish. One evening Mrs. Taskila called and said, 'Jim, before Eino died this afternoon, he said he wanted you to finish the job you started that first time he saw you. Will you come and do his funeral?'"

I thought Joey would laugh but he didn't. He simply called my attention to a higher thought, saying, "God has ways of turning our mistakes into something bigger, and it is good if we learn from Him."

I thought that was an unusual response, but it made me feel good to be working for someone like God--and listening to someone like young Joey.

"One Sunday morning," Joey said with a grin, "the weather was warm so the church door was left open. Papa was reading the Last Judgment Parable about the sheep and goats when a stray cat came sneaking into the church. Ol' Blue woke everybody up with his bark, but when he saw it wasn't a 'coon, he sort of calmed down and went over and got acquainted."

"What did your dad do?"

"He didn't do anything. Well, while he was reading, he did get the cats and dogs mixed up a little bit with the sheep and goats, but nobody noticed much."

"We had this little girl, six or seven years old, in the parish," I said. "Her name was Sandra Mae and every Sunday during the sermon she drew a picture and gave it to me after church. They were pretty good for such a youngster. This time the picture was of her sitting in church.

"'You're not smiling in the picture,' I said.

"'Oh,' she replied, 'I'll fix that,' and asked for a pencil. None was at hand.

"'Oh, I know,' she said, handing the picture back to me. 'We were singing a sad song when I drew this.'

"Another time," I continued as if listeners never became tired of hearing me, "at the high school baccalaureate, I was talking with one of my graduating friends.

"'Mike,' I asked, 'now that you're out of high school, what are you going to do?'

"'I don't know,' he replied, 'but if I could, I know what I'd like to do.'

"'What's that, Mike?'

"'I'd be the same as you.'"

Joey was silent. I watched him. He didn't look up.

"What about you, Joey?" I asked.

"I've thought about being a preacher," he said, "but...."

There was a long silence.

"But what?" I prodded.

"Well, the only preaching I know about is Papa's."

Another pause.

"And you're not persuaded that his is the only way?" I asked.

"I guess that's right," he replied with relief. "I don't know what it is, but there's something in me that says that's not the way it is for me, but I don't know any other way."

I waited and then said, "Do you think it's wrong to think the way your soul tells you to?"

"No, I guess not; that is, it might be, but I don't think so. It doesn't seem like it to me."

"I can see there is a difference between what you think is true and what your dad thinks is true, and that bothers you," I said.

A short silence followed.

"You're a sophomore in high school now, aren't you?" I asked.

"Yes."

"You'll work it out," I said. "God knows what your life will become, just as He knew from the beginning what the life of His other Son, Jesus, would come to."

As soon as I said that, Joey's whole countenance changed. He appeared to turn comfortably inside out, clean and pure. He said something that had no reference to our conversation, yet all human existence rests upon what he said. I thought he must be looking into some pre-existent past--or perhaps future--when he said:

> The sterling beauty of Christ shines in the world when I take
> your sins upon myself through forgiveness. To forgive your sins
> against me, and mine against you, is a Cross I gladly bear, for upon
> it we are crucified together, and from it new life is nourished.

Forgiveness, then, is the Lily of the Valley, the Pearl of Great Price. It is the Treasure that should never be hidden.

Glorious is the Judgment of God, for God shares Himself in Judgment. There the pure in heart see God and respond to His welcome. Fear not, for in Judgment you do not face God alone. There with you, on the one hand, stands Savior Christ, and on the other hand stand your forgiven enemies. You would not be facing God had you not forgiven them. So Christ and your enemies stand with you as you face God. When you love one as you love the other, a kaleidoscope of marvels burst forth and you become the oneness God longs for. In all creation, Judgment is the most sublime, for it exalts the pure in heart.

Your enemies must exist before you can love them, and when you love them they are no longer enemies. This is the love of Christ that fulfills you. When this love is yours, Christ is fulfilled. There is no greater love.

You are Christ's gift to God. You have been presented to His Majesty on the wings of faith and love. Christ's faith is in you. His faith in you and His love for you have no limits. They join you and your adversaries together as one, for God is love and in that love stand your adversaries. In this, you become the will of God, for God wills oneness with him in Christ--oneness for all humankind. The will of God, then, is you *being* the will of God.

God does not call us to confession, nor to repentance, forgiveness, salvation or baptism. He calls us to Christ.

With that, the transpersonal phenomenon disappeared from Joey, suddenly and naturally, the way it came.

There was a silence. We all took deep breaths.

"I'll tell Papa you want the wood," Joey said, standing up. "We will probably bring it up when he gets back from fishing."

"Joey," Vi said, "we will keep all this in your trunk."

"Thanks," he said with a smile.

He got up and left.

How does Joey know these things! But then, how does a six year old Mozart write an ever-living symphony, while others spontaneously compute mathematical equations in their heads?

I thought of Jesus in the Temple, twelve years old, astounding the religious leaders of his day.

I wanted Joey Balaam to bless me.

Chapter 30

Youth Chatter

Christine Hampton is the daughter of Bill and Addella Hampton, our friends in a former parish. She has always been a charming little creature. You'd think she is brazen; you'd know she is bright. In confirmation class she had an insatiable curiosity about what she called X-rated stories in Scripture. Here is our response to a letter we received from her yesterday:

Dear Christine,

Thanks for your letter. It was a super surprise which made us old folks real happy.

You asked what the kids here in Arkansas are like. The answer is, "Just like they are in Michigan." Here is an example:

Last Sunday night we went to the church pot luck supper. When we arrived, there were only two places available and they were at a table of young people like yourself. We asked if we could join them.

"Wondered if anyone would dare join us," said James, whose family had recently moved into our community.

Mary Jo jabbed him in the ribs with her elbow, muttering under her breath, "You're weird."

James said, "If you think I'm weird you should have heard what Joey said in the gym Friday. He made a foul in basketball and Wayne said, 'God will get you for that,' and Joey said, 'God has more important things to do than track down my mistakes.' And Wayne asked, 'Like what?' and Joey said, 'Like figuring out what's in your heart.'"

"Joey's weird, too," Lois said.

"I don't think he is," defended Rose Ann, sitting across the table.

"You wouldn't," retorted Lois. "But he is, anyway. So is his friend, Nation."

Rose Ann receded as Rose Ann always does.

"Who's Nation?" James asked.

"Oh, he's that Indian kid that hangs around by himself. He dropped out of school 'cause he's so dumb," replied Lois.

"He's only got one pair of pants and they don't have no zipper," she added.

"No zipper!" exclaimed James.   *"What keeps his, you know--flap, closed?"*

"I don't know," Lois replied with a snicker, *"but it's closed."*

"We were talking about prayer in school the other day," Mary Jo said, *"and Mr. Brown said if Christians were allowed to pray in school, so could all other religions."*

"Even Satan cults?" James asked.

"That's what he said.   He said we shouldn't even teach the Lord's prayer.   And then Joey said, 'Teaching is not praying.' And Mr. Brown asked him what he meant, and he said, 'Teaching to pray is not praying any more than telling how to drive a car is not driving.   So maybe we could be taught to pray without praying."

"What did Mr. Brown say about that?" asked James.

"He said, 'Well, Joey, if you can teach us how to pray without praying, that would be legal.'"

"That's about all he could teach," said Lois.

"He makes pretty good grades," James said.

"But he ain't no good at sports or anything," returned Lois.   *"Not like Rudy Mercer."*

"Rudy's a big bully," said James.

"You wouldn't say that if he was here," Lois counteracted.

"I would, too," James replied, without too much conviction.

Rose Ann returned to the conversation by saying, *"Nation's a better person than Rudy Mercer."*

Everyone turned to her.

"So is Joey," she added, and then got up and left the room.

"What got into her?" asked Lois.

They were silent for a minute, then James said, *"If you think Joey is weird, what about Tag?"*

All of them laughed.

"Who is Tag?" I asked.

"Oh, he's Rudy's idiot brother," came the reply.   *"He's always with Rudy and repeats everything he says.   Nobody likes him, but Rudy will beat up on anybody that is not good to him."*

That's the way the evening went, Christine.   You might call it food for thought at a church supper.   Not much different from Michigan kid gatherings.   I hope this responds to your query about what Arkansas kids are like.   They wear the same kind of clothes you Michigan kids wear.   Their music thump-thumps and wild hair-do's are the same as up *north. The girls try to get the boys to date them and the boys play hard to get--sometimes. I don't know, Christine, I'll have to ask their parents what goes on. On second thought, they probably don't know any more about it than I do.*

Let's keep in touch.

Sincerely,

Rev. and Mrs. Hilliard

P.S.:   Hope to see the Hampton Family here in Arkansas this summer.

Chapter 31

Rose Ann's Innocence

The day was comfortable, especially for August. The temperature stabilized at a mild eighty-three and the humidity dropped to seventy-two. This combination stirred life-movement in the Ozarks, especially around Dogwood where the river humidity normally competes with the thermometer for the highest position beyond ninety.

At six o'clock sharp that morning, Lem Hill suddenly shattered Rose Ann's slumber. Her father's voice came to her just as the boy of her dream was about to.... This recurring dream had never let her know what he might actually have done, but her awakening fantasies often filled in the slack--vaguely but satisfactorily for the time being.

"Rose Ann, you get yourself outta that bed and get me some breakfast in a hurry," yelled her father from his bedroom. He had a way of interrupting important things in Rose Ann's life.

This burst caused Rose Ann's mother to sit up in bed. Half asleep and half awake, she tried to sort out this unusual awakening of her husband, but she did not ask about it. Lem never woke up until she called him a little past eight after she and Rose Ann had synchronized the breakfast fixin's with his routine.

For almost a year, now, Lem had worked steadily, part-time, doing odd jobs at the Dogwood General Mdse. store. The Hills made much of this "steady" work, for it had raised their self-esteem considerably from their previous existence. Lem was "somebody" now, and Ida May Hill's woolgathering wove that importance far beyond its worth. Yet, who is to say? Steady work, even part time, no matter how low on the scale, can be a great treasure.

However, there were some trade-offs for Lem. An unprecedented discipline required him to be out of bed, dressed, fed and sometimes shaved, ready for work at the store promptly at nine. He endured this trade-off because the privilege of working for Constable Lou Mercer, proprietor of the Dogwood General Mdse. store, added a new dimension to his lifelong role as "The Big Bully of Dogwood."

This new status decreased Ida May's morning ritual of mutterings and grumblings. It had also diminished her spouse-inflicted body bruises.

Rose Ann shared none of these betterments. None of her father's income filtered down to her rough little hands. She still had to "make do" with worked-over garage and rummage sale clothes. There was no money for common things like facial makeup, not that her father would have allowed her to wear it even if she had any of these feminine commodities. No, none of that steady income spoken of so proudly by her mother, ever affected Rose Ann. However, her mother and father had more things to do now. They had other ways to spend some of their time, so this left Rose Ann to her solitude more than ever. She sort of liked that, but dubiously she did not think it was exactly the way things ought to be. Her parents did not notice that she left the house more frequently. Rose Ann liked the extra freedom, but she never knew what to do with so much idle time.

Five years ago the Dogwood school system incorporated with New Autumn. Rose Ann was grateful that school took her away from home and the confines of Dogwood on school days, but this did not help her to relate with other people. She neither accepted her peers nor was she accepted by them--nor anyone else for that matter.

"Her mother was always like that," somebody said.

However, Rose Ann had developed a technique that shielded her from outright rejection much of the time. She learned to recede immediately into absolute privacy like a turtle shelling itself.

Her escape from house boredom was taking long walks--by herself. She would walk through the woods where there were trails, sometimes where there were none. She would saunter down the road along the river or up as far as Copperhead Pass, but she never walked the street of Dogwood or along the river like the other kids did together on summer evenings.

Rose Ann's diversion from these segments of life came from the bus service of the New Autumn United Methodist Church. Its mission of picking up people for church services and youth activities was faithful. Sometimes it even made rounds to take kids to a school function. This service accommodated Rose Ann and a couple of other kids in the Dogwood area. Sometimes Joey would catch a ride, too.

On this Thursday morning when her father called her out of her deep sleep and amorous dream, she and her mother prepared his breakfast mechanically. After her father left, her mother looked out of the window and mused, "Wonder where he's going," and forthwith flopped back into bed. Rose Ann went outside. She had no thought where to go, why, or how long she would be gone. She just went. Her steps led her to the nature trail, on past Greasy Bottom. Here she stopped for awhile and watched an armadillo scratching for grubs. All was quiet at the Balaam house as she went by. Ol' Blue was sleeping under the shade tree. He raised his head, but when he saw Rose Ann he returned to his favorite devitalization. She paused and looked at him, and wondered what he had been dreaming about.

"I wish I was that ol' dog," she said to herself. "He gets treated better than Joey does."

"Or me, either," she added after walking a few steps farther and looking back at Ol' Blue.

After a time, she stood at the brink of Soaring Bluff. She had been there many times, and each time thought to herself, "I wonder if the story they tell about that Indian squaw flying off into space from here is true. I wonder if it happened right here where I'm standing."

Her mind picked up the notion that she, too, might one day step out and maybe fly away.

"Nothing like that would ever happen to me," she thought with an audible sigh. Again she walked on in silence, unaware that she had been standing almost directly over Nation Skreigh who heard her sigh, but kept to his silence.

A short time before this, Nation had come to Soaring Bluff to think about what he could do about himself, his life. He had stood on the brink of that high cliff, overlooking the expanse that lay beyond him. The distant visions which met his eyes seemed much closer than those which entered his mind. He wondered indeed if God worked in mysterious ways as Brother Jake had once said.

He almost smiled as he recalled having told his great grandmother that. He was glad she had agreed, because he sort of thought so, too. Today he still thought so, even though there was little solid evidence in his life to convince him.

He felt better as he looked around to make sure no one was on the trail or anywhere around, he walked over to a spread of prickly pear cactus growing nearby on the edge of the cliff. Carefully he took a stick and shoved some of the cactus vines aside and stepped through the prickly mess, down onto a very small ledge just below the cliff's edge. Quickly he replaced the thorny cactus so that it again covered the bare spot he had made with the stick. Then he crawled under a slab of rock overhang which afforded just enough space for him to sit upright comfortably. Here no one could see him from above or below, nor from either side unless one happened to step through the prickly pear entanglement onto the little ledge to the left. Even then one would have to stoop very low to discover the modest sanctuary which blended in perfectly with the entire cliff. Nation never sat with his legs hanging over the edge because this might signal his presence.

Here Nation sat when Rose Ann stopped on the cliff above. He thought he recognized her footsteps as she approached. When she sighed aloud before leaving, he knew for sure it was she.

He returned to his silent considerations about himself.

"I wish I could be a school teacher like my ancestor who wrote that document about Ultimatessence," he mused. "But I guess I'm too dumb," returned the familiar downbeat.

Nation's thoughts played tag with each other in this manner for some time before he fell asleep. He dreamed that he heard The Screech his great grandmother had mentioned so often.

Suddenly the sound of voices awakened him. He recognized them as Rudy and Tag Mercer. They stood on the edge of the cliff.

"I'll be glad when school starts," said Rudy.

"When does it start?" asked Tag.

"In a couple of weeks; the week before Labor Day."

"That won't be long," replied Tag, proud of his ability to verbalize this wisdom.

"I want to see more of those New Autumn chicks," Rudy said, expressing his yearning as he looked down through the valleys.

"Yeah," snickered Tag. "You sure know how to handle them chicks."

"I want you to remember this, Tag," admonished Rudy. "When I get a girl alone I want you to make yourself scarce. If you want to go places with me, then keep quiet and keep away while I got a girl. And I don't care how long you have to wait, just don't you come telling me it's time to go like you did last Saturday night."

"I won't Rudy," promised Tag.

"If you do a thing like that and watch me doing what I was doing, you can't come with me anywhere, and I won't stick up for you when you get in trouble."

"I won't, Rudy."

In the meantime, Rose Ann had come to the mile-long loop of the nature trail near New Autumn. She stopped short when she heard shrieks of laughter and delight from kids at the swimming hole by the bridge. After a short hesitation, she walked on until she could see them through the brush. She wondered what it would be like to laugh and play, even yell, with someone like they were doing. However, when she thought of things like that it only sharpened her pain of isolation which she did not understand, so she retreated back toward Dogwood.

When she approached Soaring Bluff, Rudy whispered, "Shhh, somebody's coming."

He took Tag by the arm and pulled him back across the trail toward the brush.

"It's Rose Ann," Tag said.

"Hello, Rose Ann," said Rudy, stepping from the bushes.

Tag repeated the greeting.

Rose Ann's reply was a simple, "Hi," as she started to pass on without stopping.

"Come and talk to us a minute," said Rudy.

"Guess I ain't got much to say," responded Rose Ann.

"Well, come on anyway; we can talk about something."

"What do you want to say?" asked Rose Ann, wavering whether to stop or go.

"There's lots of things to talk about," replied Rudy with a grin. Then he added, "You're a nice looking girl. You got a nice figure."

"I have to go," said Rose Ann, moving onward.

"Wait a minute," interposed Rudy, stepping in front of her. "Don't you ever get lonesome for company? Like I do? Let's sit down here and look at the view."

"I've seen the view already. I have to go," said Rose Ann.

"Well, OK," said Rudy. "I'll walk with you. Tag and me, we were on our way home, anyway."

Nation was uneasy, but he remained hidden. He didn't like Rudy and Tag any better than Rose Ann did. He tried to recollect his thoughts about his destiny, but they escaped to the infinite realms beyond. Eventually he crawled out of his secret "eagle's nest." Cautiously he looked up over the ledge and searched the area, up and down the trail. When he was sure no one was around, he took his stick and moved the prickly pear leaves aside, then stepped upon the ledge and through them. With the stick, he replaced the cactus and stepped over onto the trail.

Suddenly he heard a scream. It came from down the trail toward Greasy Bottom. When the second scream reached his ears, he recognized it as Rose Ann's. His first thought was that some wild animal had attacked her, and he was almost right. Without thinking, he dashed down the trail.

He had gone less than a quarter of a mile when he heard Rose Ann sobbing and struggling. The sounds came from some bushes just off the trail. Nation dashed through the brush just in time to see Rudy standing, zipping up his pants.

Rose Ann was struggling to free herself from Tag, who apparently was holding her arms trying awkwardly to force her down. However, she jerked free and ran down the trail toward Dogwood.

Rudy looked up and saw Nation looking at him.

"What the hell you doin' here, Injun?" he blurted. "How long you been standing there?"

Nation said nothing. He turned to walk away.

"Wait up," Rudy called, demandingly, "I want to talk to you."

However, Nation had disappeared into the swamp.

"You say anything about this," Rudy yelled after Nation, "and me and Tag, we'll say it was you that done it, not me! You hear, Injun?"

"Tag!" he exclaimed suddenly, "We gotta go catch Rose Ann."

The two of them started to run swiftly down the path. Shortly before they reached Dogwood, they found her, exhausted and weeping, leaning against a rock near the river's edge.

"Don't y'all come near me, you beasts!" Her statement had the qualities of a cornered tiger.

"We ain't a-goin' to," said Rudy. "We just want to warn you, Rose Ann. Don't you ever tell anybody about what happened back there 'cause if you do, me and Tag will say it was that Injun that done it and we'll tell how we've caught you and him at it lots of times down in the swamp. And you know what'd happen if that word got out. He'd deny it, but it'd be mine and Tag's word against yours and his. We could make things a lot worse than that, even. So don't you say anything at all about it."

Rose Ann was numb.

"Are you going to promise you won't say anything about it?" demanded Rudy roughly.

She made no response. Perhaps she was unable to do so.

"Besides, your ol' man would beat the hell out of you if he knew you was going around throwing yourself at boys, especially that smelly Injun. And you know how he hates Injuns. He'd make you sorry you ever said anything, all right."

With that he and Tag turned on their heels and walked homeward.

"Do you think she'll say anything?" Tag asked.

"Naw, she won't breathe a word of it," replied Rudy. "She'll be sorry if she does."

"She'll be sorry if she ever does," affirmed Tag.

Chapter 32

Joey and Nation

The early Saturday morning freshness of late October added its intoxicating zest to the camaraderie of Joey and Nation as they walked up the valley toward Saber Mountain. They stopped on top of a rise and sat with their backs against some oak trees. From there they looked down across the valley which stretched out far and wide. A breeze from the stretches below gently pushed upward against them on its way to some unseen heights.

"You going to do anything this Halloween?" asked Joey.

"Naw," replied Nation.

"You know that old goat that Butch Simon has?"

"Yeah."

"Well, I heard at school that some of the kids are going to take it over to Brockwell's saw mill and they're going to pile stacks of lumber up and put the goat on top of it. Then they will stack a higher bunch of boards alongside of the first one and put the goat on it. And then they'll keep doing this as long as the lumber lasts. Then they'll take down the stack of boards that the goat is not on and hide it somewhere, leaving the goat up in the air on top of that lumber. Thirty feet high, they say."

"I wonder what Mr. Brockwell will think when he comes down in the morning and sees it," mused Nation.

"A lot of the kids are going trick or treating, but most of the older ones won't," said Joey. "Trick or treat is for little kids. Papa never did let me go out on Halloween. He says the way it's celebrated is a desecration to Christians who have died."

"What did he mean?" asked Nation.

"He said that Halloween means 'hallowed evening' when we're suppose to honor the Christian saints. Papa says we should go to church and pray with the saints like the Apostles' Creed says about the 'communion of saints.' But he says the satanic evils have taken over and that's why people dress up like devils and witches and have bats and black cats and do evil things at night. He says he doesn't know why Christians have chosen this hallowed evening to do all those unhallowed things."

"I have heard that ghosts come out on Halloween more even than at full moon," Nation said.   "Do you think they are the ghosts of those saints--that have come to protest, maybe?"

"I don't know," replied Joey. "Do you believe there are ghosts?"

"Great Grandmother always said believing in something is a beginning which should always find an ending. One time she said, 'If you believe in ghosts, then find out if ghosts exist. If you find that they exist, believe in them. If not, then do not.'"

"Did you ever see any?" Joey persisted.

"My great grandmother comes back and visits me sometimes--at night. But I do not know if that is what a ghost is. It does not seem right that it should be."

"What does she do?"

"She just makes me feel...good...OK."

"Do you see her?"

"I never thought whether I do or not. It is like closing your eyes and thinking of someone. You do not see them, but it kinda registers what they look like. No, I do not think I actually see her, but she is there."

"Does she cook supper or say anything?"

"No. She does not do anything or say anything. She just sort of, you know, communicates. Like when I begin to worry about what I will ever do or become, she makes me know that it is going to be all right."

"I wish I had somebody like that," said Joey. "All I have are things like Papa's nightmares about Jakey-Boy and the razorback that killed him. He thinks I was the cause of it, but I don't see how I could be. When he has these nightmares he wakes up Mama and me with his groanings and caterwaulings. It sounds terrible, like Rose Ann Hill says about the banshees she's heard down in Creepy Crossing.

"One time Papa had a flat tire down that way when we were coming home from a prayer meeting somewhere, and those black men came walking down the road, and he thought they were going to attack him, and all at once he thought they were big razorback hogs coming to get him and Jakey-Boy. It was terrible the way he carried on. The blacks, there were only three or four of them, they turned and ran. When Papa settled down, he sweated and trembled like a leaf in a rainstorm. Mama took care of him."

"It must have been awful for him to see his son torn to pieces by a razorback boar," said Nation.

"I'll tell you something, Nation," Joey said. "It's something Mama told me not to think about, but they say when Jakey-Boy was attacked, Papa didn't try to defend him at all. They say he fired his gun and then ran for the nearest tree and climbed up in it and stayed there until Ol' Peg came by. Ol' Peg happened to be hunting and heard the ruckus and Papa's gun shot. They say Ol' Peg helped Papa get down from the tree, and then Peg took off his shirt and wrapped up the pieces of Jakey-Boy in it and took them home. When they got there, I was already born...all by myself, with Mama."

The boys were silent, hearing nothing except the rustlings of the oak leaves.

Then Joey, his heavy heart somewhat lightened, added, "I think Mama and Papa wanted me to take Jakey-Boy's place, but I never could. Mama didn't blame me, though."

"Does your papa really blame you?" asked Nation.

"He has told me that Jakey-Boy never would have been killed if he hadn't had to go get that midwife for me when I was born."

"Yes." Joey continued after a brief pause, "I think he blames me for Jakey-Boy's death."

Then Nation said, "Joey, I wish Great Grandmother would visit you."

"It wouldn't do no good," replied Joey. "Papa says I'm not a believer."

"I think you are," Nation said with genuine support. "It is just that you do not believe like your father, and that only makes you an un-believer in the way he believes. But you are a believer about what you believe."

"Trouble is," Joey responded, "I just can't find out if what I believe is real, like your great grandmother said about finding out if ghosts are real. Papa says they're the devil and I don't want to believe in the devil."

"Rose Ann Hill says she believes in the devil," Nation said. "She says if God and Satan are warring against each other, Satan will win because he is the strongest. She said that is why there is more evil in this world than good, and since she has never been on the winning side in this life, it would be kinda nice to experience it in the next one. And that is why she believes in the devil."

"I don't think Rose Ann is evil," responded Joey. "She's kinda odd, but I guess I am, too, but her dad gives her a rough time. The kids at school do too."

"Shhh," Nation said suddenly, reaching over and gripping Joey's arm.

"Panther," whispered Nation, slowly raising his .22 rifle. "He is stalking something."

Tensely the two boys watched the animal as it moved slowly, cautiously, crouching through the grass and brush across the swale that lay below them.

"Look!" Joey whispered, "there's a deer browsing. See him, through those bushes?"

"Yeah," whispered Nation. "It is a yearling. The panther is trying to shield himself with that clump of blackberry bushes. See?"

The buck jerked his head up. The cougar sprang. His dinner was spread.

Chapter 33

"That Can't Happen to My Kid!"

"Ain't you gone to school yet?" asked Ida May Hill as she passed by Rose Ann's bedroom door. "It's past eight o'clock and I bet that bus has already come and gone."

"No, Ma," replied Rose Ann weakly. "I don't hardly feel like going to school today."

"What do you mean, you 'don't hardly feel like going to school today?'" mimicked her mother. "I've got to wake your pa up and when I do he will want to know why you're laying around."

"I'm sick."

"You're sick! What's the matter with you; you were all right last night."

"My stomach hurts and I've been wrenching and retching but nothing will come up."

"Good heavens!" exclaimed Mrs. Hill. "Let me take a look at you, girl."

"No, Ma; I'll be all right."

"Turn over and take off them clothes," ordered Ida May with enough alarm in her voice to cause Rose Ann to do as she said, "No, Ma; I'll be all right. I shoulda gone to school."

"What the hell's going on in there," yelled Lem from his bedroom. "Ain't my breakfast ready yet?"

"It'll be ready by the time you get ready for it," called back Mrs. Hill.

By this time she had examined Rose Ann enough to recognize the symptoms.

"Morning sickness!" she hissed. "Rose Ann, you're pregnant. How long have you gone without your period?"

"What do you mean?" Rose Ann asked.

"Your period, child! How long has it been?"

"I don't know what you mean," Rose Ann replied innocently.

Mrs. Hill looked at her.

"How long has it been since that drainage stopped from your...your private?" she inquired, motioning toward Rose Ann's vaginal area.

Rose Ann looked puzzled for a moment, then guessing what her mother meant, said, "You mean that infection that I had?"

"Yes, yes," replied her mother impatiently.

"I ain't had nothing wrong with me that way since last summer," Rose Ann replied, wondering how her mother knew about her infection down there. She had told no one about it, but was glad when it had stopped.

"Get my breakfast ready!" Lem's voice sounded unusually surly, so Mrs. Hill told Rose Ann to lay still, and went to attend the more urgent matter at hand.

After Lem left the house, Mrs. Hill returned to Rose Ann and belatedly she tried to explained about the birds and bees. However, her mumblings were not coherent even to herself, so she gave up before she got to the real point.

This quick lesson in sexuality bewildered Rose Ann all the more. She simply knew she was going to have a baby. This gave her a sudden exhilaration and hope that she had never experienced before.

"Linda Jean, she had a baby, and the government gives her money every month," was Rose Ann's reply.

A calmness blanketed Mrs. Hill's anxiety momentarily. She wondered just how much the government paid daughters for having babies. Then reality broke in upon her pondering.

"Your pa!" she exclaimed. "What will he do!"

There was silence.

"Maybe he won't do nothing if the government will pay."

"Do you suppose they'd give me enough to go live by myself?" asked Rose Ann.

"I don't know, girl," was her mother's exasperated reply. "Maybe I can find out. Maybe if Lem knew you'd get money he would settle for that, but I know he won't want no baby screaming night and day around the house. So maybe you could live somewhere nearby and that would save him the money he spends on your upkeep."

"I know he never did want me," said Rose Ann, "so now maybe he can get rid of me and everything will be all right."

"We'll see," responded her mother. "We'll see."

With that Ida May let Rose Ann return to bed.

"But you'll have to be up and out for a walk or something when your pa comes home this afternoon," she admonished. "And don't come in till it's school bus time so he'll think you've been in school."

"I'll do that, Ma," Rose Ann said, and gratefully fell on the bed. She was kept half-conscious by the hope, a hope such as she had never dreamed of.

.   That afternoon when Lem Hill returned home from his steady part-time job at Dogwood General Mdse. store, his wife tried to approach the matter of Rose Ann's predicament.

"They say the government pays that Farnsworth girl every month because she had that kid unmarried," she said.

"All kids are unmarried when women have 'em, ain't they?" Lem said with his apathetic mixture of humor and sarcasm.

"I mean she wasn't married when she had the kid. And the government gives her money for it," Ida May tried to emphasize the money.

"You said she had the kid unmarried," Lem said testily.

"Well, you know what I meant."

"It takes awhile to figure it out," was Lem's reply. "Besides they say she's gonna have another bastard, and from the looks of her I guess it's true."

This did not deter Mrs. Hill's sales pitch.

"I wonder if Rose Ann had a baby, would she get paid every month by the government?" she asked.

"Rose Ann can't have no kid yet. She ain't married and she's too young," was Lem's irritated response.

"But I mean, *if* she did."

"What kind of woman talk is that, '*if* she did?'"

"Well, it helps out them Farnsworths, her having the kid."

Ida May felt she was losing ground in the conversation. She always felt that way with Lem.

"If Rose Ann could do that, we'd have more money," she reasoned, or at least tried to reason it through.

"What the hell you talking about, Woman?" Lem exclaimed, getting a little more than weary of the subject.

"Lem," Ida May swallowed, the pitch of her voice rising. "Lem, Rose Ann's gonna have a baby."

The sudden stillness was choking. Not a breath stirred.

"This is the way it felt just before that tornado struck in 1980," thought Ida May.

Now, as then, she knew what was coming.

Ida May Hill did not question the various forces of power. There were some things and some people with lots of strength who could handle themselves in most situations. She was not one of them. So she was dependent upon those who had the willingness and tolerance to maintain her existence. Lem had lots of power and he knew how to use it. Sometimes he used it against her, but most of the time, if she was careful, it sustained her and guarded her from the alternatives. She supposed she would surely die of starvation or worse if she did not have Lem.

At this crucial moment, as in many others throughout their lives together, she watched Lem closely. She was not intelligent enough to read his thoughts, but from experience she knew to anticipate his overt reaction. She was ready, now. She would not try to dodge his flailings for she could not. Nor would she cower from them for this only increased their velocity. She was never able to out-talk her husband.

Ida May watched Lem go through the first contortions common to a father when the news of his unmarried daughter's pregnancy penetrates his comprehension. She stood in front of him innocently with that weaponry all females possess and often use. Then, abruptly, the unexpected happened. Something in Lem's mind cross-switched. It bypassed the urgency of the immediate issue. Lem saw Ida May in the moonlight, standing just like she was that first night he saw her under the sycamore trees after the dance over at Owensville. She was beautiful, and without warning Lem's adulthood became primed with robust mettle.

Lem had one drawback that night sixteen years ago. He had never had a girl. His prowess had been limited to fallacious boasting, and he had the brute strength to convince the other boys of the dreamed-up performances of which he spoke. In his younger years, few people thought of Lem as a bully. If that is what he was, he handled it well. The boys, and even girls, thought of him as a protector, though if asked, no one could have identified just what or who he protected. His peers, and some adults, liked him, but at the same time they feared him. It was good to have Lem on your side if you were young and sometimes reckless. Besides, Lem never had to work.

"You'll never catch me pitching hay," he would boast. "Milking cows and slopping hogs is for girls, not men. Pa and me don't ever weed the garden, that's Ma's job."

These boasts caused the other boys to silence their complaints. They did not admit that these very jobs were imposed upon them in their homes.

Lem was an excellent fighter, and that was the only thing he ever did well. By the time he was eighteen, he could pin down any man or boy in the whole county and make them cry "uncle."

When the mind dissociates with one thing, it then searches for an immediate replacement. When Lem disconnected his mind from Rose Ann's pregnancy, it became absorbed into that night of nights when he saw Ida May in all her fullness. All that he was became transfixed again upon that forever moment when the moonlight beamed through the tree branches, spotlighting her beautiful auburn hair. Farther down her body, the light of the moon pressed against Ida May's feminine form tingling and exciting Lem's surging desires. Then, with no need for instruction, he marched forward to the drumbeats of instinct to take possession.

However, Lem Hill did not take possession. Ida May did.

As a child, Ida May was unaware that she was not as bright as the other kids. This may have been the reason she was a bit "stand-offish". No one ever questioned it. Most of the kids thought of her as being different, and that's about all.

"Her family is on welfare, so what can you expect," they said.

Ida May had some wants, but she never gave much thought to them because the things she wanted were impossible for her to get. However, she did want Lem Hill.

She got him.

She also got Rose Ann.

Neither Ida May nor Lem wanted Rose Ann, but she came along in the same package of togetherness. Rose Ann's coming into their world, created a real dilemma for Lem. It was either take Ida May and what she had to offer, or take nothing at all. He took the package, though his thoughts were dictated more by a young man's fancy than the considerations of fatherhood.

Rose Ann came into this world as excess baggage, and that was the lifestyle her parents imposed upon her. It became the caricature her life portrayed.

Things began to sour for Lem about the time he was old enough to vote. His parents died and his inheritance amounted to little more than the shack they lived in. Lem had no skill or inclination for working. Ida May was even less job oriented, so more and more their daily living took on the characteristics of the rags they wore.

Lem began to get ugly. His personality changed. People began to shun him--whenever they dared.

More and more often Ida May was so bruised and despondent that she would not leave the shack they lived in for days. Rose Ann grew up in this environment, never thinking that life might be different. She gave no thought that there might be another way for her to live. If she supposed anything at all, it was that family living was much the same everywhere, and while she resolved not to be this way when she grew up, the die had already been cast for her life. She treated her dirty old home-made rag doll very much the way people treated her. One time Lem saw her blacking the doll's eye with a piece of charcoal taken from the stove.

"What you doing that for?" he asked.

"To teach her a lesson," replied the six year old daughter.

"Well, I guess she needed it," was Lem's reply.

And now....

"I said Rose Ann's gonna have a baby," repeated Ida May.

"I heard you," he snapped, doubling up both fists like steel balls ready for a shot-put.

There was instant silence.

Then, like a bull, he bellowed, *"That can't happen to my kid*!! Where is she? Who done it?"

He bulldozed his way toward his daughter's bedroom.

"She ain't home from school yet," Ida May said, running along behind him. "I found out before she went to school this morning."

"Here she comes now," yelled Lem looking out the window. "That little whore; I'll take care of her."

"If she's a whore, so am I," intercepted Ida May. "Just you remember, Lem Hill, you did the same to me, and that's why I had to marry you."

Lem did not hear.

"The government pays that Farnsworth girl for having babies," Ida May said.

Lem heard.

Quickly he pondered money. Then his mind picked up on a squalling kid around the house. Another brat to feed and clothe.

"No," he muttered, shaking his head, "that won't do."

"She'll marry the guy and then he'll have to take care of her," came his second reasoning. "I'd be farther ahead that way, anyway."

Rose Ann entered the kitchen door quietly.

"You gonna have a kid?" bellowed her father.

His question threw her into helpless defense as his attacks always did. She hardly knew what to say. She was ill.

"You gonna have a kid?" he repeated.

"I...I guess so. Ma said I am," she stammered.

"Who's the father?" Lem demanded.

"I don't know. I don't know what you mean," replied Rose Ann, almost in tears.

Somewhere in the depths of her confusion there stirred the possibility that having a baby might not be as disengaging as she had hoped while she was taking her walk.

"Who's responsible for this? Who you been going out with, sneaking around in the bushes?" Lem was getting angrier.

Ida May interceded, "He wants to know who you slept with, who you've been with, Rose Ann."

"I ain't slept with no one," answered Rose Ann, utterly confused in genuine innocence.

"He means, who did you lay with, who did you have sex with?"

"I don't know, Ma. I ain't laid with nobody. I don't know what you mean, 'who did I have cess with'."

"Who the hell jabbed you between the legs with your dress up, girl?" demanded Lem in a loud voice.

"Oh, you mean....?" Rose Ann was trying not to cry. Some vague understanding began to clear away her confusion.

"Yes, I mean!" boomed Lem.

"It was...it was..." Rose Ann was trying to remember what to say. Rudy had said something about Nation. Yes, that was it, Rudy said to say Nation and then everything would be all right.

"Who was it? Who!" screamed her father, grabbing her by the shoulders with a steel-grip of his hands.

"It was Nation," said Rose Ann, body and voice shrinking under the grip.

"*Nation*!? You mean that Injun?"

The father--and the mother--were stunned.

Rose Ann nodded affirmatively, and fell to the floor.

Her father let her fall. Then he kicked her in the stomach.

"Damn Injun whore!" he muttered.

He grabbed his hat, left the house.

Ida May helped her daughter to bed. She put a wet warm towel on her stomach.

The next morning Ida May found the baby fetus on the rough wooden floor, still attached to its mother who lay unconscious beside it. Ida May severed the umbilical cord and managed to get Rose Ann back on the bed. Then, in the back yard she buried the little mistake, using a plastic grocery bag for its coffin.

Lem was out all night. When he came home at eight o'clock the next morning to get ready for work, Ida May fixed his breakfast as usual. She asked no questions, nor did she give any information since none was solicited.

The grapevine was busy like an invisible Tarzan swinging from vine to vine. Brother Jake tapped into it. He made his pastoral call on The Hills that Saturday afternoon. Then he went home and did something he seldom bothered to do. He prepared for his sermon the next day.

Chapter 34

Holy Racism

Who knows what prompts an action. A placid stream takes the path of least resistance as it flows along giving nourishment and growth to all for which it is responsible. Then a single overnight flood destroys everything.

For centuries a volcano will create and caress a Mount St. Helen. Suddenly in one burst of power it destroys the handiwork of its creation.

A field mouse darts leftward for a succulent morsel of food. Had it gone to the right it would have escaped the quick jaws of the fox.

Causes and effects seem to govern nature--and politics. The search is to pre-determine a cause so that thereby one may govern the effect, or at least alter it. Eruptions are not always stabilized immediately, but given time the flood will recede, the volcano will become dormant, and the mice will continue to procreate. Who knows--maybe someday the lion will lie down with the lamb.

In the meantime, let's face it: the witch hunts did not stop at Salem.

Some obscure notion prompted Vi and me to attend church in Dogwood this morning. Brother Jake was edgy. The sermon fitted the old frontier-preaching stereotype:

> Tell 'em what you're gonna tell 'em,
> Tell 'em what you're tellin' 'em,
> Tell 'em what you've told 'em.

Brother Jake did not name the subject, but it was blatantly clear: Racism! And believe me, there was no variation in his telling.

Double-fisted and balloon-faced, he pounded his pulpit and propounded his gospel. "The supremacy of God's white man over all them blacks and reds and yellers and whosomever else (I think those are the words he used) that falleth under that there curse of Esau back in the year 1844 B.C. which means that many years before Christ was born to that Mary-girl who was a virgin. It's right here in black and white in God's Word, Book of Genesis, chapter 25 and verse 23!"

Wow! I heard more Scriptural interpretation in that one sermon than I did in three full years of post graduate seminary!

Brother Jake spelled it out for us, and he spoke as one with authority.

"We ain't got no Blackskins around Dogwood here," his voice whipped on, giving evidence that he was God's own lightning striking out at every known god of evil, then backlashing all the unknown ones. "We ain't got no Blackskins around here," he repeated, "but there's some others...."

Here he paused to give the congregation opportunity to ponder.

They did. At least I did.

"But there's others around that's a-molestin' our women, our innocent young girls. They ain't Blackskins, but there's some Redskins around and they're all the same and right here in God's Word He says *and the elder shall serve the younger*, and *we* are God's elders of the church, so we gotta do what He ordained or His wrath will be upon us quick as a coyote after a cottontail. Yea, verily I say unto you, Brothers, the wrath of God is quick and terrible."

He paused again, eyes darting, heart churning the hot lava of hell's fire. Even now one could almost see it flowing from the corners of his mouth.

In this reflective pause, he composed himself. We sensed that he was about to reveal the secrets of Hades.

"We got one treed."

Heads jerked to attention. There was a long, silent pause. Even Ol' Blue stopped thumping his tail on the floor and looked up.

Then Brother Jake moved in for the kill.

"Yes sir, we got one treed. Though he don't know it yet. But he will. 'Cause some of us do. And we're gonna see that God's justice is laid on that degenerate, and he won't ever molest another innocent girl. No sir, not as long as he lives."

Nobody talked to us after the service. The half-dozen worshipers, huddled unto themselves, watched us from the church door as we went to our car.

"I think he was serious," Vi said as we drove away.

"Sure seemed like it. What made me uncomfortable was that the people were, too," I replied.

"Seemed like he had someone in mind; I wonder who."

"Who knows. Nobody we'd know," I said. "Where shall we go for Sunday dinner?"

Chapter 35

Vigilantes

The single light bulb hung from the ceiling of the dingy back room in the Dogwood General Mdse. store. It offered little light to the thirteen men who crowded the room. However, it may have complimented their purpose, for it is written that men love darkness more than light.

"Men," Constable Lou Mercer said, calling order to the muffled conversations, "we're here on a moral mission. One of our Dogwood daughters has been raped by a no good Redskin. Now what are we going to do about it?"

The men uttered various responses, none compassionate, none complimentary, none printable.

"Rudy, you tell us again what happened," Lou suggested.

Rudy stood and passed the jug from which he had been sipping to the man next to him. He puffed out his chest and looked around like a young rooster about to crow.

"Like I told Lem here, Tag and me, we wuz down in Greasy Bottom huntin' cottontails last summer when we heard the most gol-darndest scream you ever did hear. 'Panther!' I said to Tag, motioning him to keep down and be quiet. But it wasn't no panther. We soon found that out, 'cause this girl's voice kept on screaming and we could hear her say, 'Let me go.' We began to tear our way through the brush and then right there under that oak tree we saw them. By that time it was too late. He'd done it to her. It was Rose Ann, and she scrambled to her feet and dashed off into the brush. It was Nation all right, wasn't it, Tag?"

Tag nodded and started to say something but Rudy continued loudly, "It was Nation all right and he saw us just as he stood up, and quick as a wink he zipped up his pants and tore off down into the swamp. We chased him, but couldn't make no headway much 'cause he'd got the jump on us. When we came back, Rose Ann had disappeared, too. She went home, I guess."

Brother Jake turned to Lem Hill and said, "Lem, you're her father. Supposin' you tell us what happened after that."

"When that girl of mine got home that day, her clothes were all messed up and tored, and she was scratched and bruised till I almost didn't know who she was. But she wouldn't tell me nothing. She said she saw a bear and thought it was after her so she ran through the brush and stuff and that's why she was all scratched up and tored. That happened last August, but it wasn't till just the other day that her ma found out that she's gonna have a kid and all that. So we began to ask questions. I had to beat some hell out of her before she finally admitted the truth about what happened and she said it was that Injun buck, Nation Skreigh. So that's what happened. It's like young Rudy here, says. It was him, all right."

"Let's go get him," someone yelled.

"Where does he live?" asked another.

"I know, follow me," Rudy called as he burst through the door, the mob surging after him.

Earlier in the afternoon of the same day, Brother Jake said to Sari Jane, "I've got to go to a meeting tonight, so get supper ready early."

"Can I go to the meeting with you?" Joey asked.

"No, this ain't for no kids," replied his father.

After supper Brother Jake left for Dogwood. Joey walked up the trail to Soaring Bluff. He sat for a long while contemplating some of the things his father had said last Sunday and the hints about Rose Ann being raped. Everybody seemed to know who the offender was, but Joey had heard no names mentioned. He couldn't make heads or tails out of it all. As he sat on the edge of the cliff, he thought about other things that seemed to be going on around. Soon his meandering thoughts turned to prayer.

"Lord, here on Soaring Bluff," he prayed softly, "is where you hold the whole world together, and sometimes here is where you put my thinking in order. But now, Lord, everything is falling apart and I don't know what to think. I'm scared, Lord. I don't know why and I don't know what to do."

Here his prayer began to wane as his thoughts turned to wondering if God really cared if people hurt and have troubles.

"He probably does care about most people," Joey half-mumbled, "but I'm nothin' for Him to bother about."

Questions without answers pressed upon his mind and heart. He sat there a long time, looking out across the vast expanse that lay before him.

Suddenly his mind picked up his own voice, saying, "It's Nation! That meeting is about Nation. They think Nation raped Rose Ann and they'll get him tonight!"

He stood up, tense, alert. "I've got to go warn Nation. They'll kill him."

Joey ran down the trail, took a shortcut across a little stream, up over to the next hollow. The cool November shadows began to descend upon the lower valleys when he reached the road to Copperhead Pass near Nation's cabin. Breathless and preoccupied with the urgency of his errand, and wet with perspiration, he did not see Rose Ann until she was about thirty feet from him and asked, "Where you going so fast, Joey?"

Startled, Joey stopped, a short gasp came from his throat. Quickly he pondered whether or nor he should tell Rose Ann. Then he said, "Rose Ann, some men in town think Nation is the one that raped you. But Nation told me how he caught Rudy and Tag at it--at what they did to you. Rose Ann, they're going to come and get Nation tonight. I know they are because they're in town at a meeting right now, and I know they'll come, and they'll kill him so Rudy and Tag won't get blamed. You just gotta tell the truth, Rose Ann; you just gotta. They'll kill Nation if you don't; I know they will. Please tell them the truth."

Rose Ann made no reply.

Joey said, "I guess you won't," and started on in a trot. "It's too late, anyway," he added.

"Maybe they won't," Rose Ann called after him. "Maybe they won't come."

It was almost dark when Joey made his way up the narrow road to Nation's home. When he came within sight of the cabin, he called to Nation, who was sitting on the porch, cleaning his .22 rifle. He had heard Joey coming up the road and wondered why he was in such a hurry.

"Hi, Joey," Nation called.

Joey's breathless approach alerted Nation.

"What is wrong?" he asked.

"Nation, you've got to get out of here right now! They're going to come and get you 'cause they think you're the one who raped Rose Ann."

"What do you mean? Who is 'they'?"

"Those men in Dogwood. My pa went to a meeting tonight and I know it was about you and they'll blame you for what happened to Rose Ann."

"I did not do it," objected Nation.

"I know you didn't. But the people around Dogwood think you did 'cause that's what they want to think, and they're having a meeting right now and I know they're going to come up here and get you."

"Well, let them come; I did not do anything."

"That don't matter," responded Joey. "Look, Nation, it all came to me on Soaring Bluff awhile ago, so I know it's the truth. You caught Rudy and Tag doing it to Rose Ann and now I'll bet they have spread it around that it was you so they wouldn't be blamed."

"But Rose Ann knows it was them."

"I think she must have said it was you."

"Why would she say that?"

"I don't know. Maybe Rudy told her to. But my dad went to a meeting tonight and he thinks it was you. At least I am pretty sure he does because of the way he talked in his sermon Sunday. And there's other funny things that's been going on. Nation, I know they'll get all jugged up at that meeting tonight, and no telling what they'll do."

"What should I do?" Nation asked.

"You gotta get out of here 'cause I know they'll come looking for you."

"Where could I go? Even if I went somewhere, I ain't got nowhere to go."

"Well, I don't know, but they'll come and get you," Joey said. The gravity of his statement hit both of them at once. Joey's message suddenly registered with Nation. He understood.

"What can we do?" both boys said at the same time.

There was a pause, a short silence, and suddenly Joey burst out, "We'll stretch a wire with a pulley from your house out to a tree and tie a pillow and some blankets on it and when they come we'll pull it and they'll think it's you running away, and they'll know they can't find you in the woods in the nighttime, so they'll go home."

"Naw, that wouldn't work. Besides, I ain't got no wire," Nation said.

"You could hide in the outhouse."

"Ain't got no outhouse."

"Where do you go, then?" asked Joey.

"I ain't going nowhere," Nation replied.

"I mean when you gotta...go, where do you go?"

"Just out there," Nation said, waving his hand toward the ample choices among the trees and bushes.

"Well, you gotta do something," Joey insisted.

"I know what," he added with sudden inspiration. "When they come I'll meet them at the door and tell them you're not home."

"They would not believe you," Nation said. "Besides, they would arrest you for protecting me if they say I am a criminal."

"You ain't no criminal," Joey defended.

"Tell them that."

"I will."

"Maybe they will not come," Nation said vaguely.

"No, they're coming all right," Joey said with unswerving conviction.

Just then both of them saw the car headlights turning up the winding road.

"I will just have to face them," Nation said. "Joey, you go on home the back way so they will not know you have been here."

"Let's get inside," Joey said.

Both boys went into the cabin and closed the front door. Nation blew out the kerosine lamp.

A half-dozen cars came to a jolting halt, their headlights focused upon the house and grounds. At first nothing happened; nobody moved to get out of the cars. Then suddenly the silence of sanity ceased as the men jumped from their cars into an undisciplined hubbub of noise and confusion. Immediately the evil of mob-frenzy took command.

"Let us get out of here before they surround the house," Nation said. He pushed Joey out the back door. "Run, Joey," he whispered hoarsely. Then he turned toward the front door to face the men. Joey, supposing Nation was behind him, ran bent over from the back door toward some bushes among the trees. By this time the men had spread out, and some of them had gone around the corner of the house. Rudy and Tag dashed behind a growth of sycamore trees thirty feet from the back door. Tag spotted Joey bent over, running from the house toward the trees and bushes.

"There he goes," he whispered to Rudy, thinking Joey was Nation.

At the same time, Brother Jake came around the other side of the house. Terror struck him when his eyes picked up the running figure of Joey in the semi-darkness.

"There's that Redskin," his voice rasped and immediately his mind flashed back into the horror of the old familiar razorback nightmare.

"This ain't no dream!" he exclaimed hysterically, and in one movement he jumped into a tree branch. "That big demon of hell, coming right at us again, Jakey-Boy. But it won't get you this time! Hold on, Jakey-Boy, he ain't gonna get you and tear you to pieces like he did before!"

His rifle cracked.

Neither Rudy or Tag saw this action of Brother Jake. Concealed behind the sycamore clump, Rudy had grabbed Tag's rifle. His shot rang simultaneously with Brother Jake's.

Then all bedlam broke loose.

Raccoon hunting is a common experience with these men. They say the camaraderie of 'coon hunting on those full-moon nights has no equal. The men recognize every dog's bay and discuss it as they sit around the campfire listening. The dogs intensify the tone of their baying when they pick up the trail. No music will excite the tension of a listener more than these notes reaching the ears of 'coon hunters under the open skies of the Ozarks.

While these men stand around listening, one of them breaks the silence, saying, "They'll tree him over just this side of Sassafras Ridge."

"Naw," argues another, "Ol' Spot's got the lead, and I know how he works. He'll lead the pack around the Ridge and they'll intersect that ol' coon at that big pine tree half-way up Saber Mountain."

These speculations continue until the rhythm of the baying suddenly bursts into a crescendo of frenzied disunity.

"By gosh, they've got him treed over at Creepy Crossing!"

"Yep, sounds like it."

The men rise from their haunches and reach for their rifles. Hurriedly, quietly they kick dirt over the fire, listening intensely, and as one move rapidly through the milky sheen of the moonlight night. When they reach the scene of activity, they gather around and watch the dogs for a time. Some of the men dash in among the dogs and in accelerated excitement they skip and jump and fall over one another.

Suddenly somebody yells loudly, "I see him."

The thrill and excitement subsides somewhat as others ask, "Where? Where is he?"

"About three-quarters of the way up," yells the spotter. "See that branch sticking out there?"

"I don't see him."

"Look! See that branch sticking out on the left? He's just about half-way out from the end."

"That ain't no 'coon; that's a bunch of mistletoe."

"Look farther up," says someone else, "way up towards the moon. Ain't that him?"

"Aw hell, that's an old eagle's nest. I've seen it a hundred times."

In the meantime, the dogs continue barking, yipping, howling, and jumping over and across one another, some even trying to climb the tree. 'Coon-hunting frenzy possesses them.

"I just seen him move," somebody shouts.

At this point, a primordial action takes over, for they have indeed spotted the quarry.

Rifles bark.

Time stops.

The animal loses its grip.

The body begins to tumble downward. Slowly. It bumps against a branch. Thud! Another branch.

It hits the ground.

Moonlight madness, "lunar-tic," falls upon the men as they rush in, competing with the dogs to climax the orgy of the 'coon-hunters' tradition.

Such was the action of the men when the shots were fired and the body of Joey Balaam slumped to the ground. His body fell into the shadows of some bushes. Darkness covered it.

"I got him!" yelled Rudy, running forward triumphantly. "I got that rapin' Redskin!"

The queen of heaven hid her face in a passing cloud. She wept that night as the men stumbled around in the darkness of their victory.

"Is he dead?"

"Get a flashlight."

"This ain't Nation," a hushed voice said.

After Nation had shoved Joey out the back door of the house, he rushed to the front room window and looked out. In the moonlight he could see the melee of men running around from both sides of the cabin. Suddenly he heard the shot.

"Or was it two shots?" he thought.

The shouts and commotion in the rear of the house drew him back to the kitchen window just in time to hear Rudy say, "I got that rapin' Redskin!"

Somebody brought a flashlight. The men crowded around.

"This ain't Nation," the hushed voice repeated.

"No, it ain't," someone else gasped. "This ain't that rapin' Redskin. It's that Balaam kid."

Nation, alone inside his darkened home, also realized what had happened. He did not scream; he did not panic. He just stood there, suspended in a moment too horrible to accept.

Just then Brother Jake came down from the tree, gun in hand, wild-eyed, grinning and muttering incoherently that he had finally gotten that devil from the underworld of hell. "Finally got him with my own rifle," he said with the jubilance of making the final point of a sermon.

Rudy, suddenly aware now of what had happened, quickly picked up on the opportunity.

"You killed him, Preacher," he said loudly, accusingly. "You killed your own boy."

It took a minute for the others to realize what had happened. Then they all turned to Brother Jake, who continued to savor his victory in the Word.

"He killed my boy, this demon did--my Jakey-Boy!" Brother Jake was shouting. "An eye for an eye and a tooth for a tooth. The Word of the Lord has been fulfilled. The Lord took my Jakey-Boy, and now the Devil takes his own. Both of them have taken their own, just like the Word of God says. God took my Jakey-Boy and the devil gets this demon. Mighty is the Word of God; let it be praised forever. Hear now, my friends, not one sparrow falls to the ground that the Lord God does not know, and the demons of this world will be slain by the hand of the Lord for the mouth of the Lord hath spoken it, just like it is written right here in the Word of God."

He thumped his gun with the same vigor as he thumps his Bible in the pulpit.

Then waving his hands at the stunned men standing around he shouted, "Put on the whole armor of God, so that ye be able to withstand the wiles of the devil, for he comes in the dark and takes away the Word from your hearts so that you will not believe and be saved. Like a roaring lion he prowls around, looking for someone to devour. Hold fast, therefore, my brothers and sisters, hold fast to the Word of God."

His body began to sag, but his voice kept on, "Seek ye the Lord while he may be found. Escape from the snares of Satan. Resist the devil and he will flee from you."

With each quotation, he thrust his gun skyward in defiance as if it were his old ragged Bible, visual evidence of the protecting Word of God.

Then the burning flames left his eyes as they glazed over. Some far-off sense of reality quieted him. His body slumped slowly to the ground. Then, in weary monotone he said, "Destroy the devil who has the power of death. Destroy...for they know not what they do."

With that, Brother Jake fell.

"We better get him home," somebody said.

"Yeah, whatta you think, Lou?" another voice said. "Lou? Where the hell is Lou?"

"I'll get him," Rudy said as he turned and went around to the front of the house with his flashlight. There he saw Lou cautiously stepping through the front room into the kitchen as one would when stalking a dangerous criminal.

"Pssst, Pa," Rudy whispered.

Lou whirled, gun poised. Instantly he recognized Rudy and motioned him to be quiet and follow. Tiptoeing into the kitchen, he saw the silhouette of Nation against the window. Nation was so intent upon what was going on outside, that he did not hear them.

"You're under arrest," Lou said.

"They just shot Joey," Nation said in stunned monotone, directed to no one in particular.

Slowly, numbly, he turned toward Lou and Rudy who had the flashlight beamed into his eyes. A quivering, guttural sound came from his young throat.

"They shot Joey," he repeated with momentum.

Then in a wild frenzy of emotion he screamed frantically, "*Lou, they shot Joey! Joey is dead!*"

There was a quick moment of dead silence before the wild scream burst from its pent-up primordial source. Something like lightning seared Nation's soul. His body shuddered like deep thunder rumbling from a dark hollow with no place to settle. A vacuum sucked out Nation's life.

"Let's see that there gun of yours," Lou said, reaching for the rifle Nation clutched in his hand. "Maybe it was you that shot Joey."

In dazed silence Nation handed the rifle to Lou.

"Yeah," chimed Rudy. "It must have been him, all right, 'cause Brother Jake wouldn't kill his own boy."

Lem Hill called from the front door, "Lou, are you in there? We need to know what to do about Brother Jake. He's gone off his rocker."

"Well, I can't do anything about that right now 'cause I've got myself this here prisoner here."

"OK," replied Lem, "I'll tell them to take Brother Jake and Joey home or something."

"Yeah, you tell 'em that," Lou said. "Then you meet me at your car 'cause I need you to help with this Injun."

"OK, Lou," Lem said.

"You pull your car up here to the porch," Lou called to Lem. "I can't take no chances with a prisoner like this, wanted for raping a young innocent girl and murdering his best friend."

When the car pulled up, Nation overheard Lou say to Rudy, "If this SOB tries to escape we'll have to shoot him."

Rudy chuckled and said, "It sure would save the county a lot of money, wouldn't it--court costs and all."

Life began to return to Nation. The gravity of his situation began to reach his consciousness. He knew that he would indeed have to escape or he would be dead before they reached town. "If I make a dash for it now," he thought, "they will shoot me for sure, and if I die, Rudy's crimes will be buried with me."

On the way into town, before reaching the main road, Lou said, "Lem, you'll have to stop. I gotta relieve myself."

"Me, too," replied Rudy.

"Me, too," replied Tag who had sat in the front seat.

"No, Tag," said Lou. "You and Lem stay in the car."

Lou picked up Nation's .22. He and Rudy began to get out of the car, and required Nation to do likewise. During the process, Lou dramatized caution.

"Ought to get some barb wire and tie his hands," Rudy said.

Tag repeated, "Yeah, some barb wire would hold him good."

When they had withdrawn far enough so the men in the car would not hear their voices, Lou pulled Rudy aside a few steps and said to Nation, "Now boy, when I count to three, you make a run for it."

"I do not want to run. I did not do anything."

"Are you standing there telling me you didn't rape Rose Ann Hill and shoot your friend there in cold blood tonight when he was trying to run away from you? There's a lot of witnesses here that say you done it, and I aim to do that same thing to you, Boy, so get going."

Nation stood his ground, knowing that if he did start to run he was dead for sure. However, if he did nothing, perhaps nothing would happen, though he knew it would.

"I'm waitin', Boy," Lou said. "When I count to three either you start running or I start shooting."

"We'll shoot you with your own gun; how do you like that, Injun?" Rudy chimed.

"You'll shoot me whether I run or not."

"That's right, even if shooting is too good for you. But who knows, you might get lucky if you start running. Since you're such a nature boy, those bushes and trees might protect you."

"One," Lou began.

In the star-sprinkled moonlight, a grimacing grin spread between the set jaws of Rudy, who knew his father meant business.

"Two."

Lou's eyelids narrowed. His muscles were tense with readiness.

"Thr...."

A blood-curdling screech pierced the night. The men's heads jerked around as if pulled by puppet strings.

"What was that?" Rudy exclaimed, his voice quivering. Quickly he grabbed his father's arm.

Lou was so startled he did not notice when Rudy knocked Nation's gun from his hand. His first thought was that Lem had sounded the car horn as a signal.

"Why the hell did you do that?" he called to Lem.

"Do what?" returned Lem.

"Honk that cock-eyed horn," Lou replied irritably.

"I didn't honk no horn," said Lem. "That was a damned old screech owl."

"Screech owl hell. I never heard no screech owl sound like that," retorted Lou.

Then remembering his mission, he turned dumbfoundedly. "Where the hell did that Injun go?"

"I don't know," replied Rudy, remaining close beside Lou. "We better get out of here."

"Didn't you see where he went?" Lou demanded. "I thought you was watchin'."

"I, I *vas* watching, Pa," responded Rudy, "but I can't see anything."

"Hey, what did you do with my gun--his gun?" Lou asked, bewildered.

"What gun?" answered Rudy. "I didn't see no gun."

"I had that Injun's .22. You know I did. Where is it?"

Rudy looked around on the ground briefly, then replied, "It ain't here."

"That sneakin' SOB grabbed it," Lou exclaimed. "Why, I'm gonna get that thieving...."

Before he could finish, Rudy turned and said, "I'm getting in the car before he cuts loose on us."

Both men moved rapidly to the car. Quickly they jumped in and closed the doors.

Lou said to Lem, "Get to hell out of here as fast as you can!"

Then he added as calmly as he could, "There ain't no use looking for him tonight, but you can be sure I'll be on his tail tomorrow. We'll get the bastard."

Chapter 36

Crisis on the Move

"Good grief," Vi said as she stirred the breakfast oatmeal. "I heard 'Jolly Ol' St. Nicholas' on the radio this morning and Thanksgiving isn't even here yet."

"Yes, Christmas hawking gets earlier every year," I replied opening the morning paper--to this:

"DOGWOOD MINISTER ACCUSED OF KILLING SON," the caption read.

"Vi, look at this," I said, reading on, "'Brother Jacob Balaam, minister of the Dogwood Community Church, fatally shot his son, Joey, 16, during the midnight arrest of the boy's friend, Nation Skreigh.

"'On Nov. 18, Lou Mercer, a local constable, organized and led a posse to the home of Skreigh, 16, who is accused of raping a young teenage girl. The name of the girl is withheld. When the posse surrounded Skreigh's cabin in the woods, Balaam, a member of the posse, allegedly shot his son, mistaking him for an attacking razorback hog.

"'Skreigh, a Native American, lived alone in the cabin. Mercer apprehended him, but he escaped during his transport to the county jail. Pastor Balaam is under house arrest at his home near Dogwood pending further investigation. Funeral arrangements for Joey Balaam are incomplete.'"

The article went on with details of Brother Jake's flashbacks of terror when the razorback killed Jakey-Boy. It spoke of the "unique community of Dogwood," and the fears of the people regarding "that gun-totin' Indian."

I wanted to cry. Vi did.

That night I made a print-out of all the notes I had in the computer about what Joey had asked me to store in his trunk. The next day, Saturday morning, I drove to Dogwood. At the General Mdse. store I inquired for the residence of Mr. Leonard.

"Hey, Lou," the large, somewhat unkempt man called toward the back room in the store, "somebody wants to know where Leonard lives."

There was a silent hesitation.

"He don't live here," came the reply.

"He don't live here," repeated the man.

"Yes," I said, "but can you tell me where I might find him?"

"This guy wants to find him," the man called to Lou.

"Who the hell wants to know, and why?" asked Lou as he emerged from the back room.

I introduced myself, saying, "I have something to give him."

"If you're from the Feds, you won't find him here," was the response as Lou stood, head cocked, hands on his hips.

"I'm not...."

"And even if you ain't from the Feds," Lou interrupted, "you still won't find him here."

"It's a personal matter--rather important," I said.

"Well, Mister, if it's information you want, then go to one of them information stops you musta seen when you came to Arkansas, 'cause we ain't in the hand-out business, even information."

I thanked him and left the store.

Down across the street, a lady was hanging clothes on a line stretched from a porch post to a front gate post. I walked over to her, introduced myself, and said, "Some time ago Joey Balaam gave me something for Mr. Leonard, but I don't know where he lives."

"Oh, poor Joey!" she burst out, almost in tears. "He just never was right ever since Maybelle Sutherland cast that spell on him when he was a wee thing. And then last fall when my husband and them was out 'coon hunting, they heard him wailing up there in the moonlight up around Soaring Bluff. They said it sent chills right down the spine. At first they thought it was that Indian kid that people hear, but Rudy Mercer, he saw Joey Balaam right there in the middle of the night. Said he saw him plain as day howling at the moon, but none of the others saw him. Anyway, nobody wanted to go look for a better see at him."

"Mr. Leonard?" I asked to remind her of my quest.

"No, he don't 'coon hunt; just fishes. If he'd been there, though, you can be sure they would have found Joey--if it was Joey. Some didn't think it was. Anyway, people have seen Joey go down to Mr. Leonard's cabin and they sit and talk, sometimes for a long time. Heaven knows what they talk about. Probably demons like Joey's dad always does, except they say Joey never was like his dad at all when it comes to Christian beliefs. Leonard's pretty savvy about things like that--that is, if you can get him to talk at all, and I guess Joey could. He's savvy, all right; that's proved by his fishing. Nobody can fish as good as him because Jesus tells him where the fish are just like he told those disciples when he said, 'Cast your net on the other side of the boat.' Joey's kinda like that, too. Or at least he was. But I'm not too sure about all this stuff. Not sure at all."

"Where does Mr. Leonard live?" I asked directly.

With no further hesitation, she said, "You just take that trail down by the river a little way and you'll see his cabin over on the left, up on a knoll."

I thanked her and walked down toward the river.

Leonard was in his yard, repainting his boat. A comfortable relationship was established in no time. He expressed gratitude for the print-outs, saying, "Joey said you would do this."

Chapter 37

Death Tells Its Tales

Today is Sunday, November 22, 1992. Windsor Castle is burning in London, President-elect Bill Clinton and the Reverend Jesse Jackson are attending Mass together in a Little Rock Catholic Church, tornadoes are devastating Louisiana, and the funeral service for Joey, our enigmatic upside down heart, will be held in Dogwood this afternoon.

The morning *Democrat-Gazette* has not arrived yet. Little matter because it only serves to repeat what we've been hearing on television the past few days and nights where they tell the news before it happens, then it is repeated while it is happening, and yet another repetition when it's overwith--much like Brother Jake's sermon outline.

That's all right with Vi and me because news in this our fourth year of retirement fails to awe us like it did when we were in the fast lane of achievement. AARP knows that about its constituents, so it candidly intersperses its publications with items of social security, arthritis and those "good old days." They do this masterfully, snagging our attention so that we will adjust our trifocals and take a second look at the items they are promoting for our short-term benefit. The gains are mutual.

As I said before, age and retirement are for those who appreciate them. Vi and I do.

Early this morning, before getting ready for church, I walked the loop of the nature trail. Along the way I watched a deer browsing here and there. "My thoughts are like that," I mused, "wandering here and there, from one thing to another." I thought again of the morning radio newscast; i.e., the media's concern over whether the Queen or the State would pay for the fire damage of Windsor Castle, the political overtures (or rather, the campaigning finesse) of Bill Clinton and Jesse Jackson attending a Catholic Mass together in Little Rock, and what Vi and I ought to do about going to Louisiana to volunteer our help for the tornado victims.

Most of all, I thought of Joey. Dead now. Vi and I will attend his funeral this afternoon. The church will probably be full. They will be there for many reasons, but Joey himself will not be one of those reasons. Joey never meant that much to any of them.

I finished two brisk walks around the trail and returned to the house. As I entered, Vi said that Brother Jake had called, so I returned the call.

"Brother Hilliard," Brother Jake said, "Sari Jane's cousin, Brother Jenkins, was on his way here from Lorensville to do Joey's funeral, but he had an automobile accident and landed in the hospital. The funeral is at two o'clock this afternoon and Joey liked you pretty good, so can you come and lend a hand?"

Here I was, ready to leave for our own Sunday morning worship and ....

"Yes, I'll be there," I replied. "Two o'clock, you say, at your church in Dogwood."

Well! That established the sudden Who, What, Where, When and Why for the day. Now for the How! How in the world could I get a funeral service together for my young friend Joey by two o'clock! The first step was to begin, so that is what I did, loosening my tie and briefly thanking God for the computer word processor.

The clock hands pointed to one-fifteen when Vi and I dashed for the car and headed for Dogwood. "I hope Brother Jake leaves Ol' Blue at home today," I muttered as we backed out of the driveway.

It is difficult to concentrate on a funeral message while driving to Dogwood. The scenery, even in November, draws your attention into the spectacular dimensional views of depth and beauty. However, Vi helped.

"Remember the letter we received from Joey wanting us to be his think-tank?" she asked.

"Thought-trunk," I corrected absent-mindedly. "He needed an outlet for his thoughts after his dad destroyed his notes which he had hidden in his trunk. He wanted us to be the storage source for his thoughts. We've kept them on the computer."

"One of the things he stored with us," Vi continued, "had to do with life and death. He seemed to think neither ends, so one does not cancel the other. Life is the result of death, and death is the result of life. Both depend on the other, and you can't have one without the other any more than you can have light without dark. In that case, a person can't be dead unless he's alive."

I smiled and said, "Remember the time when he suggested how much better off people would be, especially we Christians, if we looked upon our spiritual maladies like we do our physical ones. Like when we have a headache, we say so and take an aspirin. If we have appendicitis we let it be known and have an appendectomy to correct the matter. But when we have a spiritual defect we don't even recognize it, and even if we did we wouldn't say anything about it because we'd be looked upon as odd-balls."

"What do you think he meant?" Vi asked. "Do you think he was referring to himself when he said that?"

"He was talking to us."

"Where do you think all those ideas of his came from?" Vi pondered, looking out across the valleys as we sped along.

"Certainly not from his dad," I replied in abstraction, trying to focus my thoughts upon the sermon I had in mind.

A clear declaration of fact resounded in her voice when she said, "I think they came from God."

"If that's true, then why would God waste all that information on Joey's sudden death?" I asked. Then added, "If they came from God, then surely Joey would have lived, been educated and become a super St. Paul, thrusting Christianity forward into its fullest."

Vi never argues, but sometimes she comes close to it, like now when she said, "Aren't all things possible with God?"

"Well, a person has to live long enough to bring them into fruition," I replied.

"Christ didn't."

"But Christ had others to carry on his teachings," I said.

"So does Joey," Vi replied.

A quickened silence fluttered between us.

"Good grief!" I exploded.

Another pause, and I almost shouted, "Of course! You've got it, Vi! That's it!"

The sermon fell into place!

We passed by Greasy Bottom, then up and around Silver Mountain. At one-fifty-five the car coasted down the steep grade into the village of Dogwood. Brother Jake's Community Church was ready for Joey's funeral.

The sun provided comfortable weather, lower seventies. Outside the church some people stood around, men and women, indicating that the pews inside were already filled. There was no parking place reserved for pastors, so we parked down the road a bit. Brother Jake and Sari Jane were sitting in their pickup behind the hearse. They joined us as we made our way through the bystanders and walked toward the casket which was already at the door.

Somebody on the sideline whispered, rather loudly, "What's he doing here? I thought Brother Jenkins was to do the funeral."

With great ceremony, Lou Mercer slowly opened the church door. As soon as he did so, Ol' Blue started to dash in.

Lou called to Lem Hill, "Grab that dog!"

Lem did, then while struggling to hold onto Ol' Blue's collar he called out to Lou, "What'll I do with him?"

"The Reverent will put him in the pickup," Sari Jane said quietly.

Whereupon we waited until Brother Jake did so.

The pews were all full, including the few extra chairs set up in the back. There was no music. No flowers.

"Everybody stand up," Lou announced as the funeral director started the casket down the aisle toward the chancel of the church. Following the processional, the folks from outside filed in and stood along the walls. I proceeded to the pulpit chair and turned around just as Lou, standing in the aisle at the front pew, whisper, "Roger, you and Prissy, you get up and stand over at the side 'cause we gotta have this place here for Brother Jake and Sari Jane and the preacher's wife."

He then went to the back of the church where Vi was standing and brought her up to the front pew.

"Y'all scoot down some more," he said to the people in the pew as he seated Vi.

I sat down and waited for a cue, supposing someone would explain why the Reverend Jenkins was not here. The congregation waited, too; I looked at them, they looked at me. It was quiet, probably the quietest that little church had ever been. Then when someone whispered, "I guess this is the way they do it up North," I realized that I was to do something besides preach, and the time to do it was now, so I stepped down and asked Brother Jake if anybody else was to do anything or if there was any music. He said, "You just preach to them. They know 'When the Roll Is Called Up Yonder I'll Be There.'"

I was grateful for this guidance, so returned to the pulpit and read the normal funeral introduction, John 11:25, using the New Revised Standard Version of the Bible.

Hardly had I finished when someone said to her pew-companion, "I don't think he's using the right Bible."

There was no hymnal at the pulpit, so I stepped down and asked Sari Jane for one and the number of "When the Roll Is Called Up Yonder."

Brother Jake replied, "It ain't in the book. You just sing it."

So we sang it.

I began the sermon by reciting John 11:2: "Jesus said, 'I am the resurrection and the life.'" Then I went on to say how Joey showed me that Jesus is resurrection in our present lives, coming to us and resurrecting us from the unfulfilled lives we Christians, or anybody else, now live.

"Have you ever wondered why God chooses unlikely people to carry out his real, hard-core work?" I asked. "People like the stammering Moses, the boisterous Simon Peter, the sneaking Judas, the murderous Paul. Why did God choose youthful Jeremiah who did not know anything about God? Then when he began to say the things God put in his heart and soul, his family and friends thought he had a screw loose and began to dissociate from him. Yet, of all the prophets, Jeremiah turned out to be the closest to the teachings of Jesus Christ.

"'I *am* the resurrection,' Jesus said. Yes, sure, we say with Martha at the grave of Lazarus, or here at the funeral of Joey Balaam, 'resurrection at the last day.' But can't you hear Jesus saying, 'No, Martha; hear me: I *am*....'

"Folks, I am not talking about a conversion experience whereby we accept Jesus for what He is. I am talking about a resurrection beyond rebirth, so far beyond it that only a few, very few, enter into it because the gate is so narrow and the road so hard. I am persuaded that Joey Balaam crossed that threshold, and that is why, like Jeremiah, he seemed so different from the rest of us. Had you ever thought that?"

I paused to let the thought penetrate, expecting no answer, but suddenly a woman's voice said, "I always thought Joey was kinda God-like, but I never was sure. He said a lot of things that--well, I wondered how a kid like that could think that way. Like one time he asked me, he said, 'Edna, do you think Jesus suffered more while He was growing up than He did on the cross?'"

"What did you tell him?" I urged.

"Why, I didn't rightly know what to tell him--not a kid like that, leastwise so he would understand," replied the lady whom Joey had called Edna.

"Here's another question Joey asked," I contnued, "'Do you think Jesus did more for people when He was alive on earth, or has He done more since He died?'"

"Well," said an elderly matriarch at the end of the third pew, "Jesus did a lot of great things while He was alive, but surely to goodness He does even greater things *since* He died. And surely He said so right there in John 14:12 in King Jameses Holy Bible--which is God's. I never heard of anybody being saved before Jesus died, but I, for one, have surely been saved since He did die."

A man in the back pew stood up and said, "He has done a lot more since he died than those few years when he was alive."

"And keeps on doing them," a woman's voice added.

Witnessing was no new thing with these people. They love it, so of course it continued.

"I know my life has been changed since He died," an elderly man said. "And that ain't been so long ago," he added, invoking a few chuckles from the congregation.

"This is great, Folks," I said, getting caught up in the enthusiasm, and stepping down from the pulpit to the same level with them. "Jesus taught a lot of things that came from God, and they helped a lot of people. Then after He died the things he said came alive, just as if Jesus Himself were alive saying them, and they keep stirring people to life, including all of us who are speaking here today, isn't that right? Does anyone else wish to talk about something *Joey* might have said?"

Leonard stood up and said, "I believe that young Joey Balaam quoted God just like young Jeremiah did. One time after Jeremiah had grown up, he said that God will put His law in our hearts, and then we will know Him and it will be something that will not be taught by any man. I think Joey was like that. God put His law in Joey's heart, and it was the Word of Christ, but Joey didn't have time to digest it all and to understand it. Another reason I believe that, is because in the eighth chapter of Hebrews the Bible says that prophecy is possible.

"Joey never did expose our sins and shortcomings," Leonard continued. "His questions and conversations always pointed toward the greater aspects of Christ's mission for this world, just like the prophets of old did."

"That he did!" exclaimed Sari Jane with uncontrollable emotion.

"What do some of the rest of you say?" I asked.

Silence. The silence of God.

Then, "What'd he say?" came a frail voice in the rear.

"He said Joey's on God's list, Aunt Bertha," came the hushed reply.

I wasn't sure I wanted to expand on Leonard's testimony, so to everybody in general I asked,"What about Joey?"

A blond lady threw the question back at me, saying, "Now that I think about it, Joey did say a lot of thought-provoking things when he was alive. Do you think all of those things ended with his death?"

"I don't see how they could if they're from God," was my shifty reply.

"But how do we know they're from God?" somebody challenged.

"The only way I can think of," I replied, "is that tomorrow and the days to come you folks keep discussing with one another the things you've heard Joey say. Think about them and discuss them with each other, and see what develops. That's what the people did about Jesus after his death.

They even wrote them down and that's how we came to have the Bible today. I'm with the lady who just said that if they are from God, then God will follow through with whatever plan He had in mind when He spoke to Joey. And I am thoroughly convinced that you people here in Dogwood are to be a real part of that plan. What do you think?"

"God ain't no shirker," someone said. "He finishes what He starts."

"Amen!" came from five or six corners.

"Awhile ago," I said, "we were wondering how-come God chooses people like the whimpering Elijah, the youthful Jeremiah, the stammering Moses, the cursing Peter, the ailing Paul. None of them were likely candidates for the blood and guts it takes to speak the Word of God in the raw, resurrected power of Jesus Christ, do you think?"

More "Amens. You're right on, Brother. Thank you, Jesus," from various members of the congregation, both male and female voices. There was no response from Brother Jake. Perhaps he did not understand what was being said.

"But let me suggest something and see what you think," I continued. "Isn't it possible that even today Christ chooses certain individuals for His risky tasks? I say risky, because people react when they are told that their religion is lacking. That's why Christ singles out the ones who will put before us the difficult parts of His ministry. We do not understand these hard-to-accept things, and so we refuse to explore them because that's the easy way out--it's the slacker's way. But for those who do search them out, it must be like unto a spiritual Star Trek adventure. None of us are qualified for them, so God necessarily chooses unqualified people. Then He qualifies them. The task of these people is not the same as your everyday Christians like myself who teach Scripture and promote salvation. They are those rare persons that Jesus can depend upon to stand firm against any adversary. 'Few there be that enter,' Jesus said. All people are welcome to God's grace and salvation, but Jesus *chooses* those whom He will bring forth to withstand the rigors of these greater things."

"That sounds pretty far-fetched," a voice called out.

"You're right, it does sound far-fetched, because Christ's ultimate goal for us seems so unlikely to our reasoning. But since when have the things of Jesus not sounded far-fetched? For example, didn't He say there would be those who will not taste death before they see the kingdom of God? I think Joey Balaam was one of those persons and I'll tell you why I think that. These persons are true and they are exact because God's Word is in them, and God's Word is true and exact. These people do not prove anything nor do they make any boast. It's like someone just said--they trust God who will complete what He started. He chooses them and then He qualifies them. Joey was qualified because whatever came, he stood with Christ. And I say to you today, what God started in Joey, God will finish in you folks!"

"Let it be, Lord, let it be!" Sari Jane said with conviction, loud enough for Jesus to hear. Brother Jake looked at her but she remained steadfast. The room resounded with Amens .

"Folks," I continued, "you make it clear what you think about this matter. It is obvious, and we regret, that we under-estimated Joey Balaam. Let us not underestimate Almighty God."

Resurgence of Amens.

"Joey, so like Jesus, raised some jolting questions about our died-in-the-wool assumptions about this this Christianity we proclaim. Surely some of you have heard him challenge things that we commonly accept as 'good Christianity'. Joey always wanted Christianity to be improved because he wanted the very best for Jesus. Now I want to hear from some of the rest of you. If you ever heard Joey speak of things that you think Jesus wanted him to say, speak up and tell us about it now because we really should know."

A young lady, junior high school age, stood up and said, almost tearfully, "Sometimes Joey tried to tell me things about God and how he felt and everything, but I didn't want anyone to see me listening to him, even if I did want to know about what he said. I think I tried to do what a lot of people did, and that is dump my sins off onto Joey like those people in the Old Testament did when they dumped their sins on that goat and sent the poor creature out into the wilderness."

She burst into tears and sat down.

"Folks," I said, "let me pick up on what this young lady just said. Did we exile Joey into a wilderness--a wilderness of loneliness? None of us knows how lonely life was for Joey--and painful. One time he told me he didn't think he could stand it any longer. This caused me to wonder if that is why so many young people take their own lives today. One time Joey asked, 'Was Jesus' greatest pain on the cross or in His daily living?' I had no answer, but Joey knew. His questions often contained their own jolting answers."

Leonard's booming voice spoke up, asking, "Brother Hilliard, what do you honestly think about Joey Balaam?"

"There were times," I replied, "when I thought Joey might become a real twentieth century prophet searing the world once again with the firebrand of God's holy Word. I guess I was wrong. Joey died. Surely

God protects his own. At least that's what the devil told Jesus during the temptation. Of course you can't always believe the devil.

"The fact is that God did not protect this young body that lies here before us today, so let's face it: Joey Balaam was no prophet, he was not a leader like Billy Graham--not even a religious stimulant because he just didn't have what it takes to get people to listen to him. After all, he was only a kid, a mild fanatic. Why should anyone pay attention to him? He was not aggressive enough for football--not slender enough for basketball. He always struck out in baseball. So nobody liked him very much. He was no more of a candidate for God than...than...Moses was.   Or Jeremiah, or Peter, or Paul."

"Hold on there, Preacher!" a man interrupted. He stood up and I sensed he was ready to come forward with doubled up fists. "I've been hearing that Joey had the stuff God 's made of, so we're going to get together, we people here in Dogwood, and we're going to find out about these things he said."

"Amen! That's right, Wallace! You bet we are!"

The responses were so spontaneous and enthusiastic that for a moment I felt the South was going to win at last!

Another man spoke out saying, "It's like you were saying, Preacher-- the world paid more attention to Moses and Jeremiah, and Peter and Paul *after* they died than before, so maybe we ought to pay more attention to Joey."

It was my turn to say, "Amen," so I did as enthusiastically as ever it had been said.

The man continued, "Let me tell you something, folks: It's what I think, anyway, and that is God's Word is going to be fulfilled right here in Dogwood, and it is going to be fulfilled in the resurrection of Joey Bal...."

The man never finished the sentence because Rose Ann, who had been sitting on one of the extra chairs in the rear of the nave, suddenly jumped up and began to wail, "He didn't do it! Joey told me to tell the truth but I was too scared, but he didn't do it, so I'm tellin' the truth, it wasn't him, and Joey wanted me to tell the truth so I am, and it wasn't Nation."

I stood dumbfounded, thinking first that one of those old fashion "Shouting Methodists" had cut loose. Then a large man, it was Lem, Rose Ann's father, grabbed Rose Ann. I saw him clasp his hand over her mouth and whisk her out the door as she struggled and continued to scream, kicking hysterically "Joey said tell 'em; Joey told me to tell the truth; Joey knew who done it and it was...."

That's all I heard.

A few followed the commotion outside, while those who remained looked wide-eyed and whispered to each other. Ol' Blue came dashing in, too elated with all the commotion to settle in his usual place in front of the pulpit.

"Folks," I said after we had regained some composure, "let us go now to the cemetery for the interment."

At the graveside, during the committal, a car drove up. A man walked rapidly over to Lou Mercer and talked briefly. Then they both left hurriedly, leaving mouth to ear whisperings from one person to the next as the committal proceeded. When the final Amen was pronounced, the entire gathering disappeared, as if "poofed" by Tinkerbelle's magic wand. Even Brother Jake left, though Sari Jane remained. Greatly troubled and puzzled, her eyes remained fixed upon the gray casket.

Vi and I stepped over beside her as they lowered Joey's body into the ground and began to fill in the dirt.

"The Reverent said you would take me home," she said softly, without looking up.

Yes, we took her home--to that empty, silent house where both of her two young boys had been returned to her in sudden tragic death, their blood still dripping, as friends placed their remains in her arms. Home, where nothing was alive any more. The house looked so terribly lonely.

"Joey was like that," she said softly as she got out of the car. "He was like you said."

Then, softly, she closed the car door, and with strong faltering steps climbed onto the porch. There she hesitated briefly. Her body shuddered, and she stepped forward, opened the door and went inside.

We sat in the car, Vi and I did, and wondered all the more what Joey Balaam was like.

"There are so few Joeys in the world," Vi said as we started home.

"Maybe," I said, "maybe they're dormant within us."

"Like Christ?"

Chapter 38

The Big Fisherman

Leonard of Dogwood is a huge man measuring six feet, four inches, from the top of his head to the soles of his feet which support a good three hundred pounds of solid bone and muscle. He has a voice to match. However, he seldom uses any of those assets except his ability to fish. He isn't married. His last name is never mentioned; though it could be Leonard, for all anybody knows. It may be listed on the tax records if anyone bothered to check.

Leonard of Dogwood is a "loner" who is not always alone except when he fishes. He does not go to church. Every Monday night he meets with "the boys" in the back of the Dogwood General Mdse. store. They play poker, drink moonshine and smoke the somewhat cured, home-grown tobacco furnished by the proprietor, Lou Mercer. The bodies of these men have yet to acknowledge that the tobacco is just as hard on their systems as the moonshine.

Early Monday morning after Joey's burial, Leonard stuffed Joey's "trunk papers" in his tackle box and put them in his flat-bottom boat. Then easily he loaded the boat with its contents into his old brown pickup truck and drove up the winding back road to a little hidden cove where Greasy Bottom slides into the river. There he unloaded the boat and embarked upon an exercise of catfishing and mind boggling never equaled in these backwaters of the Ozarks.

Leonard's fishing techniques have reached the fine-tuning of a Serengeti lioness on the prowl. As for the fish--school lets out when he drops anchor. The big ones send the little ones downstream with their mothers. Then these huge dominant males gather around and watch curiously like the wildebeests in a nature film when the tail-twitching stalker crouches within sight but beyond reach. Also, like those wildebeests, these granddaddy fish are intensely aware of the danger, yet unable to resist temptation, a mysterious phenomenon that extends beyond simple curiosity.

As Leonard prepared for the morning's agenda, his casual movements belied the intensity of his purpose. True to his pattern of preparations, he arranged the tackle box and selected the bait for the exact time of year, month, day, and hour. He re-calculated the weather conditions, and ascertained exactly where and how to place his rod and reel and net. Overhead an eagle circled and watched with envy as it tried to compare its soaring perfection with the polished sensitivity of Leonard's fishing technique. An oncoming tornado would have suspended itself in mid-air and marveled at Leonard's symphonic movements.

Deliberately, exactly, Leonard synchronized all of these essentials to perfection. Then he relaxed. Now his hunches, both inherent and developed, took over like the automatic pilot of a 747. He did not tease the fish; they would come. Neither did he look at his watch, for he had none. He came here this morning for one basic reason, and that was to reflect upon the entanglement of things the minister from New Autumn said yesterday and to peruse Joey's trunk papers. On consequential matters, Leonard could concentrate best while fishing his best. So he was ready now, to give his full attention to the printed information stuffed in his tackle box.

However, he did not immediately extract Joey's papers. Such a movement and sound would disturb the ingrained discipline of this fisherman at his task. Rather, he sat without movement. Once or twice he reached down, and touched the papers as if he expected the genie of Aladdin's lamp to appear and clarify the perplexities that were stirring his consciousness like a recurring dream.

However, no genie appeared.

Years ago, until his health and his doctor warned him to change life styles, Leonard was a coal miner in Kentucky. Today he reflected upon his hasty departure from that area. "That miner's young wife might have had something to do with my leaving when I did," he admitted silently, smiling as memories bobbed his head in confirmation.

That was twenty-three years ago. He spent eleven of those years on the seasonal operation of the Great Lakes ore boats. Then he drifted aimlessly westward and finally south to Dogwood. Here without the permission of the natives, he built his little cabin on a knoll up from the river where he lives unto himself and his fishing, offering and receiving no give or take with the folks around him.

The Dogwood people, being notional toward strangers, viewed him with suspicion for two years, but since he gave them no cause to develop their reservations, they surrendered and began to consider him as part of the surroundings. No doubt his catches of fish had something to do with this unusual relationship because many sought to learn his secret. However, Leonard gave no secrets and asked for none.

Shortly after his arrival in Dogwood he received a notice to register for taxation on his cabin. After that, folks began to call him Leonard.

Twelve years ago during the great tornado and flood disaster, as Leonard stood on his porch watching the rising water surround his cabin, he looked downstream and saw the car of Constable and Mrs. Mercer suddenly disappear from the road. The force of the tornado had rolled it into the river. Immediately, not withstanding the beating wind and rain, Leonard jumped into his boat and rowed to the rescue. He discovered Lou unconscious. Mrs. Mercer was unable to push the car doors open against the pressure of the water, and she was too hysterical to open the windows. The floodwaters were rising rapidly. With his super strength, Leonard opened the passenger door enough to get Mrs. Mercer out of the car as the waters rushed in. He lifted her into the boat. Then with considerable effort he tugged frantically at the unconscious body of Lou, and with great effort pulled him from under the steering wheel, across the passenger seat, out of the car into the swirling water. However, it was impossible to lift the limp body of this huge man into the boat. The water was rising fast. Leonard pushed the boat ahead with Mrs. Mercer in it, while he pulled Lou by the hair of his head to the safety of his cabin.

In the cabin, Leonard's application of mining town emergency techniques soon had Lou's wounds bound and his consciousness awake. Mrs. Mercer noticed these techniques. The next week, at her sewing circle, she posed the possibility that, "Mr. Leonard might be a doctor."

"If he is, what's he doing here in Dogwood?" questioned one of the ladies.

"Maybe hiding from his past?" proposed another.

Today, on this particular Monday morning, Leonard sat in his boat, periodically glancing at the papers in his tackle box. He continued to reflect upon his past, his earthly origin. Leonard had never seen his father, nor had he ever heard of his activities except through his mother. His father had been a preacher, an itinerant evangelist with some success for a short time. His mother held no animosity toward him. She always referred to him as The Reverend, and endorsed his enthusiastic vigor for the Lord. She said nothing against his passion for women. After all, she felt the same way toward him. "What happened, happened," she rationalized. Leonard knew that all of her life she had longed to see him again and fulfill the unwavering desire to be his wife. She had told Leonard that he had some of his father's qualities.

"Same passions as your father," he remembered her saying.

Leonard interpreted this to be favorable. These "passions" seemed to include both sex and religion, though religion was common household talk while sex was not. Leonard grew up a firm believer and church-goer. He even enrolled in a short-term seminary with the intention of becoming ordained in his church denomination, but he was turned off by their insistence that he believe only as they believed. Since some of their doctrines were not adjustable to his frame of religious reference he left that institution of rote response. The experience caused him to begin searching out the "truths" that pulpits, radio and television ministries often propounded. His search afforded him more than average knowledge about Scripture. It revealed that people often fuse Biblical declarations with denominational doctrine. This, Leonard determined, creates a hybrid result that serves no purpose beyond self-gratification. As a result, Leonard discarded many proclamations commonly accepted as "gospel truth."

The sun was an hour up when the big fisherman reached into his tackle box and took out Joey's trunk papers. He looked at them curiously as if wondering how he should begin to examine them. Caution warned him; anticipation urged him. His hands shook a little as he unfolded the first one.

Time left him alone as he read. So did the fish.

At last, he spoke softly. "All my life I have asked these same questions and thought similar thoughts. There *is* something beyond ourselves that enters ourselves. This kid, Joey, had insights to things that perplex a lot of us."

He sat motionless for a time, giving his mind freedom to ponder. Then again he looked at the crudely worded documents on the print-out of Joey's trunk. "What are the genesis beyond the genes that penetrate humankind?" Leonard asked aloud as though he expected an answer.

The fish did not answer, but a morning dove sounded its peculiar response as it took wing from the nearby bank.

"Maybe we are created more in the image of God than we dare to think. Could it be that our roots come from two sources, one from our evolutionary development on this little planet with its primordial survival of the fittest, and the other from a realm beyond of which the primordial knows nothing? Could this, then, be the transfusion which the ancients described so thoughtfully in the Creation story? After all, other people did co-exist with Adam and Eve; Cain married one of them. Might it be that during the evolutionary process of *homo sapiens* God implanted Himself into our development, and from this arose the Adam concept, differentiating a moral difference between right and wrong out of which has grown the ethics of judgment and love?"

Leonard's gaze swept the downriver scape, but his soul pushed his mind onward.

"The maturity for mankind," he mused to himself, "the final goal of Christianity, must surely reach beyond the repetition of current tradition, experience, Scripture and reason. Christianity in its fullness will be a new thing under the sun."

Leonard sat for a time, rocking with the rhythm of his boat. His thoughts began to review the things Jesus taught when He was on earth as they are recorded in the New Testament. Leonard began to compare these things with Joey's trunk notations. Perhaps the similarities were weak, but they were not absent.

"What is it that will push humankind over the threshold into what obviously is our goal--the original goal our Creator set for us?" Leonard pondered. "The teachings of God's Incarnate Son has guided us to that threshold of possibility, but it has not carried us over. Furthermore," Leonard mused, "it is *not* going to carry us over because we, ourselves, are the threshold through which we must pass. If that is true, then we are going to have to *force* ourselves *through* ourselves in order to get there."

A stimulation began to quicken Leonard's consciousness. He looked again at the papers in his hand. His eyes fell upon one of Joey's notes. It read, "First Corinthians 2 speaks of God's Spirit imparting wisdom to us. In John 14:26 Jesus said the Holy Spirit would teach us all things. This Spirit of God--what is it? What will it teach and how will it teach it? Papa says the Bible is the only source of teaching Christians need or will ever have."

Then Leonard's eyes fell upon Joey's postscript: "O God, You're trying to get me to understand. Please help me where I can't. It hurts so bad. I believe! Help my unbelief!"

Steadily, like the sun coming out from behind a slow-moving cloud, revelation began to penetrate Leonard's perception. The comprehension picked up momentum like the first tricklings of a flash flood, and very quickly the questions bursting from Leonard's mind began to answer themselves. He felt the vibrations tingling and awakening his mind like the vigor his body felt when he jumped into the cold sparkling pool beneath the waterfall after a long hot day in the coal mines in Kentucky. His soul stirred the very core of his being, awakening him to a dimension far more fundamental than fishing for fish. There came upon him a Mind-to-mind communication, and with it the sensation of belonging to some distant beginning from which he came. Titillations flashed across his mind like lightning opening up darkened skies in the dead of night. It was the Word of God, the Light that shines in darkness, signaling a new dawn.

"I am calling you," the Imprint began to be more specific. "There have been moments when you would have risen up at once and left all to follow me. Do so now."

Resistance! Never had Leonard struggled so fiercely within himself.

"Dammit all!" he suddenly exploded, "You know I have sinned just as my father did before me; therefore, I'm unfit for anything like this!"

"My concern is not with your fleshy naughties you call sins, Leonard; nor is it with those of your father," returned the Cognizance. "The social order to which you allude is essential for human relationships in your world, so it is well to observe those laws. However, social mores do not relate you to me, nor me to you. I call you beyond things of the world even while you live there."

There was a pause as Leonard tried to assimilate what was taking place. He was not surprised that these communications carried the synthesis of Joey Balaam.

Suddenly new creation surged in upon him. It was *resurrection!* coming like thunder rolling across the skies from horizon to horizon. Leonard's soul stood naked before God. This was Judgment! Astonishment, humility and elation flooded in upon him.

Then there was silence. Leonard knew that this was Christ; that He was enlisting Leonard into *His* Christianity.

Leonard's eyes fell upon the paper he had been holding in his hand. However, he did not see the paper.

"Are you--is Joey Balaam with you?"

"Leonard," came the Imprint, "the time will come when the Church will be at one with its Founder. When it does, it will take the sins of the world upon itself. When it takes the sins of the world upon itself, it will die."

There was absolute silence.

Suddenly, with a burst of comprehension, Leonard exclaimed, "Joey?"

"Yes, Joey is the epitome of that which is to come."

That evening Leonard went to the men's Monday night card game early. He entered the back room of the Dogwood General Mdse. store just as Lou was placing a four by eight sheet of half-inch plywood on bags of seed corn. Soon the usual eight men gathered around it, sitting on stools, a couple of chairs, kegs and other available posterior support. Their interest lay not in comfort, but in the fellowship of dealing cards and telling tall tales. Also it afforded the opportunity to ante up any gossip that might be wandering around unguarded.

The cards flipped and the deals made their rounds. The tobacco smoked and the liquor choked, all in harmony with the groans of loss and the buglings of victory.

Lou tried to keep the deals moving and the money rolling as rapidly as possible, for ten per cent of the winnings went to the house "for expenses."

"What was that preacher from New Autumn talking about yesterday at that Balaam kid's funeral?" asked Ol' Peg. His leg had been shot off in World War Two at Iwo Jima. Or was it the Civil War at Shiloh? He couldn't remember. Nor could he remember the question he had just asked because when he looked at his second card it was a second queen!

"I don't know what he was talking about, but he didn't sound like no preacher I ever heard," replied Zig. "Raise you ten cents, Peg."

"I call," Lou Mercer said, "and sweeten the pot another dime." Then he continued, emphasizing his Ozark twang, "Guess I ain't reeligious 'nuff to know about them thangs. Nobody kin unnerstan them Yanks, enway. You'd thank they'd larn ta speak America."

"Wish I knew more about it," came the voice of a third man as he threw in his hand. "The more about religion I hear the more confused I get. Yet seems like there ought to be some sense to it, but there ain't none."

"There is a lot of sense to what that funeral was all about," Leonard said.

An intensity in his voice caused the men to stop studying their cards and look up at him.

Slowly he laid his cards on the table.

"Let me tell you what happened this morning while I was fishing," he said, his eyes magnetizing the attention of the men. Calmly he related his morning's experience. He spoke from his heart with authority, and as he spoke, the Breath of God mingled with the tobacco smoke in room. Every man among them accepted what they heard even though it was impossible to understand this burning bush. There in that dingy back room where Nation Skreigh's life had been condemned to death, Joey Balaam's life was brought forth as Lazarus from the tomb.

Leonard finished as suddenly as he began. Silence prevailed until Lou shuffled his cards, cleared his throat and tried to revive the card game. He was not successful.

"I always knew that kid had something in his head besides marbles," said Wallace Enright.

"Yeah," responded Al Leffer, "he was different, all right, and it wasn't all bad."

"Come on, you guys, let's play poker," urged Lou. "Ain't that what we came here for?"

"Yeah, Lou, that's what we came for," replied Vince Cleat. "But I think Leonard here has something. I been kinda wondering about that kid ever since he got shot."

"I wondered about him before he got shot," replied Lou with a sarcastic grin.

Except for Lou and Lem, the men were in no mood to continue with the cards, so the session ended early, and for once everybody was sober.

Edna Enright looked at the clock when Wallace came in the back door.

"You're home early," she said, raising her head for an explanation.

Wallace made no reply as he hung his cap on the nail just inside the kitchen door.

"Anything wrong?" she pursued.

"No," he said. "Leonard got us thinking about Joey Balaam; some of the things he said before he got shot."

"Like what?" Edna asked.

"Well, you know. Those religious things he was always saying."

"Nobody paid attention," Edna responded.

"That's just it, but they're paying attention now. Anyway we did tonight." Meanwhile down the street, around the corner, Bertha Leffer was pressing Al for more information. Al was reluctant to talk about what had been said at the poker session, for he knew Bertha's skill at gossip.

"But this is not gossip," retorted Bertha when Al reminded her of the habit. So briefly, Al related further what "the boys" had said. However, he did not tag any specific name to the vague bits of information. He knew that she would stretch whatever he said like a balloon before it bursts.

Maxine Cleat was sitting in the living room with her hair in curlers reading a magazine when Vince came in. He bent over and kissed her. She knew from his vibes that something unusual had happened.

"Tell me about it," she said, her eyes dancing.

"What do you mean?" he replied, knowing very well what she meant.

She simply smiled at him lovingly. That's all it took to get him talking.

"Darndest thing happened at the poker game. Leonard said he had a conversation with God."

"A conversation with God? You mean he prayed?"

"No," replied Vince. "This morning while he was fishing something happened to him. He seemed to know exactly what it was. He was mighty convinced that some sort of insight came to him and it explained some of the things that Joey Balaam has said."

"What sort of things?" asked Maxine, sitting up in her chair.

"Well, you know. Those things that New Autumn preacher said about Joey coming alive."

"You mean Leonard has seen Joey alive? Don't tell me there's another Elvis Presley hovering around."

"No, nothing like that, but the things that Joey said and lived by came alive in Leonard, and as he told us about them it just seemed like they came alive in us, too."

Maxine's interest was intense. She leaned forward and asked, "What's this all about? What did he say?"

"Well, while he was fishing he said he read some things Joey had written and he tied them in with what was said yesterday at the funeral, and suddenly it all made sense to him. Then tonight he talked about it and it made sense to the rest of us. These are things we've all wondered about, and Joey had asked the same questions we all asked ourselves but never mentioned them to anyone else."

"I'm going to call Edna Enright about this," exclaimed Maxine.

"Aw, why don't you wait till morning; it's nine o'clock," Vince suggested.

"No, I just gotta know if Wallace has told her anything about this."

When Wallace answered the phone, Maxine said, "Wally, Vince has told me about what Leonard told you men tonight, and I'm wondering if you said anything about it to Edna."

"Well, yes," replied Wallace. "We're sitting here now drinking coffee and talking about it. Why don't you and Vince come over."

"We'll do just that," Maxine said and hung up the phone.

They walked briskly over to the Enrights.

Chapter 39

The Mercer Hearing

On Tuesday after Joey's funeral, the County Sheriff arrested Rudy and Tag Mercer for allegedly raping Rose Ann. The Assistant Prosecuting Attorney duly filed the charges with the Circuit Court. A minimum bond was posted. Their hearing was scheduled for December 21 in the county court house chambers of Judge Gerald Lando.

At the hearing Judge Lando perceived Rose Ann as a befuddled kid. She admitted having told her father that the act of rape was committed by Nation Skreigh, but the night Joey was killed he told her to tell the truth, and then at his funeral she said it was Rudy.

Turning to the girl's father, Judge Lando said, "Lem, what about this? Has anything been said around the house that would lead you to suspect this unfortunate incident was exercised by anybody other than Nation?"

"No siree, not a thing," replied Lem confidently. "When her mother found out that she was gonna have a kid, she admitted that Indian had raped her last August like Lou's boys here sez."

"What about you, Lou," the Judge said turning to Constable Mercer, "I presume you've made a thorough investigation and have evidence that this dastardly act was not committed by your sons?"

"I have, Jerry, and there is not any question about it. The Injun done it."

The Judge looked at Rose Ann. "Well now, Rose Ann, when were you telling the truth--when your mother found out you were pregnant or was it at Joey's funeral?"

Rose Ann looked down. Her hands were grappling with each other in her lap. Her whole body was rigid, shaking vehemently.

"Well, speak up, Girl. Didn't you tell me it was Nation Skreigh?" rasped her father.

The Judge waited momentarily for the silence in Rose Ann to explode. Then he asked, "Did you tell your father it was the Indian? Yes or no."

Frightened, her eyes darted from the Judge to her father.

Her trembling voice replied, "Yes."

"I guess that takes care of matters, Lou," said the Judge. "Sorry about all this inconvenience. This hearing is adjourned. You boys are cleared of this allegation."

Suddenly Rose Ann did explode.

"But Joey told me to tell the truth, so now I am," she cried out. "It wasn't Nation at all. It was Rudy here! Joey told me to tell the truth and it was Rudy!"

"This hearing has been adjourned, Young Lady," snapped the Judge. "However, tell me this: when did Joey tell you to tell the truth. Joey has been dead for a month."

"He told me that night he was killed. I met him going up Copperhead Pass that night he was killed. He was going to see Nation and warn him about those men coming to kill him."

"Had you been sneaking up there seeing that Injun?" demanded her father.

"Why no, sir," said Rose Ann, fear and frustration surging from her surprise.

"Then what were you doin' up on Copperhead Pass at that time of night?"

"It wasn't night, Pa; it wasn't even dark yet."

Judge Lando intervened. "Sit down and tell us about meeting Joey, Rose Ann."

All of them resumed their seats. Rose Ann, looking at the floor, began, "Sometimes I walk up that way, and that evening when I was coming back home, Joey was coming up the road, hurrying and all out of breath. He said he had to go warn Nation because some men were coming to get him. He said, 'Rose Ann, you just gotta tell the truth that it was Rudy and Tag and not Nation.'"

"He told you to say it was Rudy and Tag?" the Judge asked.

"Yes, and he said to say it wasn't Nation."

"Well now, Judge, I guess that wraps it up a second time, don't it?" said Lou, arising from his chair.

"Guess you're right, Lou," Judge Lando replied.

When the Mercers arrived home, Lou took his two boys for a walk. When they came to an isolated place by the river, he stopped and turned to his sons.

"You raped Rose Ann, didn't you." He stated it rather than asked.

"I couldn't help it, Pa!" Rudy said, trying to sound apologetic. "Tag and I had been over in the Greasy Bottom area looking for varmints when Rose Ann came along and.... Well, we done it before we realized.... And just then that Injun came running toward us like he had war paint on, and before I could zip up he was on me. I grabbed him and held his arms behind him and told Tag to hold Rose Ann which he did. After we all calmed down, I told them both that if anything was said about this, Tag and I would swear it was Nation who done it and that people would believe us and not that Injun, and he would go to prison while Rose Ann would be dubbed as a whore for Injuns."

"Well," said Lou, "that was pretty good thinking, but you did it and I ain't awful proud of you. At first only the three of you knew about it. Then that Injun came along and made it his business, which he ought not to have done."

Nobody said anything.

"On the other hand," Lou added thoughtfully, "maybe it's a good thing--that he came along just then."

"Why, what do you mean, Pa?" asked Rudy.

"Well, you caught him at it didn't you," said his father sternly.

"Well, oh, yes. Well, yes. Yes we did," stammered Rudy.

"We shore did," chimed Tag with a snicker.

"What are you going to do now, Pa?" Rudy asked.

"Yeah, Pa, what you gonna do?" repeated Tag.

"I ain't too sure Joey knew about it. I think he might have got wind of our posse going up after Nation and went to tell him that, but he didn't know the reason. But even so, like you say, Rudy, it's still our word against that Injun's. Yeah, it's a good thing that he butted in on you boys' fun when he did."

"What about Rose Ann?" asked Rudy.

"She won't say anything 'cause she knows what Lem will do to her if she does. Right now I bet she ain't able to say anything to anybody because of what Lem has done to her already for making those false accusations about you. Now, I want you boys, both of you, to know this: those are false accusations that she made against you. The Judge said so. And if anything further is said about it, just remember the Judge said that what she said was false. That Injun did it. The Judge said so. You understand?"

"Yeah, Pa," said Rudy.

"Yeah, Pa," said Tag.

"And if Joey did tell anyone--well, nobody paid any attention to anything he said. Besides, he's dead. And even if he had said anything, it would only be what that Injun told him, and anyone would think he was saying it to protect his friend."

"Great, Pa," replied Rudy. "They'll think Nation said we done it to save his own skin."

"Yeah, great, Pa," echoed Tag, "That's what they'll think."

"People will talk, especially people outside of Dogwood. If anyone asks you about it, you tell them what we've said here. At the hearing the Judge proved you were innocent, and even Rose Ann's own pappy said the Injun done it. Just don't go around talking about it."

"We won't, Pa," said Rudy.

"We won't, Pa," said Tag.

"One more thing," the father added. "Lay off Rose Ann."

Chapter 40

Observations of a Father's Daughter

The day after the Mercer hearing we received a Christmas card and letter from Bill and Addella Hampton, our Michigan friends. Bill said his daughter, Christine, shared with all her friends the letter we wrote last June comparing Arkansas kids with those of Michigan.

"Tuesday night at Christine's pajama party," Bill wrote, "the girls were giggling about what you folks had written about Nation's trousers not having a zipper. We fathers have always wondered what our daughters talk about at these girl-parties. Now we know."

Vi whooped and hollered with enthusiasm, for she thought surely this evidence would clear Nation. She could hardly wait until Wednesday morning to see the District Attorney about the matter, for by this time the story was abroad that Rudy and Tag had come upon the rape scene of Rose Ann just in time to see Nation zip up his pants.

"If Nation's pants didn't have a zipper," Vi reasoned, "then that proves that Rudy's story is false, so Nation is innocent!"

The next morning Henry Granger, our District Attorney, made notes of the information we offered.

"However," he informed us, "the Mercer boys have already been tried by Judge Lando and found innocent, this information about the zipper would be irrelevant. The only thing we can do is file it for possible reference in the future."

"Do you mean," Vi protested, "that even if the Mercer boys are guilty, they cannot be brought to justice because of that hearing of a Justice of the Peace?"

"We must abide by the law," replied the District Attorney.

On our way home we discussed Nation, wondering about his health and how he was surviving.

"I think he can make out as long as he is well and has ammunition," I said, somewhat dubious about the truth of my hope.

"Maybe we should take some canned food, fresh vegetables, vitamin pills and cough syrup, and leave at his cabin," Vi said "Surely he returns there periodically."

"And we'll have to get some .22 shells," she added.

"I imagine they keep a pretty close check on his cabin," I replied, "but if you will get the stuff together in a plastic bag, I'll get the shells and leave every thing at the secret place Nation showed me up on Soaring Bluff."

"Will this constitute aiding and abetting a criminal?" Vi asked.

We thought not, though the local authorities might view it differently.

Anyway, yesterday I took the vegetables, a can of pork and beans, some ammunition, Robitussin cough syrup, and aspirin, and left them in a plastic bag at Soaring Bluff. We also included this note: "Nation: The Great Spirit helps in His own way; we in ours."

We did not sign our names. He would know.

It's hard to know if we did the right thing, but we still feel good about it.

Chapter 41

Christmas at Dogwood

Christmas Day began as usual for Leonard of Dogwood. However, it did not end that way. He never fished on Christmas, and he never attended a church service. Rather, his routine was to walk along the shore of the river, and then somewhere along the way take a sashay up a deer trail. As he walked, he contemplated the men called Buddha, Confucius, Moses, Jesus, Mohammed, Martin Luther, John Wesley, Joseph Smith and others who established their forts of inspiration along the frontiers of religious complacency.

Early on this Christmas Day of 1992, Leonard packed a lunch and retreated to a remote cave which he had discovered last spring. He went upriver by boat to a little cove where last summer he had more than filled his license with a nice catch. A large tree branch overhung the water where slabs of limestone sloped comfortably up from the ripples. Here he pulled his boat ashore and began to walk through the brush, taking his usual long forceful steps. Shortly before noon he approached the location of the cave. The blackberry bushes surrounding the area were armed with seasoned barbs. They had been full of blossoms and potential fruit when he saw them last spring. By instinct, Leonard stepped quietly as he approached the cave, thinking that if a bear were hibernating inside, he could handle the situation since he was wide awake and the bear would be sleepy.

No bear, however, had taken shelter in the cave.

Suddenly Leonard stopped, all senses alert. The odor of stale smoke was faint but unmistakable. He heard nothing as he squatted down among the thorny bushes, easing his way over behind a large rock. He listened-- and watched.

Nothing.

Slowly, carefully he made his way around through the bushes and rocks to the side of the cave's mouth and waited. He could see nothing, hear nothing. There was no movement other than the natural movements of the grass and trees, but his sixth sense told him that he was not alone.

His only weapon was his patience, brute strength and pocket knife, which he drew from his pocket and silently opened the larger of the two blades.

He waited. Obviously the presence was waiting, too; possibly watching him.

Then with the nimbleness of a cat, he sprang through the small entrance of the cave and ducked behind a slab of rock that had fallen from the ceiling.

Silence. Silence as can be felt only in a remote cave.

Leonard thought of calling out, but refrained when he thought how foolish that would make him feel if indeed there was nothing or no one around.

"Outlaws have been known to hide in caves like this," Leonard thought to himself. "But anyone would have to be desperate to be holed up way off out here this time of year."

Then he thought of Nation!

By this time his eyes became accustomed to the interior darkness. He saw a slight movement and heard a faint sigh across the floor of the cave, back from the entrance.

"Who's there?" Leonard asked.

Another movement, then the sound as if metal scraping slowly on the gravel of the cave floor.

"My name is Leonard. Who are you?"

"Leonard," came the faint response as the sound of Nation's rifle dropped to the floor.

Quickly Leonard went over to the form lying on a make-shift bed. Nation was delirious with fever. Leonard struck a match but found no candle. He found grass and wood for a fire and examined Nation's condition. He found an old aluminum sauce pan and filled it with water from the nearby spring. With the ice-cold water he bathed Nation's face and hands. This cooled the fever. From the light of the fire, Leonard found some wilted carrots and celery, and a part of a head of cabbage, some Robitussin.

The next morning the fever left Nation and he was able to talk and eat a bit of the lunch Leonard had brought with him. Under Leonard's care, Nation soon recovered his health, and by February he was able to resume his life in exile.

The Christmas day had begun differently for Edna Enright. She looked at her kitchen clock again and checked the Christmas turkey baking in the oven.

"It's been in an hour and forty-five minutes," she calculated. "I do hope it doesn't get too dry."

She basted it again and checked the meat thermometer which pierced the bird's breast.

"It's ten-thirty," she mumbled to herself. "They should be here now."

She looked out the window and sure enough, they were. Al and Bertha Leffer's car swirled into the driveway and stopped at the kitchen door. Al opened the trunk to debark their contributions for the Christmas dinner just as Vince and Maxine Cleat drove in behind them.

The women immediately went to work with the preparations while the men, after helping unload the things, drifted to the garage where Wallace Enright proffered the invitation to taste the wild blackberry wine he had processed, now ready to be unveiled for this special occasion.

"Maybe it'll help the Almighty to get through to us what we've got to do here in Dogwood," he said. After the first sip, they decided unanimously that the wine did, indeed, turn out to be worthy of all the care and labor involved.

"We'll bottle up a little jug of it and take to the girls in the kitchen and propose a toast to what this day of celebration might bring," Wallace added.

Straightway they joined their wives, and whether it was the lapse of time or the lapse of toasts, suddenly Edna gasped, "Oh, I better check the old bird again!"

She dashed to the oven.

"For a minute there, Wally, I thought you might be the old bird she had to check," drawled Al.

"Guess I'm lucky," responded Wallace with a grin. "Let's go back out to the garage and do a little more checking ourselves."

"Now this here is made from 'possum grapes," Wallace said as he tapped a second three-gallon container of black-purple wine. "Not many care for it, but I don't mind it, and Edna, she likes to go out and pick the grapes for me."

"I don't like the taste of possum grape wine too much," said Al, "but I like what it does to me."

Before long, Edna called from the kitchen, "Wally, we've got the ice cream ready, so bring in the cylinder."

"Vince, if you'll take this cylinder in and get the makings, Al and I will get the other things ready."

Wallace unrolled a large block of ice wrapped in canvass sheet and began to break it into smaller pieces which he placed in a toe sack, laid it on the concrete floor and began hammering it with the broad side of an ax, crushing the ice into small chunks. When Vince returned, they placed the metal cylinder containing the liquid cream mixture into the old cedar cask and placed the crank mechanism securely over it. They poured the crushed ice into the cask, intermittently sprinkled it with rock salt until it reached the underside of the cylinder lid. Wallace then folded three other toe sacks and placed them on top of the freezer for cushion and sat upon it.

"The rest is up to you, men," he said, "but remember, making ice cream is like making love; urgently slow, wild and calm, tense and comfortable, firm and gentle. Timing is the key for good ice cream making."

Eventually Edna, from the kitchen door, informed the men that the dinner was ready. Wallace asked Vince to offer the blessing, which he did, saying, "Lord we give thee thanks for the birth of Jesus, and for the birth of all mankind, and for the birth of this Christmas dinner. Amen."

Half-way through the dinner, Bertha Leffer said, "I declare, I do wonder what that Maybelle Sutherland is going to do next."

"What do you mean?" asked Maxine Cleat.

"Well, the things you hear, and I won't repeat them at this table, but I don't doubt they're true."

The men looked at each other, shrugging their shoulders. Al said , "Please pass the potatoes."

"Why, Bertha, what on earth you talkin' about?" pursued Maxine.

"Well," Bertha said as she took a big bite of hot biscuit spread with butter and honey. She took her time, savoring the calory-laden morsel with the moment of suspense she had created.

Slowly and deliberately she dipped additional gravy onto her mashed potatoes, knowing very well that no interruption would rob her of this high moment.

Finally she swallowed and said, almost too eagerly, "Well...."

The one word was a complete sentence, masterfully expressed with the knowledge that not a person present would show the guilt of their own gossip-mongering by offering the undisguised show of interest, "Well what, Bertha?"

Bertha was not to be hurried. She knew how to get people to wait.

However, their waiting was interrupted by a startling knock at the door, and Nelda's loud voice came to them as she entered the kitchen.

"I'm sorry to barge in like this, but I just had to talk to you."

The interruption annoyed Bertha because seldom had her gossip achieved the tight intensity and attention it had just now reached. Maxine looked at Bertha with body language that said, "What is Nelda doing here?" Bertha kept silent, wondering if Nelda visited here often.

"Come on in," Wallace called, getting up and meeting Nelda in the kitchen.

"I got a bone to pick with you--all of you," Nelda sputtered. "I've got to know what's going on around here about Maybelle."

She walked through the kitchen toward the dining room.

"Last night when Maybelle was coming home from Christmas Eve candlelight service over in New Autumn she had a flat tire and while she was fixing it, who should come along but Tag Mercer, and he was half-drunk."

Edna, who had followed Wallace into the kitchen, stepped forward and reached out to Nelda, "Come and join us for Christmas dinner. Wally, get another chair while I get a plate."

"I don't want to interrupt your Christmas dinner," Nelda said with little apology, "but I've just got to get to the bottom of this. After hearing what Maybelle said last night, I went over to Mercers' this morning and had it out with them. Almost nailed that Rudy to the wall, but that little wimp, Tag, dropped on his hands and knees behind me and Rudy pushed me backwards over him. Right there on their living room floor! Then Lou threatened to arrest me for being drunk and disturbing the peace on Christmas Day if I didn't get out of his house. Well, that would have been all right except I thought a better way would come and see you folks because Tag, the little liar, said it was you who said all those things, especially you, Bertha.

By this time, a chair and tableware had been placed for Nelda, and Edna poured coffee and passed the turkey.

"I'll just have a cup of coffee," Nelda said. Her voice had become quieter, but her eyes searched and flashed like the blinkers of a highway patrol car.

"What are these things you've heard about Maybelle?" Wallace asked with no indication that he might already know some of them.

"Now, dear," Edna interceded, "let's eat and enjoy the dinner and then talk afterwards."

However, Nelda was in no mood to wait. "Tag tried to force himself on Maybelle, but Maybelle kicked his scrawny little butt and sent him on his way, but as he was leaving he yelled some awful things back at Maybelle, saying she was a whore and that everybody knew that she and Brother Jake wallowed around in the bushes and that Trio was her kid and not mine."

Nelda paused, observing the awkward expressions on the six faces before her, and the six forks of food simultaneously headed toward their destinations.

Vince broke the silence, "Well, Nelda, we have heard some of these things, but people don't believed them."

"Oh, they believe them all right. No, I'll take that back; you're right, they don't believe them because if they did it would break down the security which they've built around their own fears. People seem to think gossip will protect them from the exposure of their own guilt."

"What in the world are you talking about?" inquired Maxine.

Her question was tagged with alarm--and the fear about which Nelda spoke.

"I don't think she knows what she's talking about," Bertha said, reaching for the gravy while the others sat immobile.

"I'm saying," continued Nelda holding onto the confidence provided by Maxine's question, "that while you may not have actually believed these nasty things, you pretended you did, creating more excitement like a ten-horn buck in rutting season."

"Why, Nelda, I think you're wrong," said Edna, sounding like a mother defending her child. "We hear what we hear, but that doesn't mean we enjoy hearing that kind of talk about Maybelle. Maybelle is a very nice woman."

"Indeed she is; both of you are, Nelda," Bertha chimed in. "Why, that time she said she fell into the Devil's Sinkhole over in Greasy Bottom and said a man climed down and helped her out, everybody knew it was a vision she had of some secret lover, maybe Mr. Leonard."

"What are you talking about. She never fell into the Devil's Sinkhole or any other hole," Nelda retorted.

"Well, she said she did," Bertha said defensively, stuffing more honey and butter soaked role into her mouth. "At least somebody said she did," she added, mumbling.

"There you go again, Bertha, with your slanderous gossip!" Nelda exclaimed.

Then she looked at all the others, saying, "And you say you don't believe it. Well, if you don't believe it, why do you pass it on?"

"Of course we hear things," Maxine interrupted, "but we don't spread it as gossip."

"Bertha just did," Nelda returned, "and none of you made any effort to...."

"I did not!" Bertha interrupted. "I just told you what happened."

A short silence followed before Nelda continued. Very solemnly she said, "I wonder if you can imagine what it must be like to live as Maybelle has, suspecting people of saying things about you that are not true, yet you have no idea what they are or who is saying them. She says she wakes up at night scared to death, but not knowing why. And then when people look at her on the street or in the store and give a quick nod and pass on by, she experiences that same fear."

"That's terrible," said Edna, "I had no idea."

"Nelda's right," Al interrupted, "and it's about time we looked at ourselves to see what we've been doing."

"Al is right," Edna said. "It's just that how, in a little town like Dogwood, can you not hear things?"

"And in this place nobody would dare to disagree," added Maxine.

"Nelda did," Wallace pointed out.

"Tell you what," Edna said with assertion, "from now on when I talk with our friends I'm going to make it a point to defend Maybelle. There is no reason for anyone to believe this kind of gossip, and certainly not spred it. Maxine, Bertha, what about you--and Wally, you and Al and Vince?"

"There is a lot of other things, like ingrown prejudices, that have gotten out of hand in this town," Wallace said, "and from now on, how about the six of us--no the seven of us--standing up for what human beings should stand up for?"

All were in agreement, even Bertha, who had stopped eating and was sitting silently, tears filtering from her eyes.

"I had those same fears when I was a little girl," she said, "and the other kids laughed at me and called me 'Fatty.' Even to this day I live in fear that they will do that, and I don't know why it effects me so. But I didn't know I was doing it to Maybelle. I think my habit of gossiping has been a false security which I used to cover up that terrible fear."

"Look," Wallace said to Nelda, "ever since Joey Balaam's funeral we have talked off and on about him. This afternoon we had planned to talk about it and get down to serious business about what he said. We thought that would be a good way to spend Christmas Day. Would you like to stay and join us?"

"Please do," Edna invited.

"Yes," Bertha added, "and let's call Maybelle and see if she will come over."

Christ attended that gathering, too.

Chapter 42

Brother Jake's Trial

Spring passed and summer came. The judge changed Brother Jake's trial more often than God changed the weather. We have heard nothing from Nation, but the several bags of supplies we left on Soaring Bluff disappeared with no message except one time a little cross made of pebbles was left in his hide-away.

Finally, August 9th, Brother Jake's trial was convened. The morning began with one of those "Dog Days of Summer," and Judge Clifford Ames' temperament was equal to it. He was not happy that the case of The State of Arkansas vs. Jacob Balaam had been transferred to him. I suppose nobody likes to judge a minister of God, lest he, too, be judged. The case was a sticky one--just as sticky as the humidity saturating our clothing, gluing us to the old varnished church pews on which we spectators sat.

Into this atmosphere the court opened its session. It convened exactly on time, indicating the judge's eagerness to get the case overwith as soon as possible. The Prosecuting Attorney, Lloyd Townley, moved rapidly through the customary openings. Willard Brace, defending Brother Jake, did not cross-examine the first minor witnesses.

Prosecuting Attorney Townley, knowing something of Judge Ames' intolerance for triviality, was irritated because he could not call Lou Mercer to the stand immediately, as he had planned, because Lou and his two sons, Rudy and Tag, had not yet arrived. This frustrated the carefully planned schedule of the entire procedure. So in order to move along and favor the judge, Mr. Townley called Lem Hill to the stand.

Lem recounted the events in which he participated on the night of Joey's demise. Yes, Constable Lou had Lem drive his own car with the prisoner. No, he did not see the prisoner escape because Lou had left him and Tag in the car as lookouts while Lou and Rudy took Nation out in the bushes because Lou had to relieve himself. No, he did not know what he and Tag were to be looking out for.

Other witnesses affirmed the meeting at the general store on the night of the arrest. Yes, they formed a posse. Yes, the posse did go to Nation's cabin. Yes, you could say it was to apprehend him. One witness recounted Brother Jake's reaction when the men realized that he had shot his son.

Just as Mrs. Balaam took the stand, a guard admitted Lou. Rudy and Tag into the courtroom. Sari Jane confirmed her husband's nightmares and frequent variety of regressions regarding Jakey-Boy's death. No, she did not know what the attorney meant by saying her husband suffered from a post traumatic stress syndrome. Yes, there had been times when he reverted into extreme reactions when he became excited. No, he was not a dangerous man--"except to coons."

Prosecutor Townley called Constable Lou Mercer to the stand and led him through a review of events; i.e., organizing the posse and leading it to the home of Nation. There, while Mercer was arresting Nation on the charge of raping Rose Ann, the shooting of Joey Balaam took place. During all that fracas, he, Lou Mercer, apprehended Nation, who subsequently escaped while enroute to jail.

Defense Attorney Willard Brace, declined cross examination

Prosecuting Attorney, Lloyd Townley, called Rudy Mercer to the stand.

Rudy affirmed that he was present at the scene when Brother Jake shot Joey. He was evasive toward some questions, aggressive toward others. Yes, he had helped his father, Constable Lou Mercer, with the arrest of Nation. Yes, the escape happened exactly as his father had told it.

Defense Attorney Willard Brace did little cross examining until Tag Mercer was on the stand. As soon as Tag settled into the witness chair, Brace walked slowly toward him, looking at him intensely.

Brace: "Tag, did you have your gun with you that night, the night Joey Balaam was shot?"

Tag: "I guess so."

Brace: "Did others have their guns?"

Tag: "Yessir. Brother Jake did because he shot Joey."

Brace: "Did Rudy tell you to take your gun?"

Prosecutor: "Objection, Your Honor. Implication."

Judge Ames: "Sustained."

Brace: "Was it your idea to take a gun?"

Tag: "No."

Brace: "Whose idea was it to take it?"

Tag hesitated. He looked at Rudy.

Brace: "Who told you to take your gun out to Nation's cabin on the night Joey was shot?"

Perspiration broke out on Tag's forehead. He remained silent as he shifted positions. Then his body began to twitch.

The Defense Attorney waited, very much aware, as we all were, that the jury members were reading the body language.

Judge Ames intervened, "Please answer the question."

"Well," said Tag, "Rudy told us all to bring our guns. He said we might catch some varmints."

Brace: "Some varmints, or a varmint?"

"Objection," intervened Prosecuting Attorney Townley.

"Overruled."

"Some varmints, or a varmint?" continued Attorney Brace.

Tag: "I...I don't know what it was."

Brace: "Tag, you've been sworn in to tell the truth today, haven't you?"

Tag: "Yeah, I guess so."

Brace: "You guess so, or know so?"

Tag: "Well yes, I put my hand on the Bible."

Brace: "And you swore to tell the truth?"

Tag: "Yeah."

Brace: "Did you shoot your gun that night?"

Tag considered the question. He looked at Rudy again. His eyes shifted to his father. Then soberly and as innocently as if he were responding to his seventh grade school teacher after throwing a paper wad, he answered, "I didn't do anything."

The Defense Attorney held his gaze into Tag's shifting eyes, and repeated, "Did you shoot your gun that night?"

Tag: "No, I didn't shoot no gun that night."

Brace: "Was your gun shot that night?"

Tag, smirkingly sure of himself now in his familiar state of denial, said, "Well, how would I know since I didn't do it?"

Brace: "Was your gun shot that night?"

"Objection! The question has been answered."

"Overruled."

Brace: "Who shot your gun that night, Tag?"

Then after a quick moment, Brace added, "Check your memory, Tag; check it carefully because we have done our homework. We have reason to believe the gun you were carrying was shot that night, and if necessary, we can get a court order to prove it. You have...."

"Objection, Your Honor; the Defense is threatening."

"Objection sustained."

Then, backing away from the stand a bit and looking downward thoughtfully at the floor, Brace said, "Tag, it is to your advantage to know what the term, 'penalty of perjury' means. The court would want you to know this, so in all fairness I must ask you this question: are you aware of that penalty?"

Tag: "I don't know what you mean."

Brace: "What I mean, Tag, is that if you do not tell the truth, the whole truth, and nothing but the truth, the court can throw you in the slammer until you do tell the truth."

Townley: "Objection! The Defense Attorney is threatening the witness _again_!"

Judge Ames: "Objection sustained."

Brace: "Very well, Your Honor. I simply meant it as a point of information for the protection of the witness, not as a threat to him."

Judge Ames: "Proceed."

Brace: "Tag, you understand that absolute truth from witnesses in court is an important part of the law, don't you?"

Tag: "Yeah, I reckon so."

Brace: "Did somebody shoot your gun on the night Joey was killed?"

Tag: "I don't own no gun."

Brace: "Did you carry a gun that night?"

Tag: "Yeah, I guess so."

Brace: "Did somebody--did Rudy or anybody shoot the gun you carried that night?"

Tag: "Well, ye . . .well, no. I don't know."

Brace: "That is all for now, Tag. Thank you."

Attorney Brace then addressed the bench, "Your Honor, I would like to recall Constable Lou Mercer to the stand."

Mercer, his irritation flashing, resumed the witness stand. He bristled as he and Tag passed, giving his young son the clear message that he had fallen short. Tag flinched.

Brace: "Mr. Mercer, it has been established in these court proceedings that you headed up the posse to apprehend Nation Skreigh on the night Joey Balaam was killed. Will you tell us more about the purpose of this activity?"

Lou: "Well, when we found out that Nation Skreigh had raped Rose Ann, we didn't want that sort of thing going on in our community, so we met and thought we'd do something about it before he fled the country."

Brace: "What did you have in mind to do about it?"

Lou: "Well, we decided to go after him, to apprehend him. We wanted it to be legal, you know, and bring him to justice."

Brace: "How did you propose to find him?"

Lou: "Well, we knew he was pretty handy with a gun, so all of us got together and went out to his cabin."

Brace: "Did you find your suspect, Nation Skreigh, at his home?"

Lou: "Not at first."

Brace: "Was there any light in the house when you arrived?"

Lou: "There was at first, when we started up the driveway. By the time we drove up in the yard and got out of the cars there wasn't any--I don't think."

Brace: "Then what happened?"

Lou: "I had the men surround the house and I called for him to come out in the name of the law. 'Nation Skreigh, you come out in the name of the law', I said."

Brace: "And?"

Lou: "He didn't come out, so I had some men to back me up while I dashed through the door and stepped aside against the wall according to standard police procedure."

Brace: "Did you have a warrant for his arrest?"

Lou: "I coulda got one easy."

Brace: "Do you mean you did not have one?"

Lou: "Since I'm the constable it wasn't necessary."

Brace: "Then what happened?"

Lou: "About that time I heard a shot and there was a lot of noise and talking outside. Then after I got that Injun arrested and secured, I went and investigated. We discovered Brother Jake had shot Joey."

Brace: "How do you know Brother Jake shot his son?"

Lou: "He said he did."

Brace: "Do you know why Joey was there?"

Lou: "Of course. He was there to warn Nation that I was going to apprehend him."

Brace: "How do you know that?"

Lou: "It was pretty obvious."

The Defense Attorney paused and looked at Lou seriously. Then in slow motion, he moved his gaze from Lou to the jurors.

Lou, in turn, looked over at the jurors and quickly added, "To me, anyway; an officer of the law, it was obvious."

Attorney Brace hesitated again, then asked, "Did Joey know who raped Rose Ann?"

Lou: "Of course. Well, he must have known. Nation must have told him."

Brace: "So you apprehended Nation for raping Rose Ann?"

Lou: "I did."

Brace: "Before or after Brother Jake allegedly shot his son?"

Lou: "After. No, before. Well, it all happened at the same time. I investigated the shooting outside, and examined Joey and found him dead on site."

Brace: "What happened after you apprehended Nation and found Joey dead?"

Lou: "After I captured Nation and was taking him to jail...."

Brace, interrupting: "Where was Nation while you were examining the shooting outside?"

Lou: "He was in the house."

Brace: "Alone?"

Lou: "I had him under guard."

Brace: "Who was guarding him?"

Lou: "Well, Rudy was."

Brace: "Then you took Nation to jail?"

Lou: "Yes. Well, no. Well,..."

Brace, quickly interjecting: "Yes or no?"

Lou: "I mean we were going to take him to jail, but on the way he...he escaped."

Prosecuting Attorney Townley: "Objection, Your Honor. Brother Jacob Balaam is on trial here for the killing of his son, not Nation Skreigh for raping Rose Ann."

Judge Ames: "Does the Defense Attorney understand the objection?"

Brace: "I do, Your Honor, and I hope very shortly to present to the court and to this jury the innocence of my client, Jacob Balaam."

Judge Ames, with a gesture that was interpreted to expedite the proceedings, said, "Proceed, then."

Brace: "How did Nation escape?"

Lou: "Well, now, this is kinda embarrassing, but on the way back to town where I was going to throw him in jail, he said he had to...well, you know...to take a leak...that is, I mean, go to the bathroom real bad. I told him to wait, but he said he couldn't. So I stopped the car so he could get out 'cause, well, you know, I didn't want him to mess up Lem's car. And then we went out a little way from the car and he stepped behind a bush which I thought was natural. Then when he never came out from behind that bush, I investigated and realized he was gone."

Brace: "Was he not handcuffed or bound in any way?"

Lou: "No. I ain't got no handcuffs, none except those my grandpa had, and they're all rusted up and won't work."

Brace: "Do you have a secure jail in Dogwood?"

Lou: "No, not a real one."

Brace: "Not a real one what?"

Lou: "We ain't got no real jail there, but there's one over at the county seat."

Brace: "Approximately what time did this happen?"

Lou: "You mean the arrest?"

Brace: "I mean the escape."

Lou: "Well, let's see. It must have been close to midnight; before midnight. Maybe after."

Brace: "It was dark?"

Lou: "Yes, it was pretty dark, all right."

Brace: "Just how dark was it?"

Lou: "Well, there was some moonlight and the stars were out so I could see him, but I couldn't see him real good."

Brace: "Are you men in Dogwood so modest you think it's necessary to step behind a bush to relieve yourself, even in the dark?"

Prosecutor: "Objection!"

Judge: "Objection sustained. Proceed, and get to the point."

Brace: "Mr. Mercer, is the court to understand that neither you nor any of the others saw or heard Nation Skreigh disappear after he stepped behind the bush?"

Lou: "Well, you know how them Injuns are; they can disappear before your very own eyes and you'd not know it."

Brace: "Tell me more about what you know about Indians."

Prosecutor: "Objection--irrelevant to the case."

Judge: "Will the Defense Attorney speak to the relevancy of this kind of questioning?"

Brace: "Your Honor, this tedious questioning is relevant because it is establishing the truth of the collocation and emplacement under which my client has been falsely accused."

Judge Ames: "Proceed."

Brace: "Mr. Mercer, please tell the court what you know about Indians."

Lou: "Why, everybody knows how dirty and smelly they are. Most of 'em are on welfare if they ain't on the reservation. And they can't learn much, not much about the white man's ways which is the America way. Just like Nation there; he goes around raping white girls--under age ones at that. They don't know no better."

Brace: "So your prisoner escaped?"

Lou: "Yessir, and I don't know how he did it. He just disappeared, like that."

Lou snapped his fingers.

Brace: "Was anybody in the car when this happened?"

Lou: "Well, yes there was somebody."

Brace: "Who?"

Lou: "Let's see, now, if I can remember who got in during all that fracas. It was Lem's car so he drove. He was there."

Defense Attorney Brace: "That's all for now."

Brace recalled Rudy to the stand.

Brace: "Rudy, who was in the car that night when Nation escaped?"

Rudy: "Lem was in there, like Papa said. Papa had him drive his car while we guarded Nation in the back seat while we was taking him to jail."

Brace: "So you were there, and Lou and Lem and Nation. Is that all?"

Rudy: "Well, there was my brother, Tag. He's always with me."

Brace: "Where were you when Nation escaped?"

Rudy: "Like I said, I was with them taking Nation to jail."

Brace: "At the moment Nation disappeared, where exactly were you located in relation to the others?"

Rudy remembered his father's testimony that he was alone with Nation outside the car. His eyes darted from the Defense Attorney, to the Judge, and then to his father.

Defense Attorney Brace stepped over to block his view. Rudy's eyes focused upon Brace. He replied, "I was in the car."

Brace: "A few minutes ago did you hear your father's testimony that he was alone with Nation when he escaped?"

Rudy looked up, alert, as if he had said something wrong.

Rudy: "Yes. Yeah, I heard him say that."

Brace: "And did you hear earlier in this trial Lem Hill's testimony?"

Rudy: "No. I came in late, my Pa and me. I, I didn't see Lem up here. What did he say?"

Brace, continuing: "What about Tag; where was he at the moment of escape?"

Rudy: "He was in the car with Lem."

Brace: "He and Lem were alone in the car?"

Rudy's body shifted. Again, he showed confusion.

Then he replied quickly, "He was in the front seat. I was in the back."

Brace: "Did you watch your father and Nation while they were out of the car?"

Rudy hesitated, his mind searching like the laser on a computer hard disk. Then he answered, "Yes, but I don't think we were supposed to."

Brace: "Did you see Nation disappear?"

Rudy: "Well, he--it's like Pa said, he just disappeared."

Brace: "Did you see him disappear?"

Rudy: "Like they say, you can't see an Injun disappear. They just disappear."

Brace: "Into thin air?"

"Objection!"

"Sustained."

Brace: "Was Tag with you when Joey Balaam was shot?"

Rudy: "Sure; he was there with us all."

Brace: "I mean specifically and exactly, was he with *you* the moment Joey was shot?"

Rudy hesitated; he looked around as if searching for an escape hatch. Then he replied, "I couldn't say. Who knows exactly and specifically where anybody was at a time like that."

Brace: "Where were you standing when the shot was fired?"

Rudy: "Around. I was standing around like everybody else."

Brace: "Were you near that clump of sycamore trees?"

Rudy: "You mean when that shot was fired? What clump of sycamores are you talking about?"

Brace: "The one where one of the trunks has a gunpowder burn on it."

Rudy struggled with his inner panic. However, it became obvious, not only to the jury but also to the spectators, as Mr. Brace planned.

"There are lots of sycamores around," he said.

Brace: "Yes, Rudy, there are. However, there is only one that had a fresh 30.06 burn on it. By the way, what kind of gun do you usually carry?"

Rudy: "I didn't have no gun that night."

Brace: "No, but Tag did. What kind did he have?"

Rudy: "Did he have a gun?"

Brace: "Yes, didn't he say he had one?"

Rudy was silent, wondering what the next questions would be rather than giving answer to the one at hand.

Brace: "We're waiting, Rudy. What kind of gun was Tag carrying that night?"

Rudy, confused and pondering a previous question, said, "If he said he had a gun, then I guess he had a gun."

Brace: "What do *you* say, Rudy? Was Tag holding a gun *just before* the shot that killed Joey was fired?"

Rudy: "I don't know; I wouldn't know."

Brace: "Tag has testified that he had a gun with him that night. It's strange that everybody had a gun but you, Rudy."

Townley: "Objection, Your Honor."

Judge Ames: "Objection sustained. The Defense Attorney will refrain from expressing personal opinions."

Brace: "No further questions at this time, Your Honor."

The Prosecuting Attorney did not wish to re-cross examine.

Turning toward the bench, Brace said, "Your Honor, I would like to recall Tag Mercer to the stand once more. However, in the best interest of justice for this case, I respectfully request to invoke the rule[7] by asking that Rudy Mercer be removed temporarily from the courtroom."

Judge Ames: "The Defense Attorney will step up to the bench."

Attorney Brace did so and whispered to Judge Ames his reason for this unusual request. "If this request is granted, Cliff, I can have this trial ended in ten minutes," Brace added.

Judge Clifford Ames, aloud to the court: "The request of the Defense Attorney is granted. A guard will escort Rudy Mercer from the court room during the interrogation of his brother, Tag. Rudy, you are ordered not to discuss matters of this trial with anyone during your exclusion."

A court attendant escorted Rudy to the hallway outside the court room.

Tag resumed the stand.

Brace: "Tag, you have testified that you had a gun with you when Joey was killed. Is that right?"

Tag: "Yessir."

Brace: "What kind of gun was it?"

Tag: "It's a rifle."

Brace: "Is it a 30.06?"

Tag: "I have to ask Pa."

Brace: "It has been established that the Mercers own one rifle and it is a 30.06. Tell the court, Tag--you're still under oath--were you holding that rifle when the shot was fired that killed Joey?"

Tag: "No, I wasn't. Rudy already grabbed it out of my hand when he saw that varmint."

Brace: "Did Rudy think that the so-called varmint was Nation?"

"Objection!"

"Sustained."

Brace: "That is all, Your Honor."

---

[7]Court phraseology for unusual privilege.

Defense Attorney Brace then recalled Rudy to the courtroom and to the stand.

Brace: "Rudy, did you see Brother Jake kill his son, Joey?"

Rudy: "Oh, he didn't kill him. It was that Injun that done it."

Brace: "How do you know?"

Rudy: "Well, it's pretty obvious, ain't it? Brother Jake wouldn't kill his own son, him being a preacher and all that."

Brace: "But at the time it was evident that he did, wasn't it--his coming forward with his gun smoking, admitting that he did it, thinking it was a razorback?"

Rudy sat mute. He was cornered--like a coon up a tree, he thought.

Brace: "Please answer the question."

Rudy: "What question?"

Brace: "Did you see Brother Jake kill his son?"

Rudy: "Well, no, but like you say, there was evidence that he did."

Brace: "Rudy, a few minutes ago you said that Nation Skreigh killed Joey; that a minister of God wouldn't kill his own son. Now you speak of evidence that this minister of God did kill his son. Is this conflict due to your knowing that *neither* Nation *or* Brother Jake killed Joey, and you know who did?"

Prosecutor Townley: "Objection, Your Honor."

Judge Ames: "Objection sustained. The Defense Attorney will either withdraw or reconstruct his question."

Brace: "Rudy, listen carefully. I also want the jury to listen carefully. We all know that Brother Jake did not kill his son...."

Prosecutor: "Objection! That has never been established."

Judge: "Objection sustained. The Defense Attorney might do well to review the fundamentals of court proceedings."

Brace: "Did you tell the truth when you said Brother Jake did not kill Joey?"

Rudy hesitated, his facial expression showed confusion. He began to perspire as his mind searched for a lie that would sound like a truth.

Brace: "Rudy, you know who killed Joey, don't you."

Prosecutor: "Objection."

Judge: "Objection sustained. The Defense Attorney will confine his questions, *and his statements*, to conventional court procedure."

Brace: "Rudy, I am going to rephrase my question because the court orders me to, and you must answer the question because the court orders you to do so. Here's the question, Rudy: Do you know who killed Joey Balaam?"

Rudy's discomfiture punctuated the courtroom silence as clearly as the perspiration punctuated his forehead.

Brace: "Rudy?"

Rudy: "Yes, it must have been Brother Jake...or Nation."

Brace: "Are you stating as sworn truth that it was Brother Jake or Nation?"

Rudy ignored the question and quickly picked up from his previous statement, "Because he did what he did to Rose Ann and then he told Joey and then he was afraid Joey would tell on him, so he killed him right there in cold blood that night we was going to arrest him for it."

Brace: "Nation told Joey who raped Rose Ann?"

Rudy: "Why yes--he must have. He did it, you know."

Brace: "How do you know Nation raped Rose Ann?"

Rudy: "Because he...because he was the one that done it."

Brace: "Do you know that for a fact?"

Rudy: "Yes! I saw him. Tag and me, we saw him do it, didn't we, Tag. And then he told Joey and then had to kill him so he wouldn't tell anybody. Yes, it was Nation. It was him, all right."

Brace: "Tell the court about it--the raping, I mean. After you have finished we will recall your brother, Tag, to verify your accounts."

Prosecutor: "Objection."

"Let the interrogation continue," Judge Ames said dryly.

Brace: "I have evidence which I will submit later that Nation did not rape Rose Ann. Right now, Rudy, I want you to concentrate upon this: ballistic comparisons have been made which will prove to the court that Brother Jake's gun did not fire the bullet that killed his son. And a .22 rifle, which is a gun owned and carried that night by Nation Skreigh, was not the caliber of rifle that killed Joey Balaam. We admit that the shooting may have been an accident. Rudy, who killed Joey Balaam."

Silence.

Brace: "It may have been an accident, so tell us quickly."

Suddenly Rudy buried his face in his hands and began to weep.

Brace, no less intense than before, continued, "Who, Rudy? Who may have accidentally fired the shot that killed Joey Balaam?'

Still sobbing, Rudy replied, "It was an accident. He didn't mean to do it, but like you say, it was an accident."

Brace, pushing hard: "Rudy, who shot Joey Balaam?"

Rudy's reply was short and muffled. "Tag. But he thought it was . . . he thought it was a varmint."

The Defense Attorney paused until the audible surprise among us court spectators became muffled. Then he said, "You mean your brother, Tag Mercer, shot Joey Balaam?"

Rudy, raising his voice in defense, cried out, "But it was an accident. You said yourself it was an accident!

Brace: "One more question for Rudy, Your Honor. First let me report to the court that witnesses are available who, if necessary, will testify that when the shot was fired which killed Joey Balaam, Rudy Mercer immediately joined the crowd in great excitement, a rifle in hand, saying, "I got him! I got that raping Redskin!" Rudy, when you joined the crowd in the darkness of that night, were you carrying a 30.06 rifle that had just been shot, and did you make such a claim?"

Chapter 43

Conclusion

The sun glows westward and the evening dusk awakens the fresh coolness of our hidden valley. The humming birds are having their last drink of soda pop; they bring their own straws. A little wren is hopping along the edge of the deck telling us good night. He loves us. The bobwhite, standing on his favorite rise beyond the trail, calls his family homeward. Very soon now, as if by the whip-poor-will's signal, twilight will squeeze the color from the skies beyond the mountain silhouettes. One by one and two by two, the last of this season's fireflies join the coolness rising from the encircling hollows along the river as it drifts through our Ozark splendor. Upstream, downstream, millions of these little twinklings beckon us all to behold the wonders of our twilight zone.

Today Vi and I took some food to Soaring Bluff and left Nation this note:

Nation: Yesterday after the court acquitted Brother Jake of killing Joey, they charged Rudy and Tag with the crime. During the trial, Tag said tht Rudy had raped Rose Ann and Rudy confessed. Nobody suspects or accuses you or Brother Jake of anything. The attitude of the people, especially in Dogwood, has changed.

We want you to come and live with us and go back to school. You can make it now, Nation, for you would have many friends. You are smart and athletic, and we would all be proud of you. School starts in two weeks and you will need to register ahead of time.

Come home, Nation; your room is ready.

--Rev. and Mrs. Hilliard

ACCESSORY ONE

Do You Hear What I Hear?

A parable is a tale that wags the truth.

It's this way or that: take Jesus by His hand or grab the devil by his tail.

He's the kind of preacher who takes the spotlight from God.

More rhetoric is used to argue Scripture as an end than is used to propound it as a means.

You are Christ's gift to God.

Christians have no exemptions from responsibilities.

He's the kind of parson you'd loan books to.

Cro-Magnon Christianity.

He spoke like he was leading you on a detour through the cemetery.

Denominational doctrines remind me of the Emperor's New Clothes.

We react toward what we have been *taught* about prejudices more than the prejudices themselves.

All Christian Baptism is by faith, not method.

If we truly confessed our sins, we would be ousted from the church-- but not from Christ.

Our minds photograph things that do not exist.

We handle life much like we do a camera. We become much more acquainted with the complications than the natural functions.

Scripture rejects a Christianity that is no more than a diversion to make life bearable or better.

We are *doing* the will of God when we *are* the will of God.

It is easier to deal with truths than with Truth. Perhaps that is why most of us "stick to the Bible" rather than Christ.

Never mind the old time religion. Keep it young, invigorating, maturing!

Our charitable giving may turn out to be an embarrassment, it's so un-God-like.

What church is not guilty of using their doctrines to teach Scripture?

It is blasphemous to preach Scripture.

Teach Scripture and *preach* Jesus Christ.

Most of our practicing Christianity is determined by social order.

One can deal with divine nature only when one shares that divine nature.

What is God like? God is like what God looks for.

Take God at His Word. That's what He does--takes you at His Word.

ACCESSORY TWO

Points of View

References:
   (A) Deuteronomy 27 and 28 where the Israelites were divided, some standing on Mount Ebal shouting curses, others on Mount Gerizim shouting blessings;
   (B) Jesus' Woe Section in Matthew 23.

One Point of View

Woe to you, **Visionaries, Dreamers,** hypocrites! For you lock people out of the Kingdom of Heaven. You do not go in yourselves, and when others are going in, you stop them. You envision bright stars of achievement for your church, but your visions and dreams vanish into the black holes of everlasting annihilation! Hypocrites! Dreamers! You see yourselves as a caring church. Do you not know that Christ alone sees the caring church? Woe to you, Blind Guides! In your visions you have your reward and Christ has no vision for you!

Another Point of View

Blessed are you, **Visionaries, Dreamers,** for you invite people into the Kingdom of Heaven here on earth. You envision bright stars for your church and you encourage others to participate in that shining glory. Blessed are you, Dreamers, for Christ has awakened you to your visions and they shall come to fruition, and the black holes of destruction shall not prevail against them. Your caring for your church makes it a caring church.

One Point of View

Woe to you, **Planning Committees**,
for you thrive on the efforts of others
and lead them into your own ministry.
Hypocrites! You call people to sow
and to tend, and you reap the harvest
for yourselves. You receive praises
for your successes while you neglect
the needs of those who give those successes to you. White-washed sepul-
chers! You bend the ears of sincere
people upon the words which are pleas-
ing to your goals and not upon the
Word to which God calls them. Woe
unto you, Blind Guides! You lead
people into the swell of big numbers
where faith is impossible! Verily, I say
unto you, the Day of Judgment is upon
you!

Anther Point of View

Blessed are you, **Planning
Committees**, for your plans are
blueprints of Christ's command
to "go ye therefore...," where
heaven's reward prevails. In
love and commitment you have
counted the cost of negligence
toward your neighbor. Your
goal is to stand with Jesus when
the role is called up yonder.
Blessed are you, for you lead
your people into the sanctuaries
of Christ's spoken Word where
faith is possible. Rejoice and be
glad, for verily, I say unto you,
the Day of Judgment came, and
you knew it not!

ACCESSORY THREE

Retirement Reflections

Retirement is...
...when more grunts do less.
...when your body begins to resemble the rolling hills that surround you.
...like the evening shades stretching long and friendly across the lawn.
...when the rocking chair fits like an old shoe.
...when hindsight becomes your friendly tag-along.
...taking waddles instead of walks.
...when there are no dull days even when the days are dull.
...when the evenings get late early.
...letting your dreams float along like hot-air balloons.
...when you can relax comfortably in a vacuum.
...when every other day is Friday.
...hearing the cheering section shouting, "You did it!" Except you're not
    doing it.

BIBLIOGRAPHY

"Cherokee Tragedy," by Thurman Wilkins, The McMillan Co., Collier McMillan Ltd, London.

"The Trail of Tears" by David Fremon, 1994 New Discovery Books, NY, J 973 .00497 F872T.

"After the Trail of Tears" The Cherokees' Struggle for Sovereignty, 1839-1880, by William G. McLoughlin, 1993 The University of North Carolina Press.

"The Cherokee People" by Thomas E. Mails, 1992 Council Oak Books, Tulsa, OK.

"James Mooney's History, Myths, and Sacred Formulas of the Cherokees,"
1992 Bright Mountain Books, 138 Springside Rd., Asheville, N.C. 2880.